A Whisper
of Bones

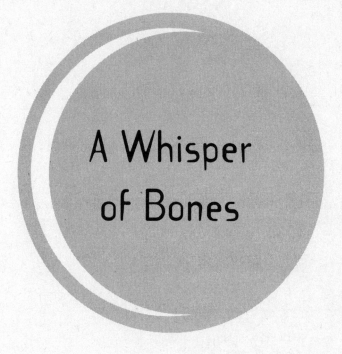

A Whisper of Bones

ELLEN HART

MINOTAUR BOOKS ✖ NEW YORK

A WHISPER OF BONES. Copyright © 2018 by Ellen Hart. All rights reserved. Printed in the United States of America. For information, address St. Martin's Press, 175 Fifth Avenue, New York, N.Y. 10010.

www.minotaurbooks.com

Library of Congress Cataloging-in-Publication Data

Names: Hart, Ellen, author.
Title: A whisper of bones / Ellen Hart.
Description: First edition. | New York : Minotaur Books, 2018.
Identifiers: LCCN 2017053460| ISBN 9781250088659 (hardcover) | ISBN
    9781250088666 (ebook)
Subjects: | GSAFD: Mystery fiction. | Detective and mystery stories.
Classification: LCC PS3558.A6775 W45 2018 | DDC 813/.54—dc23
LC record available at https://lccn.loc.gov/2017053460

First Edition: February 2018

Our books may be purchased in bulk for promotional, educational, or business use. Please contact your local bookseller or the Macmillan Corporate and Premium Sales Department at 800-221-7945, extension 5442, or by email at MacmillanSpecialMarkets@macmillan.com.

10   9   8   7   6   5   4   3   2   1

For Lee Lynch and Elaine Mulligan Lynch,
with much love.

Cast of Characters

Jane Lawless:

Owner of the Lyme House restaurant in Minneapolis. Part-time private investigator.

Cordelia Thorn:

Owner of the Thorn Lester Playhouse in downtown Minneapolis. Creative director. Jane's best friend.

Britt Ickles:

Professor of Evolutionary Genomics at Penn State. Daughter of Pauline. Lena and Eleanor's niece.

Pauline Ickles:

Britt's deceased mother. Stewart Ickles wife. Sister of Eleanor and Lena.

Stewart Ickles:

Trucker. Pauline's deceased husband. Britt's father.

Eleanor Skarsvold Devine:	Retired nurse. Frank's mother. Lena's older sister. Britt's aunt.
Lena Skarsvold:	Retired waitress. Eleanor's sister. Britt's aunt.
Frank Devine:	Tax preparer. Eleanor's son. Wendy's husband.
Wendy Devine:	Grade-school teacher. Frank's wife.
Butch Averil:	Lena and Eleanor's next-door neighbor.
Rich Novak:	Block captain along Cumberland Avenue in Saint Paul.
Iver Dare:	Pastor at Cumberland Park Lutheran. Eleanor's old friend.
Quentin Henneberry:	Renter.
Berengaria Reynolds:	California vintner.
Dr. Julia Martinsen:	Doctor of Oncology. Philanthropist.

"But surely for everything you love
you have to pay some price."

AGATHA CHRISTIE
AN AUTOBIOGRAPHY

A Whisper
of Bones

PROLOGUE

August 1978

The headlights of Eleanor's rusted blue station wagon cut through the heavy country darkness. Inside the car, with the windows rolled up, a Bee Gees song blared from the radio. "Stayin' alive," the guys sang. Ironic, thought Eleanor, since that was exactly why she was fleeing the city at such an early hour.

Clutching the steering wheel to keep her hands from shaking, she kept glancing up at the rearview mirror. She had to make sure that her sister didn't fall too far behind. Lena was driving the Ford Pinto. Eleanor had no faith whatsoever that the Ford wouldn't die in the middle of the highway, never to move again. There weren't many cops around to worry about and yet Eleanor felt like there was a spotlight trained on her. It was only a matter of time before the sound of a siren would end the world as she knew it. She tried to summon up a plausible story to tell the officer— why she and her sister were speeding through farm country at three in the morning. She could hardly tell the truth.

Slowing the station wagon and then pulling off onto a deserted dirt path, Eleanor cut the lights and then the engine. She loathed the heat, the sweltering summer nights, alive, as they always were, with creepy crawling things. A quarter moon cast its dim light over the cornfields on either side of the road. Might as well be a Hitchcock movie, she muttered, slapping mosquitoes off her arms. She ducked down next to the rear bumper, motioning for Lena to pull the Pinto into a low, flat area directly next to the road.

"Why the hell didn't you drive faster?" called Lena, bursting out of the front seat. She raked her dark blond hair away from her eyes as she rushed up the incline.

"Keep your voice down."

"Why? If you were trying to find the dark side of the moon, you succeeded."

As far as Eleanor was concerned, it was her sister's monstrous stupidity that had landed them in this mess. A decent, honest, caring person would've had sympathy for the dead body on the floor of her garage back in Saint Paul, but at the moment, all Eleanor felt was a cold, heavy knot in the center of her stomach. "We have to get the license plates off." She handed Lena a screwdriver and then crouched down behind the Pinto.

"You blame me, don't you."

This was hardly time for a debate. With a small flashlight clenched between her teeth, Eleanor set to work on the first screw.

"Judas H. freakin' Priest. You think I *wanted* this? That I'm somehow . . . responsible?" When Eleanor didn't reply, Lena said more forcefully, "Well?"

Rising from her crouch, Eleanor couldn't believe that her sister had picked this moment to start an argument. "I'm not discussing it. Get to work."

"I cried all the way here."

2

"Boohoo."

"You think I'm lying?"

As far as Eleanor could see, her sister didn't look the least bit teary eyed, though Eleanor made no pretense of understanding her. "Look. You live on the edge and dare the cosmos to push you over. Well, now it has and you've dragged the entire family along with you."

"It's *not* my fault."

"Is anything ever your fault?"

"Oh, piss off."

"And watch your language."

Lena threw her arms in the air and stomped around to the front of the car. She was back a few minutes later, plate in hand. "It's off. What do I do with it?"

Eleanor was still working; sweat trickling down inside her blouse. The final screw was rusted and didn't want to move. She'd almost given up when it finally came loose. It was times like this when she hated Steve. They'd only been married a few years when he'd been sent to Vietnam. He'd died there, his body never recovered. It wasn't his fault, and yet, awful as it sounded, Eleanor *did* blame him for leaving her all alone. He wasn't around to be a father to their child. He wasn't around to earn a living, cut the grass, fix the toilet, lift whatever was too heavy, all the millions of things that now fell to her.

After removing the gas can from the back of the station wagon, Eleanor handed Lena the car keys and the license plates. "Drive the wagon back out on the road and wait for me."

"I should do it." She grabbed for the can.

"Just this once, Lena. Do what I ask."

Eleanor waited until the wagon had backed up and was idling

along the side of the road, then began to toss gasoline all over the interior of the Pinto. Taking one last look at the quiet cornfields, the immense, uncaring blanket of stars above her, she struck a match and tossed it to the floor under the steering wheel. It caught instantly, flames crawling across to the passenger's side, then up and over to the backseat. She watched for a few seconds, mesmerized by the sight, then shook herself out of her reverie and ran for the wagon.

"Drive," she said, fixing her eyes on the windshield and the darkness beyond, terrified that, like Lot's wife, she'd turn to a pillar of salt if she dared look back.

Present Day

Just before 1:30 A.M. on a windy early December night, as the man behind the polished mahogany bar in the Lyme House pub issued his usual last call for drinks, part of a massive oak split from its trunk and crashed into the roof of the restaurant. Jane Lawless, the owner, was home in bed when a buzzing cell phone awakened her.

"You better get over here," came her assistant manager's voice.

"Why? What's going on?" She swung her legs out of bed and ran a hand through her hair. Glancing back at the woman lying next to her, still fast asleep, she got up and walked into the hall.

"I was in the bar when I heard a loud noise. I mean, the entire building shook." He explained about the tree.

That was why, at eight the following morning, Jane found herself standing in the parking lot behind the restaurant—a two-story log structure on Lake Harriet in south Minneapolis—watching a man in a boom lift chainsaw his way through the front branches, working back toward the heavy limb that was resting on the roof. Even though Jane's insurance would pay for the damage, which looked worse this morning than it had in the darkness last night, it was a headache she didn't need.

"What time do you open today?" asked the foreman, a heavy-set older guy who held a hand over his eyes, shading them from the sun.

"Eleven."

"We'll have this all removed and cleared out of here by then. You'll probably need a structural engineer to climb up and look around."

"Already called someone," said Jane. She didn't think a structural engineer would be necessary. She had a roofing company coming by later in the day to assess the damage and give her a bid on what the repair would cost.

"Windy night last night," said the foreman. "Thing is, that oak was decaying from the inside. You can't just look at a tree and determine something like that. The whole thing should probably come down."

"Up to the park board," said Jane. The wooded land that surrounded her restaurant wasn't her responsibility.

"People are like that, too," said the foreman, gazing up at the boom lift. "They might seem fine, but inside, there's nothing but rot."

Jane turned to look at him.

"I know. A bit early for philosophy."

She smiled and he smiled back.

"No, I hear you," she said. "And I agree. People aren't always what they seem." She figured he was thinking of someone specific, which was none of her business.

"Look out below," yelled the guy in the lift. He waited

until the two men on the ground moved back, then carved off a bunch of larger branches, lowering them to the asphalt with ropes. The workers stepped in and began to cut them into smaller sections, which they dragged over to the woman handling the wood chipper.

Watching the tree removal was far more entertaining than the weekly spreadsheet waiting for Jane in her office.

From around the side of the building, a dark-haired woman in a camel wool coat came into view, heading straight for them.

Jane stepped away from the din of the wood chipper. "Can I help you?"

"Are you Jane Lawless?"

"I am."

The woman was middle-aged, attractive, with a pronounced cleft in her chin. "My name's Britt Ickles." She handed Jane a card.

Gazing down at it, Jane realized it was one of her own. As weird as it might sound to people who didn't know her, she had two careers going—one as a restaurateur, the other as a part-time PI. This particular card advertised, "Lawless Investigations," and listed a phone number and an email address. On the flip side, someone had written the name of her restaurant.

"Do you have a few minutes?" asked Britt.

"Sure," said Jane. She turned and thanked the job foreman, asking him to come to her office when he was done, and then led the way up the rear loading dock, through the kitchen, and down the back steps. Instead of stopping at her office, she continued down the hall to a large foyer. Passing through the double doors into the pub, she saw that the coffeepot was on behind the bar. "Care to join me?" she asked, nodding to the pot.

"Perfect," said Britt.

"Cream? Sugar?"

"Black."

Jane poured them each a mug and then nodded for Britt to take a seat in one of the raised booths. Finally settled with their coffees in front of them, Jane asked how she could help.

Britt turned the mug around in her hands. "This is sort of bizarre, sitting here talking to a private detective."

"I'll make it as painless as possible."

She offered a hesitant smile. "I realize what I'm about to say will sound totally off the wall. You may even think I'm crazy."

Jane had heard a similar refrain many times before.

"I'm in town for a conference at the University of Minnesota. My mother was originally from Saint Paul. Yesterday, after I checked into my hotel, I had a few hours to kill, so I decided to drive over to the family home. My mother's two sisters still live there. Mom died a year ago."

"I'm sorry."

"Yeah. Thanks. Anyway, I've only visited the house once before, when I was six years old. We came because my grandfather had died and my mom wanted to attend the funeral. We stayed at the house. I'd never met any of them before. I suppose we don't sound like a close family. We're not. The fact is, I haven't seen or heard from my aunts since that visit. Apparently, there was a big fight after the funeral. I have no idea what the issues were because Mom refused to talk about it."

"Did you see your aunts yesterday?"

She nodded. "They were kind of shocked to find me at their front door. They're old women now. One is in a wheelchair. But they were gracious. Well, one of them was. Eleanor, the oldest, invited me in."

"Did they know your mother was gone?"

"I wrote them a note last year after her death. That's why I thought I could brave seeing them again." She took a sip of coffee. "We sat in the living room and talked. Eleanor had an appointment, so she didn't have a lot of time. Lena, the middle sister, the one in the wheelchair, didn't seem very friendly, so I left when Eleanor did. The thing is, as we were talking—it was when Eleanor had gone upstairs to get her purse—I asked Lena how her son was. Timmy and I were the same age. He and Lena were staying at the house that summer before the funeral, too. But when I mentioned him, Lena just stared at me. She said, 'Where did you get the idea I had a son?'"

"You're saying you remember this boy?" asked Jane.

"Vividly. At the viewing the night before our grandfather's funeral, Timmy and I stuck together. I remember this old guy whispering to us that he had lemon candies in his pocket. He gave each of us one. Timmy hated the taste of lemon, so he offered me his. And then there was a woman who urged us to go up to the coffin and kiss our grandfather. She said it would help us remember him. I was appalled. It sounded ghoulish. But Timmy said he'd do it. We walked up together. Timmy reached over the edge of the casket and touched one of our grandfather's hands. He told me later that it felt like plastic."

"You have very clear memories."

"I'm not making this up. Lena said I must be thinking of someone else. 'Wasn't there a boy down the block named Tim or Tom or Tad?' By that time, Eleanor had come back downstairs. She agreed with Lena, suggesting that I was simply confused. After all, it was forty years ago. What's strange is that, as I sat there, I began to actually think they were right, that I'd made Timmy up. I didn't press the point because, clearly, they were the ones who should know."

Jane raised her eyebrows. "But?"

"But I thought about it after I left. I've thought about little else. I'm not wrong, Jane. He was there. And that, of course, leads to the inevitable question, why did they lie? Why did they erase him? There has to be a reason."

Jane agreed that the story did sound far-fetched. "Any thoughts about that?"

"Honestly? None."

"And you're sure your memory is accurate?"

"Yes," she said fiercely. Then, frowning, she added, "At least, I think so."

"And you want me to find evidence that Timmy existed."

"Is that something you can do?"

"Possibly. Can you give me his full name?" She pulled out a pen and a small notepad from her back pocket.

"You know, I'm sorry to say, I don't know what it is. Just Timmy." Taking another sip of coffee, Britt continued, "Eleanor invited me over for dinner tonight. I was kind of surprised because Lena seemed so happy to see me leave. The thing is, if my memory is accurate, why did they lie?"

Jane shook her head.

"What if something bad happened to him?" She eased back from the table so she could cross her legs. "What if he died and they didn't tell anyone?"

"Why do you think they'd do that?"

She seemed frustrated. "I don't *know*. I realize I'm not making any sense. Maybe my memory *is* playing tricks on me."

Jane felt sorry for her. She was obviously deeply troubled by the situation. "Why don't you give it some time. Have dinner with them tonight. See what comes of it. How long will you be in town?"

"The conference goes through next weekend. I'll be flying back to Philadelphia late Sunday." She massaged her temples, took a few seconds. "Even after all these years, I can still see him so clearly. Curly blond hair. A ton of freckles. Smelled like bubble gum. He was a real ball of energy, loved to draw and sing and bang on the piano. Honestly, he was the only member of that family that I ever wanted to see again. And now I'm told he never existed."

"It is odd," said Jane. It was certainly possible that something bad had gone down that Britt's aunts didn't want to share with their niece. "I'm curious. Where did you hear about me?"

"I was at a party last night—a preconference event. I was asking around and a woman gave me your card."

"Do you remember her name?"

"Sorry. Is this"—she glanced over at the long mahogany bar—"where you work?"

"I own the restaurant."

"You own it?"

"I'm good at more than one thing."

The comment elicited a smile. "Are you expensive? Not that it matters. If I hire you, I'm only concerned with what you can find out."

"We can talk about that later, when you've made a final decision."

They spent a few minutes talking about the restaurant, then

moved on to places of interest in the Twin Cities. Britt seemed to be only half listening. Eventually, glancing at her watch, she slid out of the booth and said her goodbyes.

As Jane watched her go, she had a strong sense that she'd be seeing Britt Ickles again, sooner rather than later.

2

Eleanor was setting out a bowl of peanuts in the living room that evening when she spotted the headlights of a car pull up to the curb outside the house. Sunday night was pot roast night at the Skarsvold house. It was a family tradition, something Eleanor tried to maintain, even when the cost of the main course should have dictated something less expensive. Her son, Frank, and his wife, Wendy, usually came by to share the meal, as did the renters living in one of the three bedrooms upstairs. Because the last of the renters had given notice two days ago and moved out yesterday morning, she had extra food. Perhaps she shouldn't have invited her niece for dinner, and yet she felt ill at ease about Britt just showing up on their doorstep. She'd wanted a chance to talk to her again, just to feel out the situation.

After Britt had left, Lena and Eleanor had gotten into an argument. Nothing new in that. Lena had expressed herself in her typically crude fashion. Why the hell did Eleanor have to invite Britt for dinner? In the face of everything that had happened, wasn't it best to leave well enough alone? But no. Eleanor was too

Minnesota Nice. Shouting for Eleanor to "grow a pair," she'd rolled her wheelchair into the sunroom, which served as her bedroom, shut the French doors, and turned an old Queen album up loud enough to shatter glass. Not that Eleanor cared. She simply took out her hearing aids and got on with her day.

In Eleanor's opinion, a seventy-year-old woman wasn't supposed to listen to rock music, use the vocabulary of a sailor, or state her opinions as if they'd been whispered into her ear by God himself. Age should've taught her something, given her some dignity, some humility. Lena seemed as clueless—and reckless—now as she had when she was twenty, leaving the chaos she created for Eleanor to clean up.

It had been Lena's poisoned view of Pauline, their younger sister, that had started and ultimately perpetuated the family rift. How Eleanor had ended up with Lena in her life, the sister she'd never liked, and not Pauline, the very best of them, was nothing short of tragic. And yet, as much as she might not want to admit it, she did understand Lena's concern. Maybe she had made a mistake in inviting Britt for dinner.

Before Eleanor opened the front door, she touched the pearls at her neck and smoothed the front of her dress, realizing with some embarrassment that she'd forgotten to take off her apron. She untied it quickly, held it behind her back, and then drew back the door. The sight of Britt standing on the porch created such a wave of déjà vu that it made her almost dizzy. She's noticed the resemblance to Pauline earlier in the day, but tonight, in the dim porch light, it was more pronounced. For an upside-down moment, she thought it *was* Pauline.

"Is something wrong?" asked Britt.

"No, no, it's . . . you look so much like your mother." The

shape of her face, the soft cleft in her chin, the full mouth, and wide amber-colored eyes.

"I've been told that."

"Please. Come in." She took Britt's coat and hung it on one of the pegs behind the door. "You remember my son, Frank, right? He and his wife, Wendy, will be here any minute. Lena's still getting ready in her room. Why don't you follow me back to the kitchen? The roast is just about done."

"Smells wonderful in here," said Britt.

No hideous music blared from Lena's lair. Eleanor was grateful for small mercies. Once back in the kitchen, she wasn't sure what to do with her apron, so she put it back on. When she opened the oven door and removed the roasting pan, heat billowed out and caused steam to form on her rimless glasses. Removing them, she wiped the lenses with the tip of her apron. She didn't want to dish up the food until everyone was present. "Will you hand me that platter?" she asked, nodding to the one on the counter.

"Can I help? I'm a pretty good cook."

It was hard not to like such a well-spoken, lovely young woman. But liking was a far cry from trusting. At eighty, Eleanor's focus wasn't what it used to be, so she had to be especially careful to think through her actions, something Lena never did. "I believe I've got everything under control. Are you hungry?"

"Famished." Britt glanced around the kitchen. "I remember this room, everything but the red gingham curtains."

"I made those a good fifteen years ago. I love red gingham."

"I remember helping you make cookies. You brought a kitchen chair over to the counter so I could stand with you."

"Did I?"

"Oatmeal chocolate chip. You let me eat part of the dough."

Eleanor needed to steer the conversation away from that long-ago visit. "I forgot to ask. Are you married? Do you have children?"

"I'm divorced. No children. Friends say I'm married to my job."

"And what is it again?"

"I'm a professor of genomics at Penn State. I teach and I also do fieldwork. My postdoc was in human genetics and epigenetics."

"I'm afraid I don't know what that is."

Britt smiled. "It's difficult to put into a few words. I'm in town because I'm giving a talk at a conference of the American Society for the Study of Evolutionary Genomics. It's their annual meeting."

"I'm very impressed." Hearing the back door open, Eleanor turned to find her son, Frank, lumbering up the steps into the kitchen. She kissed his cheek, silently wishing that he'd shave more closely, then introduced him to Britt.

Britt smiled and shook his hand. "Nice to see you again. Last time we were together, I believe you were wearing shorts, a Twins T-shirt, and a baseball cap pulled over some rather long brown hair."

He ran a hand over his receding hairline. "Time flies when you're having fun." He said the words grimly, barely moving his lips.

"Where's Wendy?" asked Eleanor.

"Um, she couldn't make it. Sorry."

"Everything okay?"

"Just a schedule mix-up."

"Well," said Eleanor, returning to the pan on the stove. "Honey, why don't you take Britt into the dining room and find her a seat at the table. Then come back. You can help me put out the food."

Eleanor began to dish up the roast and vegetables—potatoes, carrots, parsnips, and onions. As she was preparing the pan gravy, Frank returned.

Standing next to her, he lowered his voice and said, "Listen, Mom. The fact is, Wendy and me, we're having some problems. Until we get things settled, can I stay here?"

She turned to face him. "Of course you can. You know I always keep your room in the basement clean and ready for you, if you need it. But . . . what's going on?" The fact was, she'd never liked Wendy and had urged Frank not to marry her. Not that she wanted to see him unhappy.

"I can't talk about it."

"You're all right though, aren't you? Can I do anything to help?"

"No worries. I'll handle it."

Telling a mother not to worry was like telling a cat not to meow. She hesitated, touched his arm. She knew better than to pry, and yet she couldn't help herself. "Won't you at least give me some idea of what's going on?"

"Maybe. But not now."

"What do I tell Lena?"

"Don't tell her anything. It's none of her damn business."

Eleanor took a moment to warn Frank away from several not-to-be-discussed subjects, things she didn't want him to talk about over dinner. In response, he offered her an exasperated sigh as he picked up the platter and carried it out to the table.

Frank and Lena were like feral cats around each other, always ready to pounce at any sign of disapproval, which, as it happened, was the normal state of affairs between them.

After Eleanor dished up the homemade Victoria sauce, a raisin and rhubarb chutney, in her favorite cut-glass bowl, she crossed into the dining room just as the French doors opened and Lena rolled herself out. She seemed exceedingly dour tonight, not looking at anyone as she maneuvered her wheelchair to the opposite end of the table. Unlike Eleanor, who took after their father and liked to think of herself as "a plump, cheerful optimist," Lena was more like their mother—thin and pessimistic. In Eleanor's never-stated opinion, Lena looked ravaged these days. Ninety if she was a day.

Sitting down at the table, Eleanor asked Frank to say grace.

Lena groaned at the suggestion, loud enough for everyone to hear.

As the food was passed around, Frank heaped his plate. Eleanor tried hard not to stare.

"So," said Lena, tapping her fingers on the table and looking straight at Britt. "Who did you vote for for president?"

"No politics at the table," said Eleanor. "You know the rule."

"Just give me a name."

"Clinton," said Britt. "Though Sanders would have been fine with me, too."

"Figures."

"Can't you be polite for five minutes?" asked Frank.

"The food is delicious," said Britt, smiling at Eleanor.

Lena hadn't taken much, and so far, she'd made no attempt to eat. "You're a scientist, Britt? That right?"

"I am. I look for new paradigms in evolution."

"That sounds like a laugh a minute."

"Actually, it's fascinating."

"You believe in evolution?" asked Frank.

"Well, I guess I don't think it requires belief." Looking across at him, Britt asked, "What do you do?"

"Tax preparation."

"Do you like it?"

"It's a job." Before he could continue, the sound of the front doorbell interrupted him.

"Honey, would you get that?" asked Eleanor.

Frank tossed his napkin on the table, rose from his chair, and left the room. A few seconds later, he called, "Butch is here."

Lena brightened as the two men came into the dining room.

"Butch lives next door," said Eleanor, introducing him to Britt. "Our new neighbor."

Butch nodded, removing his baseball cap and holding it in his hands.

"Britt's our niece. She's in town for a conference at the university."

"Are you staying here?" asked Butch.

"At the Marriott Courtyard on the West Bank."

"Well," he said, "nice to meet you. Look, I'm sorry to bother you during dinner, but when I came home a few minutes ago, I saw a couple of kids spray painting something on the side of your house."

"Those little punks," said Frank. "Mom, you should call the police."

"I chased them off," said Butch. "You do know that some of the kids in the neighborhood think your house is haunted."

Eleanor wiped her mouth on a napkin. "So I've heard."

"It *is* haunted," said Lena.

Eleanor raised her eyes to her sister and gave her head a tight shake. "Butch, you're welcome to get a plate in the kitchen and join us."

"No thanks. I've already eaten." He was a sturdy, athletic-looking man with broad shoulders, dark-blond hair, and a beard. Eleanor thought he was terribly nice.

"Well, I better get going," said Butch.

"I'll roll him to the door," said Lena with a barely concealed smirk. She gestured for him to walk in front of her.

"Nice young fellow, don't you think?" asked Eleanor.

"Seems to be," said Britt.

"He's an electrician. Good money in that." She took a spoonful of the Victoria sauce, then passed the glass bowl to her son. "He and Lena seem to have struck up a friendship."

By seven thirty, everyone had finished eating and Eleanor began to remove the dishes.

"Why don't you let me do that?" said Britt, rising from her chair.

"No, you're company. Frank will help me." Once all the leftovers had been stored in plastic containers and refrigerated, she asked her son to make the coffee while she went in search of Britt. She found her in the family room. Britt was crouched next to the wall, but stood up as soon as Eleanor entered. "Something wrong?"

"I dropped one of my earrings." Britt touched her ear. "It was a gift from my mother."

"Should I get the flashlight?"

"It's okay. I found it."

"Oh, good. Good. Now, would you like a piece of apple pie or lemon meringue? Pies are my specialty. They go pretty fast around here."

Britt pressed a hand to her stomach. "Not sure I have room for either, but apple sounds great."

"Wonderful." It was only then that Eleanor noticed how pale her niece's face had grown. "Are you sure you're all right?"

"Me? Fine. Never better."

She hesitated. "Where's Lena?"

"In her room, I think."

Eleanor groaned internally at her sister's lack of manners. "Make yourself comfortable in the living room. Frank and I will be right in." One of these days, she thought, clamping her lips shut to stop herself from saying the words out loud, that sister of hers was going to be the death of her.

3

That night, the wind picked up and the temperature dropped into the low thirties. Jane was glad she'd thought to grab her peacoat before leaving the restaurant. Early December in Minnesota was generally much colder, with several inches of snow on the ground. This year, however, the only things covering the grass were dry leaves. Unusual weather for Minnesota. As she was about to open the door of her Mini, a car pulled up next to her and stopped, its engine idling.

Cordelia Thorn, Jane's oldest and best friend, opened the passenger's door window and called, "Leaving kind of early, aren't we?"

"You checking up on me?"

"Get in."

Jane made herself comfortable in the front seat, glad for the warmth of Cordelia's new black Subaru.

"I still can't get used to your hair," said Cordelia. "Can't believe that, after all these years, you cut it so short."

"I needed a change."

"The Rachel Maddow look."

"No, the Jane Lawless look." If she'd realized how much attention she'd get because of a simple haircut, she never would have done it.

"I stand corrected," said Cordelia, looking amused.

Cordelia's entire life was a costume drama, a period piece, past or future. At the moment, she was sporting a rose-colored wig. Wigs were her new thing after finding a basket filled with them in her sister's rarely used office at the theater.

"Next," said Cordelia, throwing the car in park, "we need to work on your old sweaters and jeans."

"You mean get rid of my clothes?"

"I'm merely suggesting a wee upgrade. I'm not talking Abercrombie & Fitch or Nordstrom, just something other than Old Navy."

Glancing over at her giant friend wearing a heavy, bright red faux fur coat, Jane changed the subject, if only marginally. "Kind of early in the season to bring out the big guns."

"Without snow, it's hard to get in the mood for Christmas. One does what one can."

"How come you're not at the theater?" Along with her younger sister, the Broadway and B-movie star, Octavia Thorn Lester, Cordelia was the owner of the Thorn Lester Playhouse, downtown Minneapolis's newest antique gem. She was also the artistic director, the resident mother superior, and, when necessary, brought the force of a five-star Marine general to whatever situation might need attention.

"I have to pick up Hattie from a friend's house. Neither of them have school tomorrow, so I'm letting Hatts stay out late. Together, she and Juan are discovering the wonders of Juan's chemistry set."

Cordelia had been granted legal custody of her ten-year-old niece many years ago. They'd lived together ever since. "Lucky Hattie," said Jane.

Touching the tip of her finger to her darkly rouged lips, Cordelia continued, "I was at a party last night. I think I may have drummed up a new client for you." She explained about the woman she'd met—Britt something or other—who'd been asking around about local private investigators. "I wondered if she was gay, but I didn't get any vibes."

"So that's where she got my card," said Jane.

"You've already talked to her?"

"This morning. You must have done a good sales job."

"I always do. But back to my original question. How come you're leaving so early? I thought we might share a quick nosh together. One of your pub burgers sounds just about perfect."

"Sorry. Already eaten."

"Then join me for a beer."

"Can't. Not tonight."

"You've been spending a lot of time at home lately, Janey. One cannot help but wonder why."

"Don't start."

"Look, no beating around the mulberry bush this time. I'm worried. That woman somehow conned her way into your home. You need to look around for the coffin she sleeps in during the day. If you can't find it, call me. I'm there for you, Janey. If nothing else, we can burn your house down with her in it."

Jane took a deep breath. "There are times when I find your penchant for exaggeration funny. This isn't one of them."

"I'm not exaggerating."

"Julia's my friend. End of story."

"Is it?"

"What else do you need to know?"

"Oh, come *on*. Don't be so coy."

"You want to know if I'm sleeping with her."

"Give the woman a cigar."

"Look, Cordelia, I care about her. I don't love her, not in any romantic way. Our relationship ended many years ago."

"Did you ever wonder if this illness thingy is just a ploy?"

Now she'd gone too far. "Why don't you come over for dinner? I'll text you with a couple of dates. You can see for yourself how sick she is. But you have to promise to be decent. Friendly."

"Leave my sarcasm at the door?" said Cordelia, feigning shock. She flipped open the glove compartment and removed her stash of bubble gum. "I'll think about it."

Many years ago, Jane and Dr. Julia Martinsen, an oncologist living, at the time, in Bethesda, Maryland, had fallen in love. They'd been in a committed relationship for a couple of years, though Jane had finally ended it. Julia had played fast and loose with the truth too many times. Since then, she and Julia had continued to see each other very occasionally, although they were no longer close. Last spring, Julia had confided to Jane that she'd been diagnosed with a serious illness. Her greatest fear was dealing with it—and perhaps the end of her life—alone. Meaning, without Jane. While Jane had moved on, Julia hadn't.

In a moment of weakness—which Cordelia likened to Armageddon—Jane had promised to be there for her. Even though the love had died long ago, feelings, unlike faucets, couldn't be turned off neatly and easily. For a short time in early October, it appeared as if Julia might not have more than a few months to live. Her failing eyesight had made it impossible for her to drive. That's when Jane had invited her to move into her house. By late October, Julia had rallied and her health had stabilized. And now Jane had a permanent houseguest, which Cordelia maintained was Julia's intention all along.

"I'm the clarion call of reason," continued Cordelia, unwrapping a stick of gum. "You need to listen to me. You may think Julia is water under the bridge, but I'm telling you that unless you burn that bridge to a crisp, she'll find a way to recross it."

"I don't need all the clichés. The message was received."

"She's going to *hurt* you again, Jane."

"How? I already know she lies and that I can't trust her. Are you saying she'll hurt me in some other way? She has cancer, Cordelia, or something very close to it. I know she's not going to live long."

Cordelia raised an eyebrow. "Have you *ever* seen one scintilla of proof that Julia is ill?"

"I have. I've even spoken to a couple of her doctors." Jane had no doubt that the tumor growing behind Julia's optic nerve was real, or that the surgery necessary to remove it was not only just a partial cure, but one fraught with danger. Still, there were things she hadn't told Cordelia, mostly because she wouldn't understand.

"Janey, I say these things to you because I love you."

"I know that. And I'm grateful. But don't worry about me. I'm fine. Clear headed, feet on the ground. Same old Jane you've always known and loved."

"You're impossible, you know that? But okay, end of rant. For now. Call me when you know more about this Britt person's investigative issue. I expect a full report."

Jane could have taken a few minutes to explain what she'd

learned this morning, but she saw no point. Britt hadn't hired her. More than anything, Jane wanted to get home. "Yes, ma'am," she said, saluting. "Full briefing tomorrow at oh-six-hundred."

"I have no idea what that means. Just don't call before noon."

Shortly after ten, as she entered the front foyer of her home, Jane was greeted by two eager dogs vying for her attention. Mouse, a chocolate lab, nosed her hand, his usual earnest self, his tail wagging so fast it was almost a blur. Gimlet, a small black poodle, jumped up and down and twirled around, so excited she could barely keep her balance. How could a person not love dogs? Jane crouched down to give them each a hug and a scratch. When she straightened up, she noticed logs burning in the living room fireplace.

Coming around the end of the couch, she found Julia sitting on the oriental rug with her back propped against the couch. Next to her was a teapot and two cups.

"All the comforts of home," said Jane, sitting down beside her.

Six months ago, Julia had been fit and working hard at a profession she loved. The medication her doctors had prescribed to deal with the growing tumor had proved to be almost as bad as the disease. She'd lost a good twenty pounds off an already lean frame, mostly because the meds didn't mix well with food.

"The fire feels good," said Jane. "Chilly out there."

"I know," said Julia. "I just got home myself."

Julia had hired a personal assistant in mid-October. Carol Westin was a retired RN who'd spent the last twenty years of her working life as a healthcare educator. She and Julia had been friends and coworkers, and now Carol not only acted as chauffeur, but reader of reports and general secretary. Beyond the driving and the reading, she was also helping Julia liaise with lawyers to set up the foundation that would bear Julia's name, one that would continue the work she cared so much about: medical outreach and training in third-world countries. She worked Carol hard, but paid her well.

Gimlet pushed her way in between them, buried her nose under Julia's leg and closed her eyes. Mouse settled down next to Jane. "Have you eaten?"

Julia nodded to the teapot.

"That's not food. Let me make you something."

"No. Don't go."

"But you need to eat."

She poured the steaming liquid into each cup and handed one to Jane. "Not now."

"Soup. There's always room for homemade chicken soup."

"Maybe later."

Jane sipped her tea and gazed into the fire. She didn't want to think about her current situation too critically, but had to admit that it was nice having someone to come home to—someone who'd made a pot of tea and had built a fire. "How was your day?"

"Good," said Julia. "For whatever reason, that awful low-grade headache evaporated." She glanced over at Jane and smiled. "Now that you're home, I'm even better." She slipped her hand over Jane's, then leaned in for a kiss.

Instead of pushing her away, as Jane had for years, she let the kiss linger. Was she playing with fire by sleeping with Julia, as Cordelia feared? She didn't think so. What she'd told Cordelia was accurate. She had no romantic feelings for Julia any longer. This was just . . . what? Affection, perhaps. Whatever it was, Jane wasn't about to end it. It wasn't hurting either of them.

If anything, coming together the way they had after Julia had moved in was good for both of them. It would end one day, and Jane would have to deal with it, but until then, what was the harm?

They sat together quietly, the dogs resting contentedly next to them, and watched the fire.

"Want another cup?" asked Julia.

"No, I'm good."

"Let's go upstairs."

"Aren't you tired?"

"Not in the least."

Jane tipped her head toward Julia. "Why don't you head up? I'll put the dogs out, make sure they have their bedtime treat, and then I'll join you."

After Julia was gone, Jane spent a couple more minutes looking into the dying embers, thinking about Julia and how life often took unexpected turns. She kept repeating the thought, What's the harm? She'd said it to herself so often lately that it was beginning to feel like a mantra. As she was about to get up, her cell phone rang.

"This is Jane," she said after pulling it from her pocket.

"I want to hire you," came a woman's voice.

"Britt?"

"I found proof that Timmy did exist. Can we get together tomorrow?"

"Sure," said Jane.

"What if I meet you at your restaurant around twelve thirty? I don't have anything on my schedule until midafternoon."

"Sounds good. I can't wait to hear what you discovered."

"I'm still processing it, but I will say this much—it blows my mind."

4

Butch Averil's father was a small-town lawyer. Not exactly Atticus Finch, though if you could ignore the fact that he looked more like Pee-wee Herman than he did Gregory Peck, there were similarities.

When residents of Lewiston, Montana, couldn't afford to go anywhere else, they would often come to the house at night to talk to him. Thus Butch grew used to seeing the unmistakable signs of worry on people's faces when they arrived, and the change, the look of hope in their eyes when they left. Not that his dad could work miracles, but he did listen. He tried to make Butch understand that listening was a powerful tool, and that, occasionally, Butch might want to shut up long enough to hear what the people around him were saying. As Butch grew older, he thought about the comment a lot, realizing it was as much an embarrassing commentary on his own teenage years as it was fatherly advice. He tried, as best he could, to take his dad's advice to heart.

Shortly after eleven that night, Butch parked his Yukon in front of his house. As he hopped out, a man jogged across the street toward him. Butch stood his ground next to the driver's door, keys in hand, not sure what the guy wanted. City living, in his opinion, was very different from the quiet of the mountains.

"Thought I'd introduce myself," said the man. "Rich Novak. I'm the block captain. I live in the colonial revival." He pointed.

"Sounds like you know something about architecture."

"A hobby of mine. Anyway, I like to introduce myself to new neighbors. Ain't seen you around before." He was dressed in sweats, Nikes, and a hoodie, and had a thick, almost bushy mustache, the kind that always reminded Butch of a 1980s porn star. "So, we do meetings in my living room on the second Wednesday night of each month. You're welcome to join us."

"Thanks. I'll think about it."

"What's your name?"

"Butch Averil."

Novak walked up to the ROOMS FOR RENT sign on Eleanor and Lena's front boulevard and straightened it. "Never thought old man Hammond would sell that place." He nodded to Butch's house. "It was on the market for a good nine months. I walked through it a couple of times. Ain't in the best shape. I hope you didn't pay and arm and a leg."

"I didn't buy it," said Butch. "I'm renting."

Novak smoothed his mustache. "That right? Hammond never informed me."

Butch couldn't help but notice the guy's annoyance and figured he took his block captain status a bit too seriously. "I've spent a lot of years in construction, so I was able to make a good deal for myself. Reduced rent for agreeing to do repairs."

Novak squinted at the plates on Butch's truck. "Montana?"

"Yup."

"Never been."

"It's the most beautiful place on earth."

"If that's true, how come you're here instead of there?"

Butch shrugged.

"You an outlaw running from that law?"

"Maybe."

"I see you've become friends with Lena. She asking you to buy her booze?" When Butch didn't respond, Novak added, "I done it a couple times. Can't be much fun living in that wheelchair. Eleanor's nice enough, and I know she tries to help, but Lena strikes me as the original lost cause. And then there's Eleanor's son, Frank. That guy needs to seriously cut the apron strings."

"Meaning?"

"Meaning someone should tattoo the word 'loser' on his forehead. He needs to tell his mother to back the hell off. She's nice and all, but she can be controlling. And she babies him. Even keeps a bedroom for him in the basement. The guy's got a wife and a life. Why don't she let him live it?"

Butch had formed similar conclusions, though he didn't think it was right to share them with a stranger.

"Think about coming to the next block meeting," said Novak. "It's good to get to know your neighbors."

"Thanks," said Butch. He dug around in the rear of the Yukon until Novak had returned to his house and gone inside. Grabbing a brown paper sack, he headed up the embankment and crossed the grass to the rear of the Skarsvold house, pausing to remove a small flashlight from his pocket so he could shine a light on the stucco under one of the side windows. The kids he'd seen earlier had spray painted a single word in wavy black letters. "Evil."

Coming into the open backyard, Butch approached the sunroom and tapped on the window closest to the street, the one missing a screen. The shade went up and Lena appeared, lights on behind her. Butch pushed up on the window as Lena pulled from inside. "I should fix this for you," he said. "Make it easier for you to open." He handed the sack through the opening.

Lena passed him a twenty. "Will that cover it?"

This was the second time Butch had bought her a bottle of Old Crow bourbon. It was one of the cheapest brands, though it didn't taste too bad. He'd been living next door since mid-November. Right away, he'd seen her on the front porch and walked over to introduce himself. She'd offered him a cigarette and told him to sit. She explained that, as long as weather permitted—and sometimes even when it didn't—this was her nightly ritual. She said that her sister's head would explode if she smoked in the house.

"Want to join me for a nip?" she asked, her deeply lined face looking hopeful.

He was tired, but felt sorry for her, on her way to sit out there all by herself. "You own a good coat?"

"And wool socks and a fur cap with earflaps. Fashion is my life."

He grinned. "Okay. But I can't stay long."

"Why? You got a hot date?"

Laughing, he whispered, "Only with you."

"Good man." She lowered the window and then the shade.

After climbing the crumbling cement steps up to the porch, Butch held the screen door open as she wheeled herself out, a grocery sack in her lap.

"Will you get rid of these for me?" she asked, handing him the sack.

Inside, he found four empty liquor bottles. "Okay."

"Don't say anything to my sister."

"My lips are sealed."

Pulling a flask and two paper cups out from under her coat, she poured them each a generous inch. She offered him one of her menthol cigarettes, but Butch declined, a move that always seemed to disappoint her.

"So how's the job search going?" she asked, lighting up and looking blissful as she sucked in a lungful of smoke.

"Interviewed for a good one yesterday. I've got my fingers crossed. I should hear by the end of the week." He sat down on the wood railing, but got up when he felt it shift and then crack under his weight. "Your house could use a little work."

"More than a little," said Lena. "But there's no money. El and I live mostly on social security and what we make from renting rooms. Welcome to the joys of old age—in other words, penury."

"Do you both own the house?" he asked, settling down on a painted metal chair, more rust than paint.

"Yeah."

"Why not sell it?"

"Out of the question."

"Because?"

"It's holy. Our great-grandfather built it, that's why it sits kind of crooked on the lot. It used to rest on thirty-five acres of prime farmland. The point is, the house is supposed to be passed down through the family ranks unto the mists of eternity. I grew up here, you know. There were four of us kids. Me, El, our youngest sister Pauline, and our brother, Dan. Dan and Mom died in a car accident when I was still pretty young. I guess you could say Mom never liked driving on highways. She hit a guardrail one night when she was ferrying Dan back from a hockey game, which caused the car to swerve into oncoming traffic. End of Mom and Dan."

"You talk about it so . . . easily."

She tossed back a few swallows of the bourbon. "It happened. Nothing I can do about it now."

Butch wondered if, when he was an old man, he'd be able to talk about his life with such apparent equanimity. "So you've lived here ever since you were a kid?"

"Hell, no," she said, tapping ash into a saucer resting on the floor next to her wheelchair. "I had a life once. Lena Skarsvold was a wild child." She made her eyebrows dance. "Hard to believe that now, looking at me in this damn chair. Arthritis can end your life as you know it."

"Are you in a lot of pain?"

She grunted. "My hips, my knees, my shoulders, my spine."

"Isn't there something a doctor can do?"

"Hell. I was given a bunch of prescription forms of ibuprofen. Not only didn't they help, I ended up in the emergency room with a bad bleed in my stomach. I almost died."

"What about medical marijuana?"

"You have to be on death's door in this state before they'd give it to you for pain."

"Opioids?"

"Nah, I'd rather drink and smoke and end my life awake, buzzed, and happy."

She had a point. If nothing else, drinking was her decision, none of his business. "You know, those kids I saw by your house earlier tonight, they sprayed the word 'evil' under one of the side windows. I thought I could paint over it tomorrow."

"No, leave it there. The world might as well know who we are."

"You're joking, right?" He studied her face. "How did the idea that your house is haunted get started?"

She gazed at him over the rim of the cup. "It *is* haunted. It's a simple fact."

"You believe in ghosts?"

"You think that's crazy?" Tipping the cup back and emptying the contents, she settled more comfortably into her wheelchair. "The first time I realized something strange was going on was when I was living in an apartment over on Rice Street. I would leave in the morning, making sure all the windows were closed and locked. More than once, when I got home, I found the window in my bedroom wide open. At first, I wasn't sure what was going on. The only person with a key to the apartment, other than me, was the landlord, and he was never around, even when I needed something. And then, at night, my bedroom would get freezing cold, even in the dead of summer. The spirit world is real, Butch. Real and dangerous." She poured herself another few inches of bourbon and downed it, wiping a hand across her mouth.

"Has that happened here, too? The thing with the window?"

"No. But there's other stuff. I don't like to talk about it. It scares me." She pulled her coat more closely around her shoulders.

"But how did the kids in the neighborhood find out?"

She held up a gnarled finger. "My fault. See, someone wrote

an opinion piece in the Saint Paul paper about one of those TV shows that investigates ghosts. The guy called it bullshit. I wrote one in response, calling the *guy's* opinion piece bullshit, and believe it or not, it got published. A few weeks later, a man knocked on our door, wanting to talk to me. He was writing a book about hauntings in Minnesota. I told him about my experiences. Signed something that gave him permission to use it in his book, but then I thought better of it and asked him to exclude my comments about our house. I assumed he would. But when the book came out, there it was. People in the neighborhood began talking. Eleanor freaked. And now, we've become 'the official' haunted house."

"Have you ever actually seen a ghost?"

She hesitated. "Maybe."

"Do you think all houses have ghosts?"

"I don't know. But this one does. Another reason to drink." She held up her cup.

Butch hadn't even tasted his. He had work to do tonight and couldn't afford to get juiced. Hearing the front door open, he glanced up to find Frank standing, or perhaps more accurately, looming in the doorway.

"I heard voices," said Frank, opening the door and stepping outside.

"Go away," said Lena. "This is a private conversation."

"Are you two drinking? I smell alcohol."

"It's Butch. He's a real boozer. Show him your cup."

Butch held it up, at the same time noticing that Lena had hidden hers, as well as the flask, in the folds of her coat.

"Now, run along, Frankie." She flicked her hand at him dismissively.

"You should come inside. It's too cold to sit out here."

"Isn't it past your bedtime?"

He glared at her for several seconds, then turned and went back inside.

Lena waited until the door was closed before saying, "He's Eleanor's spy."

"You're kind of hard on him."

She shrugged. "Let me give you a piece of advice. The world consists of two categories of people: your friends and your enemies. It's your life's work to place everyone into their proper slot." She held up the flask. "More?"

"I think Frank's right. I'm cold. Maybe it's time we both turned in."

She blew smoke into the air. "Drink more. You'll warm up."

"No, really. It's late."

"Okay. You run along. I'm a tough old biddy. I'll stay out a while longer."

He lifted up the grocery bag of empty bottles. As he rose from the rickety metal chair, she touched his arm.

"Tell me one thing before you go. Is Butch your real name?"

"Pardon me?"

"Butch. Is it a nickname?"

"I don't like my given name."

"Which is?"

He cleared his throat. "Eugene."

"Ah. Got it." She nodded. "Hey, before you go, as I think about it, maybe you should paint over that graffiti on the side of our house. No use advertising our sins."

"Your . . . sins?"

"Ghosts hang around for a reason, not just because they like the cut of your jib."

He had no idea how to respond. "I'll look for some stucco paint tomorrow."

"Super duper." When he'd reached the sidewalk in front of the porch, she added, "Night night. Eugene."

5

"You're humming. For a second there, I thought you might break into a boisterous whistle." Cordelia stood framed in Jane's office doorway, hand on her generously endowed hip.

Looking up from her laptop, Jane said, "I never whistle."

"I know. So why do I feel one about to burst forth from your lips?"

Jane shut her laptop and leaned back in her chair. Eleven in the morning was the break of dawn for Cordelia. "What brings you here so early? I doubt it's to check on my general happiness."

"*Are* you happy?"

Jane thought about it. "Yes, I think I am."

"Any particular reason?"

"Stop fishing. If you have a question, ask it directly."

Cordelia entered and draped herself over the couch. She sighed, casting an eye at Jane to make sure she was watching, then sighed even more loudly.

"You're not happy, I take it."

"No."

"Any particular reason?"

"The usual."

"My advice is, don't watch the news before you go to bed."

"Hard to turn away from a political train wreck."

Jane and Cordelia had spent entire days mulling over the current state of politics. Cordelia was angry and wanted to join every march, picket every representative, and generally analyze every twist and turn. Jane's reaction was to read, to plow through books, blogs, and magazine articles to help her make sense of the country and the times in which she was living.

"So you came here to sleep on my couch?" asked Jane.

"Do I look like I'm sleeping?"

"Are you hungry?"

Her face brightened.

They settled themselves in the upstairs dining room, at a table near one of the windows overlooking Lake Harriet. Cordelia seemed intrigued by the new winter menu. "This looks so different. Where did all the adjectives and verbs go, all the sourcing info and culinary poetics?"

"I wanted to try something simpler, more direct. As for sourcing, I would hope our customers could trust by now that we're finding the best possible food and serving it with creativity and elegance."

Cordelia took longer than usual to decide what to order. She finally settled on a short rib potpie with a side of honey and ginger roasted sweet potatoes.

Jane had seen the morning fish order arrive, so she ordered the pan-seared scallops with roasted turnips and rainbow carrots.

41

She liked her scallops with nothing but a squeeze of lemon as a garnish. The vegetables were finished with cream, bacon, and freshly grated parmesan.

"Are you happy now?" asked Jane.

"I'm getting there. Hard to be cynical about food."

Jane made a habit of eating in the dining room at least once a week. She felt it was important to get a customer's-eye view of the experience, though she knew her cooks and waitstaff took extra care when she was the one at the table.

"Hey," said Cordelia, squinting and then jerking her head away.

Jane turned to look.

"No, no. She'll see us."

"She who?"

"Sylvia Moon. You know——Moon & Burroughs Creative? You met her once at one of my parties. She's been around forever. Must be in her eighties if she's a day. Did I mention I loathe her?"

"Who's that with her?"

Cordelia tapped a finger against her chin.

Jane wasn't sure, but she thought she heard the word "enchanting" escape Cordelia's lips. Turning, she motioned for the server. At the same time, she took a better look at the two women engaged in an intense conversation at a table near the hearth. "Enchanting" was hardly the word Jane would have used to describe the younger of the two. The woman had wildly curly red hair and looked as if she'd just escaped a violent windstorm. She was heavy-set and middle-aged, with weathered skin and heavy eye makeup.

When the server arrived, Jane asked for a glass of the house Chablis.

"Wonder who she is?" mused Cordelia. "Probably not a model."

"Probably not," agreed Jane. She glanced up in time to see her upcoming appointment walk through the double doors into the dining room, more than an hour early.

"So sorry," said a serious-looking Britt, a leather computer case slung over one shoulder. "I know we said twelve thirty."

Cordelia drew her eyes away from Sylvia Moon's companion long enough to look up. "Hey, don't I know you?"

Britt blinked. "You're the woman I met at that party the other night. The one who gave me Jane's card."

"Small world," said Jane.

"Look, I know I'm early," continued Britt. "I've got plenty of work to do, so I can meet you in the pub whenever you're done."

"No, no, no," said Cordelia. "I won't have it. Anything you have to say to Jane, you can say to me. We're partners in crime, you know. Have been for years."

Britt seemed puzzled. "Okay, but . . . I thought you were a theater director."

"I contain multitudes, to quote my old buddy Walt Whitman. Anyway, when it comes to detection, Jane's the brawn. I'm the brains." Removing the rhinestone-encrusted reading glasses perched low on her nose, she added, "You know, Janey, we should put that on those cards of yours. Truth in advertising."

"You mean 'caveat emptor'?" asked Jane.

"Exactly. No, wait. What?"

Clearing her throat, Jane invited Britt to order lunch. She motioned for one of the servers to bring a menu.

"Everything is good here," said Cordelia, flapping her napkin in front of her and then tucking it into the neck of her sweater.

When the server brought Jane's wine, Britt ordered a cup of coffee. "This is all I need, really. After what happened last night, I'm too keyed up to eat."

"Never happens to me," Cordelia whispered into her glass of iced tea.

Jane quickly brought Cordelia up to speed on the case. She was right about one thing: Jane did lean on her when she needed a sounding board, though at times Cordelia's snap judgments, otherwise known as her infallible intuition, sent Jane careening in exactly the wrong direction.

"So what happened last night?" asked Cordelia as her lunch was set in front of her.

Britt played with her napkin. "It was a strange evening all around. Sometimes I felt like I was in the middle of a family fight, while other times it was like being inside a Scandinavian art film. Anyway, after dinner, I had a few minutes to myself, so I wandered back into the living room. When I looked up the stairway I had this sudden memory. I recalled being upstairs in one of the bedrooms. I must have been asleep when Timmy came into the room because all I remember is his face looming over me. It was early morning. He started bouncing on the mattress and grabbed my hand. I can still hear his voice telling me to get up, to come with him. I followed him down the stairs. He put a finger to his lips, said, 'Everyone's asleep. We gotta be quiet.' He opened the pocket door into his grandfather's study."

"He was your grandfather, too, right?" said Cordelia between bites.

"Yeah, but I never met him, so he might as well have been a ghost. Anyway, Timmy ran in and said something like, 'Cool place, huh?' There were several big, overstuffed chairs, one large potted plant, books and magazines on a bookshelf, and then a roll-top desk toward the back of the room."

Jane sipped her coffee, marveling at the vividness of Britt's recall.

"Timmy hopped up onto this leather swivel chair by the desk. 'Come on, let's draw,' he said. He found a couple of pads of paper in one of the desk slots. He gave me one, along with a pen. And then he climbed down and said something like 'You draw and I will, too. And then we'll play hide-and-seek like we did yesterday. Except this time, we'll hide our drawings.' We hunkered down on the rug to create our masterpieces. We hadn't been at it for more than a few minutes when we heard the stairs creak. Timmy tore his picture from the pad and then grabbed mine. He put the pads back, and we each hopped up on a chair. We were sitting there, more or less twiddling our thumbs, trying to look innocent, when Eleanor came in. She told us that we needed to go upstairs and get dressed in our good clothes because we were all going to church. I would imagine it was the day of the funeral."

"Interesting," said Cordelia, tapping a napkin against her mouth. "But a memory isn't exactly proof of Timmy's existence."

"Just wait. The study is now a TV room. As I stood there, I remembered that Timmy had slipped the pictures we'd drawn into a crack between the wall and the baseboard, sort of close to the desk, which was where the TV is now. I eased myself behind it and ran my hand along the baseboard. When I didn't find anything, I found a paperclip in my pocket, straightened it and pushed it down into a couple of the more visible cracks. I didn't really think the drawings would still be there, but on the third try I hit pay dirt." She removed two folded pieces of paper from the pocket of her cardigan. "Here," she said.

Both pages had grown yellowed and fragile with age. When Jane unfolded the first one, she found a child's drawing of a boat with waves, a flock of birds—elongated *V*s—the sun in the sky, and a name scrawled in big, loopy letters at the bottom. "Timmy," she said, looking up.

"Let me see that," said Cordelia, reaching across the table.

"I'm not crazy," said Britt. "Timmy *was* real. He was there and so was I. Eleanor and Lena are lying about him and I need to know why."

It wasn't the kind of proof that would hold up in a court of law, though for Jane, it was more than enough.

"Can you help me? Can you find out what happened to him?"

"Of course we can," said Cordelia, studying the drawings. "No problem."

"I can't promise anything," said Jane. "But if you hire me, I'll do my best."

"Have you ever had a case like this before?" asked Britt.

"I've found missing people, but we knew they existed. And they'd left tracks. We have no idea what happened to Timmy."

"Those aunts of yours," said Cordelia, handing the drawings back. "We'll put the screws to them. Find out what's what."

Britt toyed with her coffee cup. Looking down, she said, "I got the impression that they don't want to see me again. They were happy to have me over for dinner last night, but when Eleanor said goodbye, she wished me well, like she didn't expect to ever see me again. Lena was even less friendly. Even if I wanted to go back to the house, I doubt they'd talk to me. You're my last hope to make sense of this."

"Look," said Jane, seeing the hurt in Britt's eyes, "you have to accept that, if I can find the answers you're looking for, it might not be a positive outcome."

"You mean that Timmy's dead."

"It's possible."

"Anything's possible," offered Cordelia, sneaking another look at the women across the room. "Maybe your aunts did away with him." Seeing Britt's reaction, she added, "Or maybe not."

"I want to hire you," said Britt. "Do I have to sign something? I can write you a check right now, as a retainer. Or whatever you call it."

Jane spent a few minutes discussing her process and her cost. She hadn't touched her lunch and looked down longingly at the scallops as she began to jot down some notes, enough to get her started. "I'll prep the papers and you can sign them the next time we meet. For now, the check will be enough."

Britt took out her checkbook. When she was done making the check out, she left it on the table, shook Jane's hand, and then smiling, shook Cordelia's. "Keep me posted."

"Will do," said Cordelia. "And just an FYI, we know how to apply the third degree."

Britt cocked her head. "People don't use the third degree anymore, do they?"

Cordelia smiled. "Not since the FBI developed all those wonderfully inventive junk science methods of crime scene investigation, like bite mark analysis, handwriting analysis, hair analysis. Just an FYI. We don't do much forensic evaluation. But never fear, we know how to do our jobs."

After Britt left, Jane picked up her fork and took a taste of her lunch.

"She's a real trip."

"We all are."

Cordelia stiffened. "They're coming over to our table."

"Who's coming?"

"Sylvia," said Cordelia brightly, standing and taking both of the old woman's hands in hers. "So wonderful to see you."

"Likewise, darling. This is all so fortuitous. I have someone I want Jane to meet." Waving a hand at the windblown woman next to her, she said, "This is Berengaria Reynolds. You may know the name. The Berengaria winery in Sonoma?"

Jane rose from her chair. "Of course. Russian River, right?"

"I'm flattered," said Berengaria.

"Every sommelier I've ever known adores your wines. I'd feature them on a regular basis, but we have trouble finding them." Berengaria Reynolds was a cult star in the world of wine. She'd made her name on a Cab-Syrah blend, a world-class offering that had won numerous awards. She continued to produce fine wines, though, as with many great vintages, they were made in such small quantities that they sold out quickly. "What are you doing in Minnesota?"

"Oh, a little of this, a little of that. Mainly, I'm consulting with a couple friends who own a local vineyard."

"Have you tried our ice wine?" asked Cordelia, removing the napkin from the neck of her sweater.

Casting her first real look at Cordelia, Berengaria said, "You like sweet wines?"

"I like sweet everything."

She raised an eyebrow. "And you are?"

"Cordelia Thorn. Artistic director and owner of the Thorn Lester Playhouse."

Cordelia was six feet tall. Beside her, Berengaria looked like a dwarf. "Your first name," Cordelia continued. "It's . . . big. I love big."

"You an English history buff?"

"Film. Cecil B. DeMille. *The Crusades*, 1935. Loretta Young played Berengaria and Henry Wilcoxon played Richard the First."

This elicited an amused smile from the vintner. They continued to lock eyes until Jane cleared her throat. "Would you like to join us?"

"Can't," said Sylvia. "Berengaria has an appointment in Saint Paul and we're already running late."

Tearing her eyes away from Cordelia, Berengaria said, "I'm traveling with a few of my newest vintages. If you have time, Ms. Lawless, I'd like to get your thoughts on them."

"Please, call me Jane. And yes, I'd love that." She removed a business card from the back pocket of her jeans and handed it over.

"I'll call and we'll make a date. You're invited, too," she said, inclining her head toward Cordelia. "If you can bring yourself to drink a few wines that aren't sweet."

"I imagine there will be compensating factors," said Cordelia, matching Berengaria's smile with an amused one of her own.

Jane returned to her plate of food, now cold and completely unappetizing. She reached for the breadbasket.

"My gaydar just exploded, crashed, and burned," said Cordelia, waving air into her face.

"You think she's a member of the tribe?" Had they been standing near a pile of birch logs, Jane was sure the sparks from the encounter would have ignited a conflagration bigger than the historic Chicago fire.

"I need a cigarette," said Cordelia. "I am utterly and totally smitten."

Jane buttered a piece of sourdough. "If that's true, then my advice would be, don't mention the fact that your favorite beverage is black cherry soda. You also might want to dig out your copy of *Wine for Dummies* and do some serious studying."

6

Frank paused for a moment on the stairway landing between the living room and kitchen. He'd been upstairs taking a shower and was on his way back to the basement to get dressed when he heard someone banging on the piano. The old upright sat tucked against the stairs. Gazing down at the little girl plunking away on her god-awful song and then over at a sour-faced Lena, Frank came to the conclusion that there were worse ways to make money than tax preparation.

Frank saw himself as an underachiever. His mother had encouraged him to attend college, even saying she'd do whatever she could, on her nurse's salary, to help him pay for it. She wanted him to get into a respectable, moneymaking profession—lawyer, doctor, dentist, banker—but all Frank could manage in his youth was a two-year accounting degree, which got him exactly nowhere. He knew what he wanted to do, but he also knew that it would mean he'd have to live in his mother's basement for the rest of his natural life. Accounting, at the very least, gave him a few options.

The fact that his second marriage was coming apart meant that he was about to fail on another front. He wasn't willing to admit that it was over. Wendy had given him an ultimatum yesterday: Grow the hell up or get out. Okay, so he wasn't much good at being an adult. In fact, he wasn't much good at anything these days. Something had to change and he figured that something had to be him.

After finding some clean clothes in the basement closet, he left his bed unmade, an empty, rumpled bag of potato chips peeking out from under the covers, and made his way up to the kitchen. The pathetic banging continued, the perfect soundtrack to his morning depression. His mother and Iver Dare, the senior pastor at Cumberland Park Lutheran in Saint Paul and an old friend, were seated at the round oak table, enjoying a cup of coffee and one of his mother's caramel rolls.

"Morning," grunted Frank.

Iver glanced at his watch. "I believe this is technically afternoon."

"Did you sleep all right?" asked Eleanor.

Frank got down a box of Cocoa Krispies from the cupboard. "Yeah. Thanks." He dumped the cereal into a bowl and then moved over to the refrigerator to get some milk.

"I have good news for you," said Iver.

"That would be unique."

"You know that mural you painted in the church basement?"

Of course he remembered it. It was one of the few times he'd been paid to do what he loved. Murals weren't in high demand back in the eighties, when he still thought he could make mural painting his career. All the walls in the basement were covered with his handiwork. As a teenager, he'd spent every spare minute down there learning his craft. He'd paint one mural, snap a Polaroid, then gesso over it and paint another. Until he gave up. What was the point? With the exception of his mother, nobody gave a rat's ass.

"Yes," said Frank between bites. "I remember it."

"We have a new member. His name is Walter Mann. He came to me after services last Sunday asking if I knew anything about the person who painted it."

"He wants to have me arrested?"

"No, no, of course not. He was very impressed. He'd like to talk to you. I hope you don't mind. I gave him your phone number."

Frank chewed his cereal. He would bet money that the guy would never call. And even if he did, it would be a couple compliments and that's it.

"Actually," said Iver, pushing away from the table. "He gave me his card. I think it's in my coat. Let me get it for you."

As soon as they were alone, Frank sat down next to his mother. He pointed to her ears and asked, "You got your hearing aids in?"

"Yes," she said, looking concerned.

"Listen up, then. I found Lena on the porch last night with Butch. She'd been drinking. I could smell the alcohol. She said it was Butch, but I was standing almost directly in front of her. It was Lena, I know it."

His mother's expression turned serious.

"You have to talk to her."

"I can't believe, after all these years, she'd start up again."

"Once an alcoholic, always an alcoholic. You know what she's like when she's drinking."

Eleanor began twisting the napkin in her lap. "I don't know. Maybe I should ask Iver to talk to her."

"I say we search her bedroom. Find out where she's hidden the bottles and get rid of them."

"Who's buying them for her?"

"Butch? Novak? Who knows? Who cares? She's getting it somewhere and it has to stop before she blats out something she can't take back."

Iver returned to the room and handed Frank the business card.

"Thanks," said Frank. He studied it for a few seconds. "I better get going or I'll be late for an appointment."

"Will you be staying here again tonight?" asked his mother.

"I don't know." He felt in his back pocket for his wallet.

"I'll go down and tidy up your room, just in case."

"No," he said quickly. "Please don't." The idea that his eighty-year-old mother would offer to make his bed was humiliating. He should have taken care of it himself. He sucked so bad at life. Digging into his pocket for his car keys, he couldn't leave fast enough.

Frank figured that if he kept his 1997 Chevy Suburban long enough, it might actually be worth money one day. As it was, with just over two hundred thousand miles on it, it was a rolling piece of junk. But it was big and spacious, necessary for a big spacious guy like himself. And because he could still find repair parts on the internet, he kept fixing what was wrong. The rust was a different matter.

Parking in a lot outside a one-story brick building just off Stinson Boulevard, Frank pushed the driver's door open with his foot, cringing at the sound of screeching metal. He entered through a glass security door and walked into a large waiting room. Seeing half a dozen people sitting in the room, he squeezed himself into a chair next to an aquarium. Even the angelfish had little interest in him. He felt like Eeyore, the old, gray, stuffed donkey in the Winnie-the-Pooh books. Or, put in more contemporary language, he was a walking, talking, human buzz kill.

"Frank?" said the receptionist, motioning at him. "Dr. Bachelder will see you now."

Frank had been coming to the Forrester Clinic of Family Psychology for a couple of months. His therapist, Dr. Craig Bachelder, was an older man who reminded him of Pastor Dare. Bachelder might be a decade younger, with shaggy silver hair and horn-rimmed glasses, while Pastor Dare combed his thinning gray hair straight back from a high forehead and wore wire rims, and yet beyond the physical, they were brothers under the skin. Both men were bookish, natural mediators with soothing voices and calm, almost Zen-like demeanors. Sometimes it felt to Frank as if the two men had been let in on a secret that had escaped the rest of humanity—knowledge that allowed them to negotiate life with an equanimity lesser mortals found impossible.

Frank took a seat on an uncomfortable chair with a rigid back across from Bachelder's more comfortable leather recliner. "Thanks for seeing me on such short notice."

"When you called, you said something about a fight with your wife."

"Yeah," said Frank, crossing his legs and then uncrossing them. "It was a bad one. She told me to leave. Didn't want to talk to me again until I'd had a chance to speak with you."

"I see. I wish I had more time to give you today. Why don't you tell me what the fight was about?"

"Oh, you know. The usual marital crap. Something small that escalated. But . . . we said things that will be hard to take back. She got really angry, went after my relationship with my mother. Said she was sick of living with a man like me."

"A man like you?"

"She thinks my mom bosses me around too much."

"Does she?"

"Well, sometimes. I think Wendy was also talking about my depression."

"Are you still taking the medication I prescribed?"

"Oh, yeah, of course." He wasn't. He might not be sure of much, but he knew a pill wasn't going to solve the kind of problems he had.

"You know, Frank. I've been seeing you for what"—he checked his notebook—"almost seven weeks. Several times you've alluded to something that happened in your past that continues to haunt your present, and yet, whenever I move the conversation in that direction, you refuse to talk about it. It makes me wonder why you're here."

"I—" He didn't know what to say. His wife had suggested seeing a therapist, but Wendy suggested lots of things he never acted on.

"I don't usually make this kind of blanket statement, but . . . since we don't seem to be making any real progress, I'm going to just say it. You're a very angry man, Frank."

"I am?"

"Depression is often anger turned inward. Sometimes it's easier for us to handle our anger if we can diffuse or deflect it. The problem is, you can't bury your feelings forever. They have a way of leaking out. Are you afraid of your anger, Frank?"

He took a breath, held it.

"This fight you had with Wendy. Did it get physical?"

"You mean, did I hurt her? I didn't lay a finger on her. I'd never do that."

"Good. That's good."

"Look," said Frank, leaning back in his chair. "If I am angry, it's at myself, nobody else."

"Why is that?"

"Because I'm a failure."

"In what way?"

"In every way. I don't deserve happiness."

Dr. Bachelder closed his notebook. "This . . . thing that happened. Was it a long time ago?"

"I don't want to talk about it."

"Were you a child?"

He hesitated, his eyes skirting the room. "I was thirteen."

"And your father died when you were—"

"He was killed in Vietnam. He deployed when I was a baby. I don't even remember him."

"Thirteen can be a difficult age, especially without a dad."

"Tell me about it. But knowing that isn't getting me anywhere with my wife. I need your advice. Should I stay away for a few days, give her some time to cool off? Or maybe . . . I mean, I was thinking I could bring her flowers."

"Do you love her, Frank? Do you want to work things out?"

"Absolutely."

"Does she know anything about this problem in your past?"

"No, of course not."

"Tell me. Are you generally open with her about what you're feeling?"

"I don't know. Yeah. Sometimes."

"You might want to ask yourself this question. Do you think your lack of openness makes her feel cut off from you?"

"Now you sound like my wife. I'm never going to be anybody's open book. Take it or leave it."

"There's the anger I was talking about. The truth is, Frank, it's hard to live with silence. If you give Wendy the choice between taking you with your silence or leaving you, how would you feel if she chose the latter?"

This wasn't getting him anywhere. Rising from his chair, he said, "Thanks for nothing."

"I'm sorry you feel that way," said Bachelder, rising with his notebook tucked under his arm. "I hope you'll come back so we can continue our conversation. But, as always, the decision is yours."

On his way back through the waiting room, Frank's cell phone rang. Fishing it out of his pocket, he swept a finger over the screen. "Hello?" he said, holding it to his ear.

"Is this Frank Devine?"

"Yeah?" He pushed through the glass door and stood leaning against the hood of his Suburban.

"My name is Walter Mann. I'm the executive editor at Rupert A. Wilson Publishing. I wonder if you'd be willing to stop by my office sometime in the next couple of days. I have something I'd like to discuss with you."

"Can you be more specific?"

"Give me a sec."

Frank heard voices in the background, several people all speaking at once.

When Mann came back on the line, he said, "I'm afraid I have a situation here that requires my immediate attention. Let me have my secretary call you and we can set up a time to get together. That work for you?"

"Sure. I guess."

"Wonderful. Hope to see you soon."

As Frank opened his car door and slid into the front seat, he wondered what fresh horror this guy was about to bring into his life.

7

Twilight was beginning to settle over Saint Paul as Jane parked her SUV a block away from the home of Britt's aunts, Eleanor Skarsvold Devine and Lena Skarsvold. She'd surveyed the area to get the general lay of the land, but wanted a closer look at the house before she drove back to her restaurant to begin some on-line research.

As she made her way down the cracked sidewalk, a chilly wind scattered dry leaves across her path. The closer she got to the end of the block, the more obvious it became that the Skarsvold property was terribly rundown. The house sat farther back from the street than the other houses along Cumberland Avenue. It had elements of the Arts and Crafts style, with tall gables and a broad porch flanked by large, square posts. Once upon a time it had likely been sided with wood, though somewhere along the line someone had covered it with stucco, now cracked and badly discolored. Much of the paint on the dark green window trim had pealed off long ago, revealing whole sections of rotted wood. Many of the screens were rusted. A few were missing. Around the perimeter was a tangle of vines and dead shrubs partially covering a crumbling fieldstone foundation. In a neighborhood where the rest of the homes were smaller but well tended, the Skarsvold place stood out.

Jane paused for a few seconds, gazing up at the once stately home, hands in her pockets, wondering what it had looked like when it was new. Was it poverty, neglect, or something else that had caused such a decline? Whatever the case, the house, with its low, curled roofline over an unscreened porch, seemed dark and brooding, as if the people inside were hiding from the world. And that was why the FOR RENT sign stuck into the grass on the boulevard seemed so incongruous.

ROOMS AVAILABLE
WEEKLY MONTHLY
INQUIRE WITHIN

Jane glanced up as a pickup truck rolled around the corner and pulled to a stop across the street. A workman in white painter pants, white cap, and a dark hoodie hopped out. A second later a light came on over the door of one of the houses and a woman stepped out onto the concrete stoop, calling, "We need at least three more gallons."

"Aw, crap. I only got two."

The woman in the doorway shrugged, disappearing back inside.

Seeing Jane, the man waved. He slammed the cab door and then trotted across the street. "You looking for a place to rent? The bedrooms are nice, not real big, but clean. I've seen 'em."

"You live around here?" asked Jane. The guy was skinny, middle-aged, with a bushy mustache.

"Rich Novak," he said, extending his hand. "I'm the block captain. I live in that colonial revival back there." He turned and pointed. When he saw Jane look at the house where the woman had just emerged, he said, "The wife and I are rehabbing that one. It's a Foursquare. Got it for a super price."

"You flip houses?"

"Well, yes and no. I'm a mechanic. But yeah, in my spare time, I like to stay busy with side jobs to make a little extra. This is our first try at rehabbing."

"Good luck," said Jane.

"It's a nice neighborhood, in case you're wondering. Two old ladies own that place." He nodded toward the house. "They rent out rooms to make extra money."

"You know them?"

"Oh, yeah, for sure. They're quiet. Keep mostly to themselves. Someone's always home, so if you want to look, I'm sure it wouldn't be a problem." He hesitated. "You from around here?"

"No," said Jane.

"Just traveling through?"

"You could say that." She wondered if he gave everyone the same kind of interrogation.

"Hey, come on, Richard," called his wife, sticking her head out the front door. "If I'm gonna keep goin', I need that paint."

"When the ball and chain calls, I gotta obey." He grinned. "Maybe I'll see you around."

Jane tried not to cringe. She loathed that sort of reference to a wife or girlfriend. She waited as he ran back across the street, reached into the bed of his truck, and retrieved the paint. As he went inside, she made a quick decision. The lawn sign gave her a way into the house to meet Britt's aunts. It seemed like such a stroke of luck that she couldn't ignore it.

A sign under the front doorbell said, NOT WORKING. PLEASE KNOCK. Jane rapped on the wood next to a lace-covered oval of glass. A few seconds later, a single, bony finger hooked back the lace. The door opened, revealing a plump elderly woman with a halo of white hair. "Can I help you?"

"I'm interested in renting one of your bedrooms."

The woman peered at her through a pair of rimless glasses before saying, "Please. Come in."

The interior of the house smelled like coffee and cinnamon rolls, and appeared to be in better shape than the exterior. The living room was warm and inviting, with a muted mustard-colored paint on the walls, a fireplace flanked by built-in bookcases and a mantel filled with photographs. The furniture wasn't antique, although it was old. If Jane had to guess, she would have said it was all circa 1970s. Lots of oranges, avocado greens, and golds, a color scheme so dated that it was coming back into style. The wood floor was covered by a threadbare oriental. Directly to her right were half-open pocket doors revealing a den with a TV. Jane assumed it was there that Britt had discovered the drawings. An upright piano sat against the stairway.

"Are you interested in renting by the week or the month?" asked Eleanor.

"The week," said Jane. She wasn't sure how much information she'd need to give, which could be a problem.

"We don't ask you to sign a lease. But we don't accept checks or credit. Just cash."

"That's fine." Jane wondered if she was really going to rent one of the bedrooms.

Eleanor introduced herself, explaining the various rules. "We don't allow you to use the kitchen, but there are microwaves in two of the rooms. We mostly get students because we're so close to the U of M agricultural campus." She smiled, smoothing her apron. "If you'll follow me?"

Halfway up the stairway was a landing. One side of the stairway led up from the living room, the other down into the kitchen. Making a left, they continued on up a longer flight of stairs to a second floor landing. Eleanor opened up three doors, turned on the overhead lights in each room, and allowed Jane to look around. "As you can see, two of the rooms are the same size. One has a single bed, a large dresser, and comfortable reading chair and floor lamp. The other has a double bed with a smaller dresser and a desk."

Jane was drawn to the room with the double bed. The furniture was old but sturdy, the wallpaper a light green damask pattern. The block captain had been right when he said the rooms were clean. There was something almost *Little House on the Prairie*–esque about them. Perhaps it was the lack of clutter. "Do you have Wi-Fi?"

Eleanor laughed. "We'd never be able to rent to students if we didn't provide that. My sister, Lena, she's on the . . . the Facebook all the time. I was never much of a computer person. I guess that makes me a dinosaur."

"This room would work for me."

Eleanor seemed pleased. "Oh, I should mention. We have a garage for rent. It would be an extra fee. This has been an unusually warm fall, but we're going to get snow. If you have a car—"

"I do."

"Would you like to see it?"

"Sure."

Eleanor led the way back downstairs into the kitchen. She removed a flashlight from one of the drawers, and then, lifting her coat off a hook by the back door, she said. "Our backyard light is burned out. I keep meaning to ask my son to replace it."

"I could do that for you," said Jane. "If you have a ladder."

Eleanor turned to her. "That's so kind of you. But Frank's staying here for a few days, so let me see if I can get him to take care of it."

The backyard was unfenced, the grass dry and patchy. Eleanor buttoned up her coat as she carefully negotiated what was left of the narrow sidewalk. "I used to love gardening," she said. "All I can manage these days is making sure the house is clean, and even then, I need help from a lady in my church." As she approached the double garage doors, she removed a set of keys from her pocket. "We use a padlock," she said, slipping a key into the lock and tugging it apart. "It's a little larger than your usual one stall. My father used it as a workshop back in the day. My great-grandfather built the home in 1881. It's been our family's home ever since."

Jane's cell phone rumbled inside her pocket. She removed it and checked to see who was calling.

"Do you need to take that?" asked Eleanor, turning her flashlight on the interior, revealing an uneven floor covered with a thin layer of crumbling concrete. "We used to have electricity out here, but it doesn't work anymore. I haven't wanted to spend the money to get it repaired."

Jane walked in, using a flashlight app on her cell phone to illuminate the long, battered workbench, the open shelves. Everything was covered in a thick layer of dust.

"My son painted that," said Eleanor, nodding to the mural on the rear wall.

"Wow," said Jane, walking closer. It was wonderfully colorful, filled with strange, unearthly birds and animals. "He's talented. Do you mind if I get a picture?"

"Of course not."

Jane held up her phone and took several.

"So," said Eleanor, bending down to pick up a discarded Styrofoam cup, "would this work for you? I hear we may get snow in the next few days."

"Sleet tomorrow night." Jane hated this in-between kind of weather, when the temperature hovered around freezing. It wasn't warm enough for rain, but not cold enough for snow. If she really was going to stay for a few days, renting the garage was probably a smart idea. "Yes, I'd like to rent it."

"Wonderful," said Eleanor. "Why don't we go back in the house? I'll get you a key for the padlock, one for the front door, and then we can settle your bill."

As they trudged back through the dark, Jane wondered if she was making the right decision. For good or ill, it seemed she was about to become a temporary member of the Skarsvold household.

8

Jane's plans for the evening had changed. Instead of returning to the restaurant to do online research on the Skarsvold case, she returned to her house to pack an overnight bag and explain to Julia that she'd be gone for a couple of nights.

Julia was generally home by six. Entering through the front door, Jane set her briefcase down in the foyer and then crouched to give her dogs the usual mix of scratches and hugs. Mouse carried a ball in his mouth and dropped it next to her foot, hoping for some playtime. "You are such a good boy," she said, giving his ears a gentle pull. Gimlet couldn't seem to stop spinning. "Come here," said Jane, scooping the little poodle up and cradling her. "You're a wiggle worm." She grabbed the ball and tossed it into the living room. Mouse ran after it, nearly crashing into the couch.

Walking into the dining room, Jane found Carol Westin working alone at the table. As soon as Julia had moved in, the dining room table became her makeshift office. Carol sat amid stacks of papers and file folders, typing on a laptop. Julia often sat across from Carol, but tonight, seemed to be missing in action.

Carol tilted her head toward the kitchen. "If you're hungry, I heated some of that soup you brought from the restaurant. There's a lot left."

"Where's Julia?"

"She wasn't feeling well, so she went up to bed."

"This early?" Jane lowered herself into one of the chairs. "Is the headache back?"

"Yeah. Think so."

"Did she take some of her painkillers?"

"I hope so."

Jane kissed Gimlet's head, watching Carol type. "Between you and me, how's she doing?"

Carol typed a moment more, then stopped, sighed, and looked up. "She had a meeting again with that doctor over at the university."

"I thought she was seeing Dr. Hansman at the Medical Arts building downtown."

"Dr. Reid took over in early November. As I understand it, he's more of a specialist. She never really confides in me about her illness."

Jane was beginning to get the sense that Julia wasn't confiding in her either.

"I'm not sure what Dr. Reid said, but I don't think it was good news. She went in for another CT scan last week. Did she mention that?"

Jane shook her head.

"Well, everyone handles things differently."

"What are you working on?" asked Jane, nodding to the papers.

"Foundation stuff. There's so much to do, but, little by little, we're getting there. We have meetings with lawyers all day tomorrow."

"You think Julia will be well enough to do that?"

"Sometimes I don't know where she finds the strength, but yeah, she'll be there."

"Listen, Carol, I'm going to be gone the next couple of nights. It's part of a new case I'm working on. I don't really want to leave her alone. I don't suppose you could stay. You know, just in case she needs something and I'm not around."

"Why not? I've got nothing at home but a cat who wouldn't care if I never appeared, as long as he had enough food. I wanted a sweet, friendly little guy, but instead I adopted a sleek, gorgeous Norman Bates."

"That bad?"

"He's a sociopath. Of course, you could probably make a case that all cats are sociopaths."

"Ouch."

"Oh, don't get me wrong. I love him. But being around your dogs, it just makes me realize that affection isn't his strong suit." She took off her glasses and rubbed her eyes. "I'll need about an hour to run home and pick up some things."

"Take your time," said Jane. "And thanks."

After the dogs gobbled down their evening kibble in the kitchen, Jane let them out into the backyard, watching them through the window over the sink as she ate a quick bowl of soup. When they were finished, she wiped off their paws. Knowing she had a treat, Mouse kept sniffing her hand as she climbed up the stairs. Entering the bedroom, she pointed to the dog bed in the corner and both dogs hopped in. She handed them each a Milk-Bone, whispering for them to lie down. Mouse was his usual obedient self, but Gimlet seemed more interested in jumping up on the bed to be with Julia. For some reason, pointing at Gimlet and looking stern seemed to impress the little poodle. After twirling a couple more times, she snuggled down next to Mouse and began to crunch her way through the treat.

Jane sat down on the bed next to Julia, watching her breathe softly into a blanket she'd bunched under her chin. In the dim light, her face was still so young and lovely, with a vulnerability she masked, often at great expense, while awake. The work she was doing with Carol was fundamentally end-of-life planning. After what Carol had told her, Jane wondered if there was some new wrinkle in either her health or her treatment. The lack of trust that had existed between them for so many years continued to have repercussions. Habit was hard to break.

"You're home," said Julia, opening her eyes, a faint smile on her lips.

"I didn't mean to wake you. How are you feeling?"

She turned on her back, held the palm of her hand to one eye. "Not great."

"Anything I can do? Are you hungry?"

"No."

"Thirsty?"

"I have everything I need."

"Really?" Jane brushed a strand of hair away from her cheek. "I wish I could do more." Feeling helpless, her eyes welled with tears.

"Oh, Jane. I'm fine. All I need is a good night's rest. I'll be back in the game tomorrow. Just wait and see."

"I know you will," said Jane, leaning down to kiss her.

"That was nice. Why don't you crawl in?"

Jane stretched out next to her. She explained about renting a room at the Skarsvold house, that she would be gone for a couple of nights.

"That's fine," said Julia. "Tell me about your new case." She closed her eyes.

Jane spent the next few minutes filling her in. The soft smile on Julia's face began to fade as her breathing deepened. Content just to stay in the moment, Jane closed her eyes, too. When the door opened and then shut downstairs, causing Mouse to give a low growl, she roused herself, knowing Carol had returned.

"You better go," said Julia.

"I don't want to leave you."

"I'm not good for much tonight. Besides, I need my beauty sleep."

"You hardly need sleep to be beautiful."

"Careful, Jane. You don't want to overcommit, or give the impression that you really care."

"Of course I care."

She smiled, pressing a finger to Jane's lips. "It's fine. We don't need to relitigate our dysfunction every five minutes. I'm happy to take what I can get, especially now that it includes your body."

Jane was torn. Maybe the Skarsvold case could wait.

"You go," said Julia, turning on her side, facing away from Jane. "I'll be fine. Honestly. All I'm going to do for the next eight hours is sleep. Not very exciting stuff."

Jane explained that she'd asked Carol to stay with her for the next couple of nights.

"I don't need a babysitter," came her annoyed response.

"No, but for my peace of mind, I'd like her to be here. I'll give you a call in the morning. In fact, let's plan to have lunch together."

"I think I have all-day meetings. But I can check and let you know." She reached behind her and patted Jane's hand. "You go be a superhero and save the world."

"If I had a choice, I'd rather save you."

"That's a nice thought. To be continued."

As soon as Jane swung her Mini into the driveway behind the Skarsvold house, her headlights hit the garage, revealing the word "witch" spray painted in bold black letters across the doors. She sat for a moment, nonplussed, wondering who would have done such a thing.

Backing her car up, she drove around the block and parked along Cumberland Avenue, behind a white Chevy Suburban. She pulled her overnight bag off the passenger's seat and headed up the walk. Even before she reached the steps, she could see the dark outlines of two people sitting directly to the left of the front door.

"You must be Jane," said the woman in the wheelchair, a cigarette dangling from her lips. "I'm Lena, Eleanor's sister. Welcome to Chez Skarsvold."

"Thanks," said Jane. Lena looked nothing like Eleanor. Her face was hard, covered in deep wrinkles. Her hair looked like it had been packed away in an old trunk for centuries. Wherever it had come from, it definitely wasn't real.

The burly bearded guy sitting next to Lena wore a sheepskin-lined suede jacket, jeans, and hiking boots.

Turning toward him, Lena said, "This is our new renter. Jane something-or-other."

Jane shook the man's hand.

"Butch Averil," he said. "I live in the house next door."

"Kind of cold to be sitting out here," said Jane.

"We're Minnesotans," said Lena. "That means, by definition, we're crazy."

Jane did a double take. "Listen," she said. "I'm renting the garage space, but when I pulled in a few minutes ago, I noticed that someone had spray painted the word 'witch' across the doors. I didn't want to disturb it until you'd had a look."

"Oh, for the love of—"

"I'll take care of it," said Butch. "It's the neighborhood kids. They think the house is haunted."

"You might want to call the police, make a report," said Jane.

"No police," came Lena's sharp response.

"You sure you don't want to reconsider that?" said Butch. Stuffing his hands into the pockets of his jacket, he swiveled around so he could survey the dark street.

"They're harmless," said Lena. "A bunch of kids can't hurt us."

Jane wouldn't have been that cavalier about it if it had been her garage, though if Lena decided to ignore it, that was her call. "Well, think I'll head up to bed."

"Eleanor always turns in early. If you need anything, come talk to me. My bedroom is in the sunroom off the dining room. I don't sleep well, so I'm usually up."

"Nice meeting you," said Butch, rising halfway and touching the brim of his baseball cap.

"Yeah, ditto," said Lena, dismissing Jane with a cursory wave.

Except for the ticking of an ornate clock sitting atop the mantel, the interior of the house was quiet. Each step on the stairway up to the second floor squeaked under Jane's weight. At least nobody, she concluded, would be able to sneak up on her. She felt relieved when she entered the bedroom and shut the door behind her. She switched on the overhead light and threw the bolt lock. After setting her overnight case on the floor in front of the nightstand, she sat down on the bed, testing it out. She hated supersoft beds as much as she did the extra hard variety. This one seemed okay. If Cordelia was here, she would undoubtedly find a lump that would make a good night's sleep impossible, but then Cordelia was a princess. Jane needed far less to be comfortable.

Thinking of Cordelia, Jane propped a couple of pillows against the headboard, stretched out, and took out her cell phone. She punched in the number. A couple seconds later, Cordelia answered.

"Wassup?"

"Where are you?" asked Jane.

"At the theater. Where are you?"

Jane explained about the sign on the front lawn, and about renting a room at Britt's aunts' house.

"You're inside the belly of the beast? Have to say, Janey, you work fast. Discovered any moldering bodies yet?"

"Reel in your overactive imagination for a minute and let me run something past you."

"Better yet, I could come over with my magnifying glass and jammies. We could have an old-fashioned sleepover."

"Just listen, okay. When I got here, I found that kids in the neighborhood had spray painted the word 'witch' on the garage. Apparently, it's not the first time that sort of vandalism has happened here. What do you make of it?"

"That the kids are smart. They're trying to warn the world."

"I ran into Lena Skarsvold on my way inside, the younger of the two aunts. When I mentioned it to her and suggested that she might want to call the police and file a report, she shut it down immediately. 'No police' she said. Period. End of sentence."

"She's hiding something, Janey. Clear as a bell."

Jane tended to agree. "Or maybe she just dislikes cops. She deserves the benefit of the doubt, don't you think?"

"Yours, maybe. Not mine. What else have you discovered around the place? Secret passages? False walls?"

"I haven't had much of a chance to look."

"Well, chop chop, Jane. No time like the present. Unless the inhabitants of murder mansion are milling around, you better get to it."

"Lena's out on the front porch. Eleanor's in bed."

"What are you waiting for?"

Jane wasn't sure. Something about the old house did seem to give her the creeps. Not her bedroom, thankfully. "I think I need to move into my examination a bit more slowly."

"Nonsense. Go forth and explore."

"It's late. I'm tired."

"Why do I detect reticence? You may not be as brainy as me, dearheart, but you generally have an excess of courage."

Not tonight, thought Jane. Maybe it was the starkness of the word "witch" on the garage doors. Whatever the case, she felt uncharacteristically spooked and wasn't about to leave the room until the sun was up. She'd start her examination in the morning. "I'll give you a call tomorrow."

"Do that. I want to know *all* the details. In the meantime, keep the lights burning. Evil hides in darkness. You also might want to keep a cross handy, a necklace of garlic, and a metal stake."

"They're not vampires."

"Yet to be determined."

"Goodnight, Cordelia."

"Oh, all right. Peace, Janey. Out."

9

Breathing hard, Butch banged on the Skarsvolds' front door. Holding a cell phone to his ear, he yelled for the 911 dispatcher to send the police and fire truck right away. He gave the address, told them his name, then cut the line. "Fire!" he shouted, continuing to bang on the door. "Wake the hell up in there. Fire. Fire!"

The door creaked open. Lena, looking bleary eyed and disoriented, rolled her wheelchair back so he could come in. "What . . . what's going on? It's the middle of the night." She spoke with a kind of forced precision; the way drunks did when they were trashed and trying not to show it.

"Your garage. It's burning. I called 911. Is Frank here? I saw his truck outside. The wind's picked up. We gotta make sure none of the flying debris lands on your house." Behind Lena, Eleanor descended the stairs with slow, measured steps. Frank appeared a few seconds later, rushing into the living room, his protruding stomach covered by a white T-shirt with so many holes it almost didn't qualify as clothing.

"What the hell?" demanded Frank.

"The garage, it's on fire," said Butch. "Come on. We gotta get out there."

"You called the police?" asked Eleanor, her eyes glassy with shock.

"Mom, let me handle this," said Frank. Turning to Butch, he said, "I'll get my coat and find some shoes and meet you in the backyard."

"You own an extension ladder?"

"Yeah," said Frank. "It's in the garage."

Butch noticed that the new renter he'd met earlier had also come down the stairs. Hurrying back out to the porch, he ran around the side of the house, finding that the fire had nearly doubled in size while he'd been gone. Not knowing what else to do, he rushed from one piece of burning debris to another, stomping each out. Frank joined him, huffing and puffing so hard Butch was afraid he was going to have a heart attack. They both choked on the thick black smoke, waving it away from their faces.

As the fire truck arrived, sirens blaring, Butch began to see neighbors emerge from their houses to see what was going on. Several people darted across the street to where he was standing, among them, the block captain, Rich Novak.

"Jeez," said Novak. "That garage is so old, I'll bet it was tinder dry."

Butch felt another presence move up next to him. It was the new renter. "I'm sorry," he said. "I don't remember your name."

"Jane."

"Right."

"Did you see who set it?" she asked, her eyes fixed on the flames.

"Probably the same kids who spray painted the garage doors."

"Had to be," said Frank. He stepped between Jane and Butch. "There was nothing in there that would combust on its own."

"My money's on gasoline," said one of the neighbors, an old guy in a gray bathrobe and pajamas. "An old-fashioned Molotov cocktail."

The skin on Butch's face had grown hot and raw. Two police cruisers eventually pulled up and parked in the middle of the side street, closing it off to traffic. When Butch turned back to the house, he saw Eleanor framed in the kitchen window, watching. She did that a lot. Quiet watching. Unlike her sister, Lena, who tended to insert herself and her opinions loudly into every conversation, Eleanor was more measured, less sure of herself—the kind of woman, Butch suspected, who looked carefully before she leapt.

"I wonder if the arson investigators will ever figure out who set it," said Novak.

Butch understood the deeply human pull toward fire-setting. The flames were mesmerizing, a glowing monster that owed its life to a single spark. A single *intentional* spark, Butch thought to himself. The spark itself was simple physics. No moral goal or purpose needed. The intention, however, was where the human element entered the equation. And the human element, as Butch knew so well, was a wildcard, the place where the uncertain and the unpredictable slipped in and took over the story. Like Eleanor, who sat in front of the kitchen window, a look of deep concern on her face, all Butch could do was wait and watch.

10

The following morning dawned in mist. Just after seven A.M., Jane stood in the backyard, the grass around her covered in hoarfrost, and examined the intricate pattern of icicles hanging off the charred timbers. The temperature had plummeted overnight into the low twenties. The police and firemen had stayed for hours.

Try as she might, Jane found it difficult to imagine that a burning garage would have any bearing on her case. Still, as with any catastrophe, even a minor one, it commanded both attention and explanation. Eleanor and Lena had stayed up until the wee hours, watching the scene from windows on opposite ends of the house. Jane had turned in around three, thinking there was little she could learn from the smoking ruins.

Taking out her cell phone now, she snapped a couple of pictures and sent one to Cordelia and another to Britt.

"That's gonna be one hell of a mess to clean up," called Rich Novak, crossing the hoarfrosted grass to where she stood. "You get any sleep?"

"A little." Instead of the painter pants he'd worn last night, this morning he had on a belted blue coverall. On the upper left chest was a patch embroidered with the name RICHARD. "Are you off to work?"

"Yeah, another day, another thirty cents." He grinned, but turned serious when he looked back at what was left of the garage. "We gotta talk about this at our next block meeting. One garage fire has a way of generating more. We gotta be proactive about it. Maybe it's time to organize a block watch."

They spoke for a few more minutes. Jane was a little surprised by how much jewelry Novak wore to work. Besides earrings in each ear, he had a silver chain around his neck and multiple rings on each hand.

"Well," he said, kicking at a piece of charred wood, "guess I better get going. See you around, yeah?"

"Sure," said Jane.

"You know," he added as he reached the edge of the grass, "just because you're renting don't mean you can't join our block association."

She assured him she'd think about it. As he walked away, she headed back to the house. She came in through the side door and up the three steps into the kitchen, finding Eleanor, in her robe and slippers, standing over the stove watching a pot of water come to a boil.

"Morning," said Jane.

"I was about to make myself a cup of instant," said Eleanor. "Would you like some?"

"I would. Anybody else up?"

"Just us." She motioned Jane to a chair at the kitchen table as she carried the pan over to the sink. Removing two mugs from the cupboard, she filled them with hot water and then stirred in the Folgers. "Are you hungry? I made sweet rolls yesterday."

"Sure," said Jane. "Thanks."

Eleanor took down a couple of plates. She removed the foil from a baking pan on the counter and lifted out two generous rolls, setting one in front of Jane and then bringing over the butter dish, a couple of napkins, knives, and finally the mugs.

"I'm really sorry about your garage," said Jane, taking a sip of the coffee, trying not to grimace at the bitterness.

"My son, Frank—did you meet him last night?"

"Is he the one with—" She twirled her finger next to her head.

"The man-bun? That's what you call it, right?"

She nodded.

"Yes, that's Frank. He said that someone from our insurance company would be out this afternoon. And possibly a fire investigator. They're calling it arson, you know. I can't imagine why someone would do such a thing."

Jane could. Fire was a way to hide a crime. Another possibility was always the owner of the property. A nice fat insurance settlement could motivate certain individuals to override their normal scruples. Eleanor hardly seemed the type, though Jane knew you couldn't judge people by what they said or how nice they seemed. "Your insurance should pay for the cost of the cleanup and the rebuild."

"That's what Frank thought. But we have a sizable deductible. It's not going to be easy for us to come up with enough money to cover that." Eleanor picked absently at her sweet roll. "I'm just glad you didn't park your car in there last night. Was it just luck? Or did you have some reason?"

"Your sister didn't tell you?"

"Tell me what?"

She explained about finding the word "witch" spray painted on the double front doors. "Lena and Butch were sitting on the front porch last night when I got back. I mentioned it and said I didn't want to disturb the scene in case you wanted to call the police and file a report."

She seemed horrified. "Lena didn't say a word about it." Her eyes darted around the room. "That woman."

"Have you and your sister always lived together?"

"Oh, my no. No, she left when she was twenty. Didn't come home again until our father's funeral, and then, she only stayed for a month. My husband and I lived in an apartment in Minneapolis until he went off to Vietnam. He died there."

"I'm so sorry," said Jane.

"It was a long time ago. But it was a hard time. I was lonely, and also, I felt Frank needed a strong man in his life, so I moved back in here with my dad. I never remarried. And Lena, she never wanted a marriage—at least, that's what she said. I will say, she had her share of boyfriends when she was young, although none of them ever put up with her shenanigans long enough to pop the question."

"Is Frank your only child?"

She looked away, her expression turning wistful. "My father loved children. Frank was his only grandchild. Well, except for my sister Pauline's girl, Britt. But she only visited here once— after my father died. He would've loved to have been surrounded by grandchildren, but it wasn't to be."

"You and Frank lived here alone after he died."

"We did. When I was diagnosed with cancer in my late fifties,

Lena moved back in. She knew I needed help. When I got back on my feet and returned to nursing, I thought she'd move out again, but she decided to stay permanently. I could hardly object. This has been our family home for generations. In my father's will, he made it clear that anyone in the family would always be welcome to live here."

"What did Lena do for a living?"

"Oh, mostly waitressing jobs. She never liked being tied down. She'd quit one job and then go off on her motorcycle for a few weeks. When she got home, she'd look for another."

"She had a motorcycle?"

"Oh, yes. She's led a very different life from mine. She's in that wheelchair because of arthritis, but also, in my opinion, because she burned the candle at both ends. Our father was very arthritic before he died, so I suppose there's that. I seem to have escaped joint problems, knock on wood. But Lena and me . . . we've never really seen eye to eye on much, although, over the years, circumstances have forced us to."

"You mean because she moved in with you."

Eleanor touched the pearls at her throat. "Yes. That's right. We had to pull together to keep the place afloat. She had her unsavory friends and I had my job and my church. And never the twain, as they say . . ." She let the sentence trail off. "I'm sorry if that sounds cold."

"No," said Jane. "Family relationships can be hard."

"And close quarters only exacerbates the challenges."

The front doorbell chimed.

"I hope that isn't the insurance agent. I'm not even dressed." She pushed away from the table with a sigh.

Jane quickly buttered the caramel roll and wolfed it down.

She couldn't believe how wonderful it tasted, probably because she'd had nothing but a small bowl of soup for dinner last night. She looked longingly at the pan on the counter as she washed the roll down with several gulps of the awful instant. When she came around the corner from the dining room into the living room, she found Eleanor talking to a young man. He was wearing tan corduroy slacks and an army-green field coat, a snap-brim hat pulled down over his blond hair. Hanging off one shoulder was a black canvas briefcase.

"I hope I didn't wake you," the man was saying apologetically. His eyes roamed the room. "I saw your sign outside. My name is Quentin Henneberry. I need a place to stay for a couple of weeks."

Eleanor seemed hesitant. When she saw that Jane had come into the room, she appeared to relax a bit.

"Is it possible to see one of the bedrooms?"

He spoke softly, almost reverently, which Jane found a bit odd.

"We only accept cash," said Eleanor. "No credit cards or checks."

"That's fine."

She continued to hesitate, but eventually gave him the same spiel she'd given Jane yesterday—the house rules, what was permitted and what wasn't.

He listened politely. "Would I be allowed to play the piano?" he asked when she'd finished.

"I . . . I don't know. Nobody's ever asked that before. I guess I don't see why not, as long as it's during the day and isn't too loud or disruptive."

"I love classical music. And hymns."

"Do you? Same with my father. That was his piano." When she turned to look at it, her eyes softened. "My sister plays it occasionally. And she gives piano lessons to some of the kids in the neighborhood."

"Could I see the bedroom?" he asked again.

"Oh, yes, of course. If you'll follow me."

Jane moved over to the window above the couch and looked out. The morning mist had lifted as far as the treetops. She glanced at her watch, deciding it was probably time to get to work. And yet, on her way to the front door, she paused by the stairs, wondering if she should leave Eleanor alone with a total stranger. Eleanor's life had undoubtedly been made of many moments like this. There wasn't much Jane could do to change it. Even so, she felt a stab of guilt as she trotted out to her car and slipped into the front seat. She started the engine and turned up the heat, but sat for a few seconds looking back at the house, not quite willing to leave. Instead, she sent Julia a text.

What about lunch? Early? Late?

The response came back almost immediately.

Won't work. Will I see you tonight?

Jane texted back:

Absolutely. What time will you be home?

Julia's response:

7ish. Found the fictitious boy yet? Try under the rugs.

Jane wrote back:

Funny.

Julia responded with an emoticon: a smiley face wearing sunglasses.

Smiling herself, Jane put the car in gear and headed back to Minneapolis.

11

Frank paused next to the garage, as close as he could get without actually stepping into the rubble. He refused to look back at the house, and yet even without doing so, he knew his mother was watching him through the kitchen window, urging him on. She'd sent him outside to do a visual inspection. The problem was, with so much charred debris covering the floor, what she wanted to know was impossible to find out. She was being overly cautious, in his opinion. The last thing he wanted was for a fire investigator or insurance adjuster to find him squirreling through the wreckage. Not that simply looking into what was left of the old garage suggested anything untoward.

Stop it, he ordered himself. He dithered like this all the time— back and forth, examining one side of an argument and then the other. He was sick to death of himself. His self-loathing was redirected by the sound of his cell phone. Holding it to his ear he barked "Hello." He knew it wouldn't be Wendy. He'd texted her three times yesterday and received nothing but silence in return.

"Mr. Devine? This is Caroline Millbank. I'm Walter Mann's secretary?"

"Oh, yeah," he said, moving away from the garage. He could see his mother pointing toward it. All he could do in response was shrug.

"I'm wondering if we can set up a time for you to meet with Mr. Mann."

"What's this about?" he asked, holding a hand to his other ear as a passenger jet flew overhead.

"I'm afraid I don't have any information on that. Would this afternoon be a possibility?"

"Tomorrow would be better," he said, remembering that he'd promised his mother that he'd be around when she met with the insurance guy.

"Would ten work for you?"

"I suppose."

"Good. I'll let Mr. Mann know you're coming. Have a nice day, Mr. Devine."

"Whatever," he muttered, clicking the phone off. His mother was motioning him inside. He felt like a fly struggling to get out of a sticky web. He pointed to the garage and once again, shrugged. And then he pointed to his phone. "Later," he mouthed. He didn't wait to see her reaction.

Stopping for breakfast at a local diner, Frank made small talk with a waitress he'd known for years. He spent the rest of the morning at the tax office, mostly with his feet up on the desk, reading the latest copy of *Entertainment Weekly*. Ever since watching *The Tudors* on TV, he'd had a crush on Natalie Dormer. After devouring an article on her, he stuffed it into one of the desk drawers and forced himself to work on organizing his files for the upcoming tax season. He still needed to sign up for the annual continuing education program—two hours of ethics, three hours of federal tax law updates, and two five-hour sessions on related tax subjects. As usual, he'd left it until the last minute, hoping beyond hope that one of the lottery tickets he routinely bought at the gas station by his house would pay off and he could quit his job and go live on a beach somewhere.

Before leaving for the day, he texted Wendy again, taking a different tack this time. He hadn't apologized for his behavior yesterday. Today he would.

I'm so sorry, hon. I was an asshole.
I hope to God it's not a permanent
condition. If I come by tonight, will
you talk to me? Please, please please,
Wendy. Forgive me?

It wasn't enough. He left the office and drove to a local grocery store, one that always had nice fresh flowers. He dithered over his purchase for so long that the woman behind the counter started eyeing him, as if he might be loitering for some nefarious purpose. He finally decided on a bunch of yellow daisies. Was that trite? Maybe he should have given her a dozen red roses, but they were so expensive.

Frank and Wendy had bought a house in Roseville two months before they were married. It represented a new start for him, a place apart from his mother and Lena. He was such a freakin' cliché, living in his mother's basement for all those years after his first marriage had blown up. It was just easier. He liked easy. He also thought it was fun to tell people that he lived in his mother's basement and then watch their reactions. It was better than most prime-time TV shows.

Driving up 35W, Frank took the County Road D exit. Wendy wouldn't be home for another hour. She taught fourth grade at the local elementary school. Frank didn't want to actually run into her. If she wouldn't return a text, it was even more doubtful that she'd talk to him. But he did want to leave the flowers. And maybe a note. Oh, God. A note. He should have bought a card, or at the very least, taken one of those little cards the flower kiosk gave away for free. But even if he had remembered to buy a card, he had no idea what it should say.

Fitting his key into the front door lock, Frank carried the flowers into the kitchen. He stopped dead in his tracks when he saw Wendy sitting at the kitchen island staring down at a package of Oreos. "You're home."

She raised her eyes to his. "Got one of the other teachers to cover my class so I could leave early."

He paused before reaching over and placing the flowers on the counter, pushing them gingerly toward her. "For you," he said, stepping back away from the island.

She looked at them as if they were covered in anthrax, then turned toward the patio doors.

He followed her gaze and saw that the chair he'd broken two nights ago was resting on the deck, on its side. One leg missing. "Oh, God," he whispered. "Did I do that?"

"It didn't get that way by itself."

"I didn't mean it. I'm sorry if . . . my actions scared you."

"You're sorry? So you bring me flowers. You think that's what I want?"

"I wasn't trying to scare you, hon. I threw it at the wall."

"Where I happened to be standing."

"I'd never hurt you. You know that."

She picked up a spoon and removed a tea bag from the mug resting next to the package of cookies. "I thought I did. Now I'm not so sure."

"You never answered any of my texts."

Clearing her throat, she straightened up and said, "Did you really see your therapist?"

"Do you think I'd lie about that?"

She raised an eyebrow.

"Yes, of course I saw him."

"And? Did you tell him about the fight? What you said? What you did?"

"Well, I mean, sort of."

"And what did *he* tell you?"

He scratched the back of his neck, inadvertently loosening the clip in his bun. Several hunks of hair fell free and covered his ear. Brushing them back, he said, "He said I was depressed."

"That's news? What else?"

"Well, he said that I might have a problem with anger."

"You think?"

"I'm a mess, Wendy. I always have been. You must have known that when you married me."

Pushing her glasses back up her nose, she appeared to give it some thought. "What I knew was that you were a wonderful man with a bad self-image. I thought I could help you with it."

"You can, Wendy. You can."

"I also knew that your mother was a shameless control freak whose sole mission in life was to prevent you from having a life of your own."

"Don't start," he said. "You don't know what you're talking about."

"Don't I? Where did you spend the last two nights? At a motel?"

"We don't have money to throw around like that."

"Honestly, Frank, I'd be thrilled to learn you spent them with a hooker. Anything but your mother's basement."

The skin on the back of his neck began to prickle. "I was glad I was there. For your information, someone set fire to her garage in the middle of the night. She was terrified."

That stopped her. "A fire?"

"That's right."

"Did you set it?"

"*What?*"

"Did she get you to do it so she could bank the insurance money?"

"Are you crazy? Of course not."

She shook her head, returning her attention to the contents of her mug. "I don't know, Frank. I just don't know anymore."

The silence stretched.

Finally, Frank said, "Can I come home? I love you, hon. I don't want to be away from you. Not ever."

She drummed her fingers on the counter. "I guess I'd rather have you here than think of you in that awful hole."

His mother's basement wasn't a hole. Well, technically, it was. But it was also comfortable, if a little moldy smelling. "Is that a yes?"

"No more throwing chairs."

"Promise." He took a couple of tentative steps toward her. "So . . . I can stay?"

She looked up at him with her pretty brown eyes, telegraphing, he hoped, forgiveness.

This was probably the moment when he should have moved the conversation to the bedroom. But, as with all such moments, it passed. "You feel like a pizza?"

"When don't I?"

"I'll drive."

Eleanor kept an eye on the clock as she washed the dishes in the sink. She hoped beyond hope that Frank would remember that the insurance man was coming by. Perhaps she should call Iver, see if he might be willing to stop over to give her the support she needed. Lena would be no help at all. Her gruff manner did nothing but put people off.

Hearing a sound behind her, Eleanor swiveled halfway around to find her sister wheeling herself into the kitchen. The worried look in Lena's eyes mirrored her own.

"What are we gonna do?" she demanded, her gnarled hands resting on the wheels.

"Be patient."

"I'm no good at patience. I saw Frank from my window. Why the hell didn't do more to look around?"

Eleanor had the same question.

"You should go out there, El. See what's what."

"I did."

"When?"

"Early this morning, after everyone left."

"And?"

"I didn't want to take a flashlight. I was afraid. I couldn't see much."

"This sucks so bad."

"Maybe not. Maybe everything will be all right."

"In what universe will cops and arson investigators crawling around our garage be fine?"

"It was just a fire, Lena. They'll take a look, determine whether it was an accident or arson, and that will be the end of it. Remember when old man Chung's garage went up in flames? That's exactly what happened."

"That was twenty years ago."

"So? In the end, I think it's possible that it will be a good thing. We could use the insurance money. We can hire someone to scrape away the debris. So what if we don't have a garage?"

Lena drew her eyes away. Her mouth barely moved, though she seemed to be saying something.

"What?" asked Eleanor. She turned to see what her sister was looking at only to find nothing but the kitchen table. "Lena?"

"Over there," she whispered, jabbing her finger. "Don't you see him?"

"See who?"

"He's right there." For a second or two, she seemed to be listening.

"Have you been drinking?"

"Oh, bite me."

Eleanor placed her hands on her hips, staring down at her.

"Maybe it's time we fessed up. You know? Don't you ever feel like the weight is too much to bear?"

"No," said Eleanor flatly.

"You're a hard one."

"I could say the same about you."

"Great. Let's have a fight. Perfect timing. The cops will walk in on us, hear us arguing over our sins, and send us to lower hell like we deserve."

"Will you stop it?" said Eleanor. "We have to stay strong. Stick together. It's the only way we'll get through this."

Lena wheeled herself around and headed back through the doorway, belting out the opening words to a song she often referred to as a hard rock spiritual, the Rolling Stones', "You Can't Always Get What You Want." When she came to the second line, "A glass of wine in her hand," she raised her arm and gave Eleanor the finger.

12

Jane sipped from a can of Coke as she sat in her Mini across the street from the Skarsvolds' backyard. Eleanor and a gray-haired man stood together arm in arm near the garage and spoke to a second man holding a clipboard. Since it was close to three, Jane assumed the second man was the insurance adjuster. If Eleanor's son Frank had come back for the meeting, he was nowhere in sight.

Both Britt and Cordelia had responded with texts after viewing the photo Jane had sent them. Cordelia was suitably appalled, mostly because she'd missed a dramatic event. Britt said she was sorry that it happened, but was pressed for time. She would be giving her presentation to the symposium tomorrow morning and was stressing about it. Jane sent a text wishing her luck.

Since she had no desire to intrude on the insurance conversation, Jane stayed in her car, glancing through the research she'd done on the case earlier in the afternoon. She hadn't learned much. Lena and Eleanor had lived quiet lives, so there were no criminal warrants or arrest records, no court cases, nothing that would suggest that anything had ever been amiss. All Jane had come up with were employment records, family birth and death records, and credit history. On paper, at least, the two women looked like model citizens.

Jane hadn't run anything on Frank Devine yet, but hoped to get to that soon. Because he'd been a boy of thirteen when Britt met him, it seemed unlikely that he was involved in Timmy's disappearance, though she couldn't discount it entirely. The more Jane searched the internet for information, the more she realized that she would need to find answers elsewhere.

Shortly after everyone in the backyard moved into the house, a red Ford SUV, with the words SAINT PAUL FIRE printed on the side, turned onto the side street from Cumberland Avenue and swung into the drive. A woman in cargo pants and a navy-blue jacket jumped out. She moved around to the back of the SUV, opened the rear door, and began strapping on a utility belt. Once it was secured, she hung a camera around her neck, lifted a heavy metal utility box out of the rear and shut the door. She approached what was left of the garage and began taking photos. She appeared to be most interested in the back of the garage, where the fire had done the most damage.

Setting her research aside, Jane slipped on her sunglasses and headed across the street. The woman was crouched down next to some scattered glass on the lawn, when Jane walked up. "Afternoon," she said. "Are you the fire investigator?"

The woman nodded, squinting up at her.

"I live in the house," said Jane.

"Were you here last night when the garage went up?"

"Afraid so."

"Know anything about how it happened?"

"No. Except . . . some kids in the neighborhood painted the word 'witch' across the garage doors last night. I'm told they think the house is haunted."

The investigator straightened up. "Yeah, I noticed some black paint on one of the doors. You have any idea who the kids are?"

"I'm just a renter. You should ask the owner, Eleanor Devine. She may have more information."

"What's your name?"

"Jane. Jane Lawless."

The woman looked at her quizzically. "Lawless?"

"It's not a commentary on my morals," said Jane.

The woman studied her for a few seconds, then laughed. "Good to know." She lifted the strap from around her neck and set the camera on the ground next to the toolbox. Opening the top of the box, she retrieved a pair of leather work gloves, slipped them on, and then waded into a section that was mostly sodden cinders and ash.

"The fire seemed to burn hottest toward the back," said Jane.

"Probably a single point of origin. The broken glass tells me there was a window right about here." She drew her hands apart, framing it. "Basically, you go from the heaviest burned area to the least, which gives you the direction it migrated. The front of the garage is still partially intact, and the beams have a lighter char."

"Are you positive it was arson?"

"No, not yet, but I'm leaning that way. From what my supervisor tells me, there was no electricity out here. I'll have to confirm that. The homeowner said there wasn't any stored gasoline or other combustibles. No space heaters. Nobody was refinishing a desk or a chair, so no possibility of combustible rags." She stepped around a fallen beam. "This floor is unusual. Looks like someone tried to cover packed dirt with concrete, but they didn't know what they were doing. See there, how thin it is in spots? And a lot of it has cracked." She straightened up and looked around. "It would have been easy enough to break the window and toss in something combustible. Wouldn't take much with wood this old."

Moving deeper into the rubble, she leaned down to examine what appeared to be an old hubcap.

Jane turned and glanced back at the kitchen window, wondering if Eleanor was monitoring what the investigator was doing. Sunlight glinted off the glass, preventing her from seeing inside. On the other end of the house, Jane could make out Lena's face in her bedroom window. She was about to wave when she heard the sound of breaking timber and then a loud thump.

"What the—" came the investigator's voice

Jane swiveled around. "Oh my God," she said. "Are you all right?" The woman had sunk down into a hole up to her waist.

"My ankle," she groaned, bending over.

"What the hell just happened?"

"Must have been standing on a trapdoor. Boy, I didn't see that."

Moving closer, Jane said, "Can I help you out of there?"

"Just give me a sec." She seemed embarrassed. "I'm usually more careful than this. Hey, what's that?" Pulling a small flashlight from her tool belt, she bent down, shining the light all around her feet. "There are plastic evidence bags in the toolbox. Get me a couple, would you? And while you're at it, look for a trowel."

Jane dug through the box until she found what the investigator wanted, handing them over.

With the flashlight clenched between her teeth, the woman bent over and dropped several small lumps of dirt into one of the bags. She dug around with the trowel. After a few seconds, she came up with something else, a metal object. She knocked some of the dirt off it and then placed it carefully in the second bag, making sure both were sealed before handing them to Jane. "Just set them next to the toolbox."

With her back to Jane, the woman hoisted herself up out of the hole. Jane took the opportunity to slip her cell phone into her hand, aim it at the bags and click off a few pictures. The piece of metal looked badly rusted. To come to any conclusions about what was in the other bag, Jane had to crouch down. "What are those?" she asked, bending closer.

"Bones," said the woman. After brushing off her pants, she sat down on the ground and pulled off her boot to examine her ankle.

"You think someone buried a dog down there?"

"I'm not one hundred percent positive, but I think they're human."

Jane stared at them. "But they're so small."

"Could be fingers, or bones from someone's feet. Or they could belong to a kid."

Her head snapped up. "A kid?" Turning, she saw that Lena was still at her bedroom window.

The investigator dug a cell phone out of her coat pocket. Punching in a number, she waited and then said, "It's Pittman. I'm at the garage fire on Cumberland. I need crime scene techs dispatched. You better alert the SPPD." She listened. "Yeah. I will." Stuffing the phone back into her pocket, she returned her attention to the garage.

"So, what's it mean?" asked Jane.

"I think," said the woman, pulling off her gloves and dropping them next to her, "that we may have something a lot more serious here than a torched building."

13

As the daylight faded over Cumberland Avenue, Jane stood at the single window in her bedroom looking down on the backyard. Police had set up emergency lights all around the garage to assist the forensic examiners. They'd cleared the backyard of gawkers, cordoning off the area with yellow crime scene tape, forcing onlookers to stand so far away from the activity that it was impossible to see what was going on. Jane felt she could monitor the scene best from her bedroom. She was glad now that she'd chosen the room that faced the back of the house.

Still reeling from the knowledge that bones had been found in a pit inside the garage, Jane had come into the house through the back door to find Eleanor and the man she'd been standing arm in arm with earlier sitting at the kitchen table, drinking coffee. The man stood up and introduced himself as Pastor Iver Dare, a minister and old friend of Eleanor's. He was friendly and open, and was clearly at the house because he cared about Eleanor's welfare. Eleanor said the police had informed them of the discovery made in the garage, but offered nothing beyond that. Both looked suitably concerned, if not outright worried. Jane asked a couple of questions, but it was clear neither was willing to talk about it.

Passing into the dining room, Jane saw that the French doors to Lena's bedroom were open partway. Lena was sitting in her wheelchair, staring into space, a look on her face that Jane could only describe as terror. Something seismic had just happened to the Skarsvold family.

Once back in her bedroom, Jane watched the crime scene techs package up the contents of the hole. They appeared to be removing one plastic bag after another. Slipping out her cell phone, she called Cordelia. "Are you sitting down?" she asked when her friend answered.

"Not exactly a serene way to begin a conversation," said Cordelia. "And no, I am fully upright."

"You need to be sitting down before I tell you what I just learned."

"Cordelia M. Thorn is a warrior. Hit me. I can take it."

Jane paused. "Okay. Here goes. The arson investigator sent out to examine the Skarsvolds' garage found bones. In a pit." At the sound of loud crashing, Jane whipped the phone away from her ear to keep her eardrum from shattering. She waited a few seconds and then said, "Cordelia? Are you there? Are you all right?"

More thudding. Then, "It wasn't me. I dropped the tray of food I was carrying."

"I didn't know you were carrying a tray of food."

"Now I have a heart failure *and* a mess to clean up. Oh, blither. Just a sec."

Jane noticed one of the police officers head toward the house.

"I'm back," said Cordelia. "Now, bones you say?"

"The arson examiner found two. They're small. Most likely human. And a piece of rusted metal. There's a crime scene unit over here right now digging deeper into the pit."

"*Small* bones?"

"There are lots of small bones in our bodies, Cordelia. Or, she said they could belong to a child."

"Heavens."

"Exactly."

"Have you called Britt?"

"Not yet. I want to know more before I do. She's supposed to give her presentation tomorrow morning."

"If I didn't have something vitally important on my agenda to-night, I'd be right over. You are clearly in the middle of the action."

Jane moved over to her bedroom door and opened it. Voices floated up from the living room. One belonged to Eleanor. The other was a man. She assumed it was the police officer she'd seen walking toward the house. "You know," she said, whispering now, "I think I better go. There's a cop downstairs talking to the family."

"Suck up every piece of info you can," said Cordelia. "We'll debrief later."

Jane tiptoed out into the hall and stood at the top of the stairs. Lowering her head, she listened. Eleanor was speaking:

"I've lived here most of my life, Sergeant Nesbitt. And yes, I knew about the root cellar in the garage. My great-grandfather built the house. For a time, it was a working farm. I have photos if you'd like to see them. The root cellar was a place to store veg-etables and fruits over the winter months. My dad used it, too, for the same purpose."

"Have you or your sister ever stored anything down there?" asked the sergeant.

"No. Never. When I moved back home with my son after my husband died, I asked my father to nail it shut. I didn't want my son anywhere near it. He was a normal boy. If there was something dangerous to get into, he'd find it."

"Can one of you describe the root cellar?"

Lena spoke for the first time. "Well, it had a dirt floor with some straw over it. It was—I don't know, it's hard to remember exactly—maybe seven feet deep. Dad used a ladder to get down into it. The hole was maybe six feet long, five feet wide, with a heavy wooden trapdoor to cover it. Hinged, I think. I never went near it as a kid. Thought it was creepy."

"Can you tell us more about what you've discovered?" asked Eleanor.

"I can't comment," said Nesbitt.

"But you think you found human bones?" asked another male voice that Jane recognized as Pastor Dare's.

"The cellar was definitely used to dispose of a body." He let his comment hang in the air before continuing, "Do you have any thoughts on who it might be?"

"Certainly not," said Eleanor, her voice uncharacteristically hoarse.

"When do you think this . . . body . . . was put down there?" asked Pastor Dare.

Eleanor broke in. "If you're suggesting my father or my grandfather were somehow complicit, I reject that, too. They were both good, decent men."

Patiently, the sergeant replied, "To answer your question, Mr. Dare, it takes eight to twelve years for an unembalmed human body to decompose. That means this person went into the cellar anywhere between the time the pit was first dug until the early part of this century."

"You can't be more specific?" asked Pastor Dare.

"Not at the moment."

"Will you ever be able to narrow down the time line?" asked Eleanor.

"We hope so. We've recovered . . . certain items that may help with that. Now, moving on. Has anyone in your family gone missing over the years?"

"Nobody," said Eleanor.

"Friends? Neighbors?"

"Maybe someone fell in, hit their head, and died," offered Lena.

Jane found the comment not only ridiculous, but her tone jarringly cheerful.

"If that's the case," said the sergeant, "are you're suggesting that nobody in your family ever noticed a dead body in the root cellar?"

"Lena was just trying to be helpful," said Eleanor. "But . . . are you saying that this person, whoever he or she was . . ." She paused. "Didn't die a natural death?"

"At this point, we can't rule anything out."

Silence followed the sergeant's remark.

"Will you let us know what you learn?" asked Pastor Dare.

"As much as I can."

Jane heard the sound of wood floors creaking and assumed everyone was getting up.

"Until further notice," said Nesbitt, "the garage is off limits. It's an active crime scene."

"How long will your team be out there?" demanded Lena.

"Through the night at the very least. Probably into the day tomorrow."

"We'll do anything we can to help," said Eleanor. "We want to get to the bottom of this as much as you do."

Eleanor seemed sincere. And yet, if the bones belonged to Timmy, surely she knew something about it. Jane heard the front door open and then close. She was about to head back to her bedroom when she heard Lena say:

"We're toast. All of us."

Jane stopped and turned around.

"Keep your voice down," came Eleanor's terse reply.

"Are you drinking again?" asked Pastor Dare.

"What if I am? I'll say it again. I think we should all come clean. Tell the truth. If that means they put the lot of us in jail, so be it."

"Stop it," hissed Eleanor. "We have renters upstairs. This is no place for a discussion like this."

Jane bent her head and concentrated, trying hard to make out the words, but everyone appeared to be taking Eleanor's counsel. They were whispering now. That is, until Eleanor said, "Iver, please, I've got to get out of here. Can't we go somewhere?"

"Right," snarled Lena. "You two go off and have fun. Me? I'll stay home and worry myself into an early grave."

"Perfect solution," said Eleanor. The acid in her voice was unmistakable.

"Come on, you two," said the pastor. "That kind of talk won't get us anywhere."

"Go ahead and find your no-tell motel room for the night," said Lena, her voice dripping with sarcasm.

"Take that back," demanded Eleanor.

"Why should I? You don't think I know? You've had the hots for Iver ever since you first met him."

"That's it," said Pastor Dare. "Eleanor, get your coat."

After the front door creaked open and then shut, Lena shouted, "FYI, I'm going to smoke in the house from here on out. *Deal with it.*"

14

Butch waved at the bottle-blond waitress, holding up his bill and a credit card. She smiled and nodded, mouthing "One second" as she turned back to the table of six—all men. It felt as if she'd been taking their orders for an hour, chatting them up, undoubtedly hoping for a massive tip.

Finally, striding across to Butch's booth, she grabbed his ticket and the credit card.

"I'd like more coffee."

"Sure thing." She removed his dinner plate and dirty silverware. "Be back in a sec."

Butch didn't much like Italian food, though his target sitting at a table next to the window obviously did. He'd ordered himself spaghetti and garlic bread. When it arrived, he found the red sauce watery, bland, and way too sweet. The wine list was equally pathetic. He'd nursed a glass of the house Cabernet, frowning at the flat, sour taste, until all the garlic bread was gone. Right now he was nursing his coffee, waiting until the target paid her bill. She'd come to Luigi's directly from work to have a meal with a friend. Her name, as usual, was Jenny. All of them had been named Jenny. And none of them had taken him where he wanted to go.

His newest Jenny eventually said goodbye to her friend, giving her a hug. They continued their conversation on their way out the door. Butch knew where she lived, so he didn't have to race to his car and follow her home. Even so, he took the same route she did, staying far enough behind her Nissan to not attract attention. As she pulled into her driveway, he eased to a stop a few houses away on the opposite side of the street and switched off his lights. There was a second car in her drive, an older model Dodge Charger, which intrigued him.

After she'd gone inside and he could see her through the picture window, he picked up his camera from the passenger seat, spending a few seconds digging through the camera bag for his telephoto lens. He wanted to get up close and personal without actually being up close and personal. That would come later. Clipping the lens on, he slid out of the front seat and jogged over to an elm tree large enough to obscure his presence. Holding the viewfinder to his eye, he scanned the living room until he saw her. He clicked off a few photos. She stood by a chair, talking to a woman who'd just come through a rear doorway into what looked like the living room. He clicked off several more photos, getting a good one of Jenny looking up at the woman, then giving her a lingering kiss.

Adjusting the focus on the zoom, he took a picture of the Charger's license plate, then dashed across the street and crouched down next to the rear bumper. He hesitated another few seconds, looking both ways down the quiet street. When he was as sure as he could be that nobody was watching him, he straightened up and moved quickly to the passenger's door, cupping his hands around his eyes and scanning the interior. What he found was a rolling garbage bin full of crumpled McDonald's bags and discarded soda cans. Crossing over to Jenny's Nissan, he glanced inside long enough to learn that the interior was immaculate. The two cars were owned by two very different people. The Charger likely belonged to the girlfriend.

Hurrying back to his own car, he slid in and started the engine, turning up the heat. He had such high hopes for this particular Jenny, but unless the photos caused him to rethink his conclusion, he'd wasted another evening with nothing to show for it but a slight case of indigestion.

"Bye-bye," he whispered as he put the car in gear and drove off. "Wish you had better taste in restaurants."

After stopping at a drugstore to buy a couple Snickers bars and a sack of Fritos, Butch pulled up in front of his house, ready for another night of renovations. He'd fallen behind on the work he promised to do in order to lower his rent. Earlier in the day, the owner had dropped off a cheap toilet, one he expected Butch to use to replace the even cheaper toilet in the bathroom. Butch figured it would be easy enough, unless he ran into something unexpected.

Tonight would also be another opportunity to make progress on the kitchen cabinets. In his opinion, no matter what he did, he was merely putting lipstick on a pig. Compared to the Skarsvold house next door, which might be in terrible shape but remained impressive in size and design, the puke-tan rambler he'd rented was a small, boring box.

Even before Butch got out of his car, he saw the bright lights illuminating what was left of the Skarsvolds' garage. Crime scene tape had gone up, establishing a perimeter around the backyard, which appeared to be a hive of activity. He couldn't imagine why an arson investigation would take so much manpower.

Seeing the neighbor he'd met last night, the old guy in his bathrobe, Butch jogged over to him. "Hey," he said. "Do you know what's going on?"

"Not entirely sure," said the old guy, folding his arms. "But I've heard a few whispers." He winked.

"About what?"

"Well, if you can believe it, the arson investigator they sent out found some bones buried under the garage floor."

"Bones?"

"Human bones."

Butch's eyebrows shot up.

"Hard to believe those two old ladies are capable of murder. Still, the more bones I see them bag, the more I think we've got ourselves a homegrown case of *Arsenic and Old Lace*." He wiped a hand across his mouth. "The house is supposed to be haunted you know."

"Yeah, well, I have a hard time believing that."

He shrugged.

"Looks like they've dug down pretty far," said Butch

"The pit was already there. I'm told."

"Another whisper?"

He looked over and smiled. "I'm retired. I got a lot of free time on my hands and I like to monitor the local gossip."

"Well, I guess we'll find out soon enough."

"You know the sisters?"

"I've met them."

He nodded, and kept on nodding. "Yup. Just a matter of time before all is revealed."

"What do you mean, *all*?"

In response, the man gave another wink.

Butch was repelled by how much the guy seemed to be enjoying someone else's tragedy. Love thy neighbor didn't seem to be operative along Cumberland Avenue.

Instead of returning to his house, Butch made a beeline for Lena's front door, where he knocked loudly. He was more than a little startled when Novak opened it.

"Evening," said the block captain.

"Can I come in?"

"No skin off my nose." He walked away, leaving the door ajar.

Butch removed his baseball cap and stepped inside. Lena sat in her wheelchair in front of the cold fireplace, smoking one of her menthols and tapping ash onto a plate next to her on the floor. Novak had dropped down on the couch, his legs spread wide. He was smoking, too, although it wasn't tobacco.

"Welcome to our den of iniquity," said Lena, taking a deep drag. "You know Rich, right? My mad stoner buddy?"

"I thought Eleanor wouldn't let you smoke inside the house."

"There's been a rule change around this joint," said Lena. "I'm now allowed to do whatever I want." She pulled a flask from her sweater pocket, unscrewed the cap and took several swallows. "This thing's empty. Richie, be a good boy. Go into my room. You'll see a wardrobe to your right. In the bottom, you'll find my stash. Might as well bring the entire bottle. Or what's left of it." She eyed Butch. "That reminds me. I'll need more of that sooner rather than later."

Novak jumped up and left the room.

"Okay," said Butch. "But go easy, okay?"

"Easy isn't in my nature."

He could tell that she was already pretty hammered.

Novak returned with the bottle and handed it to her.

"Who wants some?" She held it up triumphantly.

Butch shook his head.

"Nope," said Novak. "I'll stick with my blunt."

"Your loss." She set it down on the floor next to her makeshift ashtray.

"I ran into one of your neighbors outside," said Butch.

"Sit down, boy. You're making me nervous."

He looked around, settling on a tufted chair. "The neighbor said that the arson investigator—"

"Discovered human remains in our garage. Yeah, yeah. I heard all about it."

"Is it true?"

"Apparently."

"And?"

"And what? Do I know who they belong to?" She pinched two fingers together and made a twisting motion next to her mouth.

"Not to change the subject," said Novak, easing lower on the couch, his legs stretched out in front of him, "but I'll say it again. You oughta sell this dump. Move on. I know, I know. Eleanor doesn't want to. But I'll bet you could get a good price for it. Plenty of money for you and your sister to go your separate ways. I mean, somebody just burned your garage to the ground. That means you'll get a nice fat insurance settlement. It was me, I'd use it to repair the house, get it ready to be put on the market. I'll do my best as block captain to get to the bottom of the arson, to make sure it don't happen nowhere else along Cumberland. But, you know . . . maybe it's time to talk to your sis again. Raise the question one more time."

"I'll . . . take it under advisement." The cigarette dangling from Lena's lips bounced as she spoke.

Watching ash fall onto her sweater, Butch had the sick feeling that there might be another fire in her future.

"Anyway," said Novak, stretching his arms over his head. "I promised the wife I'd go pick up a pizza."

"Get one for us while you're at it." She dug around in her sweater pocket, coming up empty.

The last thing Butch wanted was more Italian food, although he did want to talk. If pizza was the price he had to pay, so be it. "Here," he said, taking some cash from his pocket and handing Novak a twenty.

"What kind?" asked Novak.

"Cheese is fine," said Butch.

"Pepperoni," cried Lena. "But none of those damn anchovies."

"Your wish is my command, yo," said Novak. "I shall return."

Once he'd gone, Lena picked up the liquor bottle and took a slug directly from the spout. "Wish I had some beer to offer you. Better put that on the list."

"What changed? You're smoking inside the house. Drinking in full view of your sister."

"She's not home. But, to answer your question, I changed. I finally grew a pair."

Which explained exactly nothing.

"Hey, Butch. Tell me something. How come you left last Friday morning and I didn't see hide nor hair of you until Sunday night?"

He was surprised she'd noticed. He should have given her more credit. "Well, see, I've got a friend with a cabin."

"On a lake?"

"Yeah, a nice one."

"What's the name?"

"Um, Big Lake."

"What's it near?"

"It's not really near any towns."

She dropped the nub of her cigarette, nearly missing the plate on the floor. "Huh. Sounds remote. What do you do at this cabin?"

He shrugged. "Sleep. Play cards. Drink."

"Chase women?"

"Nah."

"Right." She snorted. "I know what young men like."

He doubted she knew what he liked. "But . . . back to the bones in the garage."

"Can't talk about that."

"You have no idea who they belong to?"

She jerked her head toward the piano. Staring hard, she whispered, "Do you see him?"

"See who?" He looked around. "There's nobody here but us."

Her eyes welled with tears. "He's come home."

"Who's come home?"

"There's so much I never told him." She felt along the floor, found the bottle and took another gulp.

Butch doubted she'd still be awake when the pizza arrived. He decided to play along. "Tell him now." He rose from the recliner, crouched down in front of her and took her hands in his.

"Ignore the crazy old lady."

"You're not crazy."

"You don't think so?"

"No."

"Wha . . . what would I say to him? He must hate me." She flicked her eyes toward the piano. "He scares me," she whispered. Her eyes swam inside her head until she finally focused on Butch's face. "I'm a wretched excuse for a human being." None of the words came out clearly.

"Why is that?"

"You know why. I was a terrible mother."

He felt suddenly sorry for her. "That's not true."

She blinked, closed her eyes, and swayed. As her shoulders began to shake, she covered her face with her hands and burst into tears.

Butch moved closer, put his arms around her and held her. "It's all right," he said. "Don't cry. Please don't cry." She was in no shape to talk coherently about anything. He'd have to wait for another time. He continued to try to reassure her, although nothing he said seemed to penetrate. "Come on, Lena. Let me get you to bed."

He wheeled her into her bedroom. It was a sad little room, with a twin bed, a small clock radio on the nightstand next to a lamp and a bunch of pill bottles, a recliner in one corner and the freestanding closet in the other. Everything in the room was old and worn, even the old rock posters on the walls. There were books, of course. She liked to read. He opened the closet door. Inside were a few dresses. A robe. A few shirts and sweaters. Two pairs of jeans. This was her life. She wasn't starving. She lived in a warm house. She had family around her. And yet, if there was a God and he wanted to punish her, he'd done a good job.

As he lifted her onto the bed, her wig fell off. Underneath, her hair was gray and baby fine. He couldn't believe how light she was—like a sparrow, a tiny damaged little bird with a fierce heart. After patting the wig back into place, he covered her with a quilt, and then stood looking down at her. He was about to turn away when he stopped himself. Leaning over her, he kissed her forehead. "Goodnight," he whispered. "Sweet dreams."

15

The next morning, Wendy was standing at the stove making breakfast when Frank slogged his way to one of the wooden stools by the kitchen island.

"Morning," he mumbled, cringing at the sound of the wood creaking under his weight. He should have combed his long, scraggly hair and brushed his teeth before emerging from the bedroom, but the bacon's siren song was too much. "That smells good."

She glanced over her shoulder and offered him a sly smile. It was the look she always gave him after a night of wild abandon. Unlike every other man on the planet, Frank had never been all that confident of his lovemaking skills. Even more suspicious was his general lack of a sex drive. He'd been a virgin on his wedding night, a fact he hid from his few buddies and, when it came down to it, even his first wife. Last night however, he'd channeled his inner Arnold Schwarzenegger and performed admirably.

After dishing up the food, Wendy set a plate in front of him and then stood at the counter pouring them each a glass of orange juice. She pushed his cell phone toward him with her index finger, saying, "Your mother called."

"I know." The bacon tasted better than usual, which he put down to last night's hard labor.

"Six times. And she left you a bunch of messages."

After Wendy said he could come back home, he'd completely spaced on his promise to be with his mom when she talked to the insurance agent about the garage fire. Of course, she'd called twice during dinner, though devouring an extra large meat-lover's pizza with two sides of wings at the local Pizza Hut with his forgiving wife seemed far more important than listening to Mom berate him for blowing her off. The phone had been set to vibrate, so Wendy had no idea he'd been in such high demand. And then later—well, he was busy.

"You gonna call her back?"

"Eventually."

"Six phone calls seems like a lot, even for her."

"I suppose." He closed his eyes as he stuffed the second piece of bacon into his mouth. "This is so good."

"I'm a fabulous cook."

He grinned, not quite able to look her in the eyes.

"What are you up to today?"

"I've got an appointment this morning with Walter Mann."

"A tax client?"

"Nope." He wiped the grease off his lips with a paper napkin.

"You're being awfully mysterious."

"It's probably nothing." He did admit to a certain curiosity and maybe even a tiny irrational hope that the meeting would turn out to be something more than a few compliments as he was shoved out the door.

"All right," she said, between bites. "I like a man with a secret."

He stopped chewing.

"I'm kidding," she said, laughing and covering his hand with hers. "You know, sometimes I don't understand you at all."

"Count your blessings."

She finished her eggs. "Anyway, be a dear and put the dirty dishes in the dishwasher. I've got to get going or I'll be late for school."

"Can't disappoint a roomful of nine-year-olds."

She came around the island and gave him a long, slow kiss. "Duty calls."

"Mmm."

"See you tonight?"

He nodded. As she left the room, he swallowed the mass of pulverized toast in his mouth. When he heard her call, "Bye," he pushed his plate away, rose from the stool, and returned to the bedroom to get dressed. Next stop, the Rupert A. Wilson Publishing House.

Oh, joy, thought Frank, sitting down in another waiting room next to another fish tank. One tiny guppylike critter swam over to scope him out. He pressed his thumbs to his ears, stuck out his tongue, and wiggled his fingers.

The fish darted away.

"Damn straight," he whispered. "Nobody messes with Frank Devine."

Before he knew it, he was shaking hands with Walter Mann, a suave, well-dressed, older man, a dude who exuded confidence. Frank hated him on principle.

Mann motioned him to the chair in front of his desk. "Let me get right to the point," he said, glancing at his watch. "I think you've got immense talent."

"Seriously? I mean . . . thank you."

"Pastor Dare told me you've done a number of public murals."

"Well, only two. Although, if you count the ones I did at my parents' house, it's dozens."

"I like your style. Everything is so . . . so round and fat and fanciful."

"And wicked and playful," added Frank.

"Yes, that's it exactly."

"It's the world I've always wanted to live in." The only world where he'd ever felt safe.

Mann sat back and folded his hands. "Here's my question. Would you consider illustrating a children's book?"

"Excuse me?"

"We publish children's books. Picture books. I'm always looking for something fresh and new. For someone with an engaging visual imagination. I've got a particular book in mind, but beyond that, I believe I could keep you gainfully employed for many years if you'd come work for us."

"You're offering me a job?"

"I am," said Mann. "Will you think about it?"

"Hell no," said Frank, noticing that there was a food stain on his tie. Covering it with his thumb, he said, "I can give you an answer right now. I'd love to illustrate a book. As many books as you want."

"Well, that's just marvelous," said Mann, fixing Frank with an angelic smile. "I'll have my secretary set up a meeting for you with our art director."

Frank was so stunned he almost couldn't speak. "I . . . I can't thank you enough."

"We can talk money if you want, or we can wait until you've spoken with my art director and you know more about our process, what it will require from you."

"Give me a ballpark number," said Frank, forcing his voice into a lower register.

Mann launched into a discussion of advances against royalties, career-earning potential, and finished by saying, "This will be a big book. The author won the Newbery Medal, so it will be a high-profile rollout. Lots of press and interviews."

"Um, I mean, wow."

"You could be looking at a very good living down the line." Glancing at his watch again, Mann added, "Let's talk soon."

"Great."

"Can you find your way out of our maze of offices?"

"I left breadcrumbs," said Frank, rising from his chair.

Mann grinned. "Wonderful. It's going to be a pleasure working with you."

Frank walked out to his car in a daze, wondering if he was dreaming. Nothing like this had ever happened to him before. It was like winning the lottery, except that he'd have to work hard for the money. But drawing his inner world, the place he loved most, had never felt like work to him.

Feeling strong for the first time in . . . well, *ever*, he whipped out his phone and stood next to his open car door, listening to the sixth message his mother had left him yesterday.

"Frank," came her voice over the tinny speaker. "I'm worried about you. I don't understand why you won't return my calls. This is urgent. The arson investigator discovered bones in the garage this afternoon. In the root cellar. You know what that means. They've surrounded the entire backyard with that crime scene tape. Please come home. We need to talk."

He clicked the phone off and let it drop to the pavement, watching it shatter. Words could be made of concrete, too. His life had just shattered against one. He'd always known it would never end, that a single frightful night would follow him to his grave and beyond.

Steadying himself against the door, Frank closed his eyes, the word he couldn't bring himself to say out loud swirling bright and dangerous inside his mind.

Bones.

16

Jane arranged to meet Britt for a late lunch at a restaurant near the Skarsvold house. The temperature had plummeted in the last couple of hours. A storm was moving through, bringing snow, wind, and colder temperatures. Seven inches were predicted before morning.

Jane relaxed as she waited for Britt, sipping from a cup of tea while enjoying the sight of the fluffy white flakes burying her car across the street. Friends in other parts of the country often offered her humorous condolences for living in Minnesota. All that cold and snow, they'd say. How can you stand it? The fact was, Jane loved winter. She hated the heat and humidity of summer. Winter sun was beautiful, warming. Welcome. Summer sun oppressed her. Autumn was her favorite season, but winter wasn't far behind. She liked early darkness, the shorter days. All her DNA came alive in winter.

She was on her second cup of tea when Britt came in the door, shaking snow out of her hair. Jane waved her over.

"Boy, it's really coming down out there," said Britt, shrugging out of her coat as she sat down. She rubbed her hands together. "I forgot to pack gloves."

"Here," said Jane, pulling a pair of mittens out of her coat pocket. "Take these. I've got another pair in my car."

"Are you sure?"

She smiled. "How did your presentation go?"

"Good," she said, shifting in her chair. "A lot of people came up afterward and wanted to talk. I think I raised more questions than I answered. It was kind of hard to get away." She looked up as a waitress appeared with the menus. "Can I get a cup of coffee?" she asked. "Black."

Jane glanced at the menu, scanning the sandwiches.

"So tell me what you've learned," said Britt.

"Would you like to eat first?" She wasn't sure how Britt would respond to her news.

"Why? Is it bad?"

Jane waited a beat. "The arson investigator discovered human bones in the garage. Specifically, two small bones."

Britt's eyes widened.

"There was apparently a root cellar toward the back of the garage. That's where the body was buried."

She opened her mouth, but nothing came out.

"The police came by to talk to Eleanor and Lena last night. They consider the site a crime scene, and not just because they suspect arson."

"Wait, wait," said Britt. "You said, *small* bones? Like a child's bones?"

"I asked the arson investigator about that. She said there are lots of small bones in a human body. Could be from a hand or a foot. Or, she did say it was possible the bones belonged to a child."

The words appeared to hit Britt with the force of an express train. "You're saying it could be Timmy?"

"It's possible."

The waitress set a cup of coffee in front of Britt. "Would you two ladies like to order?"

"Not yet," said Jane. "Give us a couple more minutes."

"You said the police talked to my aunts. What did they say? How did Eleanor and Lena explain it?"

"They couldn't."

"Or they wouldn't." She looked down, a scowl forming. "They're lying, Jane. Just like they lied to me."

"There was a crime scene unit working in the garage through the night."

"Did they find anything?"

"As far as I could tell from my upstairs window, they were bagging up a fair amount."

"I knew it," she said under her breath. "They did something to him." She shoved her chair back from the table.

"Where are you going?"

"Where do you think? I don't care if my aunts don't want to see me again. I have to talk to them."

"Britt, wait. We don't have any proof that the bones belonged to your cousin. Let me do a little more digging before you approach them."

"No," she said flatly.

Jane stood, clutching her napkin. "Please, let's talk about this first."

Britt yanked her coat off the back of the chair and headed for the door.

Jane looked around for the waitress. Unable to locate her, she sat down and waited for her to come out from the kitchen. Growing impatient, she tossed a ten-dollar bill on the table and left. If Britt intended to accuse her aunts of murder, Jane wanted to be there. She figured the situation required a referee to prevent an explosion.

Eleanor was dusting the piano in the living room when the front doorbell chimed. "Britt," she said, opening the door, a startled look on her face. "What a . . . nice surprise."

Britt pushed past her. "Where's Lena?"

"I'm right here," said her aunt, rolling into the room. "I thought we made it clear that we have nothing more to say to you."

Eleanor shot her sister a cautionary look. Be nice, she pleaded with her eyes.

"Why don't you sit down, dear. I think the coffeepot is still on."

"I don't want any coffee. And I don't want to sit."

Eleanor was taken aback by her abrupt tone. "Is something wrong?"

"You tell me. I heard the arson investigator found bones in your garage. Human bones. A *child's* bones."

"No, no," said Eleanor. "Who told you that?"

"Oh, great," said Lena, pointing. "We have an audience."

Eleanor hadn't heard the door open, but when she looked around, she saw that one of the new renters had come in.

"This is a private conversation, Jane," said Lena. "Feel free to leave."

"No, stay," said Britt. "I need a witness."

"Britt, please," said Eleanor. "I don't know who's been talking to you, but you've been given some misinformation."

"You're saying it's not Timmy?"

Eleanor was so shocked by the accusation, she felt her legs begin to shake. Thinking they might give out on her, she sat down on the piano bench.

"Timmy who?" demanded Lena.

"Your son," Britt all but screamed.

"I don't *have* a son," Lena yelled back.

Eleanor felt dizzy. She held on to the edges of bench, afraid she might fall off.

"Tell me the truth," said Britt, her eyes fixed furiously on Lena. "Timmy was your son. I remember him. Vividly. When I was here on Sunday night, I found a picture he drew. I remembered him stuffing it into the baseboard in your den and that's where I found it. He signed his name. That's proof." She switched her gaze to Eleanor. "The only reason I can think of that you're lying to me is because he died and you covered it up. You buried his body in the garage. What I don't know is *how* he died."

"You're insane," muttered Lena. "A drawing isn't proof of anything."

"But bones are," said Britt.

Eleanor was drowning. She had to force herself to breathe.

"You think I won't go to the police with this?" demanded Britt.

"Do whatever the hell you want," said Lena, rolling her wheelchair backward out of the room. "But don't come back here ever again."

As Britt whirled around, Eleanor looked helplessly into her niece's cold, angry eyes.

"How did he die?" asked Britt. "Can't you give me that much?"

Summoning all her strength, Eleanor replied, "I know you won't believe me, but this Timmy you're talking about, he never existed. Those aren't his bones. I'm sorry. There's nothing more I can say."

Her niece's eyes had turned into two tiny slits of hate. "Fine," she said. "I shouldn't have expected anything from either of you. My mistake. Just know that, one way or the other, I'll find the truth, even if it sends both of you to prison for the rest of your miserable lives."

17

Communication had never been a problem for them. Iver understood Eleanor better than anyone ever had. He'd been her rock
for so many years that she'd lost count. When his warm hands
held hers, as they did now, she surrendered to a profound feeling
of love and contentment. At least, his touch had always produced
that effect before.

With the discovery of the bones, everything had changed.
Eleanor fought the sense of dread that ebbed and flowed inside
her. Her emotions were like a squall that hadn't quite formed
into a gale. But the storm was coming. Of that, she was certain.
She sensed a disturbing electricity all around her.

"Do you sense it, too?" she asked Iver. "It's like we're standing
on the shore, watching the waves move toward us. They're still
a ways out. But they're huge. And, oh the wind. It's picking up.
A whirlwind is coming."

"Let's try to think positive thoughts," said Iver, moving his
chair closer to hers.

The kitchen table was covered with rye bread and cold cuts, butter and mayo, cookies and lemon cake, anything and everything that seemed cheerful and ordinary. What was more normal than the two of them having a late lunch together on a snowy early December afternoon? Except today, neither of them had any appetite.

"Just because the police discovered bones," continued Iver, "doesn't mean they'll be able to prove anything. Making a case good enough to take to trial is, in my opinion, a pretty remote possibility."

She wanted to believe him. "But what if—"

"What?" he asked, his eyes full of concern.

She could hardly bring herself to say it. "What if the real threat doesn't come from Britt, but from Lena. With her brain macerated in booze, she might let something slip and not even know what she's saying."

Iver withdrew his hands and sat back in his chair. She assumed she'd upset him until she realized Lena had rolled into the kitchen. The smell of alcohol preceded her like a bad dime-store perfume.

"Well, aren't you two cozy," she said, pulling open the refrigerator door and removing a can of Coke. "By the way, dear sister, when you get a minute, I'd like to talk to you about something important."

"Just say it," said Eleanor. "I don't keep secrets from Iver."

"Never doubted that for a second," muttered Lena, rolling closer to them. "Okay, here's the deal. I've been thinking. Maybe we should sell the house."

Eleanor's mouth dropped open. "We've already talked about that."

"Rich Novak thinks that we could get a good price. He even offered to help us get it ready to go on the market. I'm sure Butch would kick in some time, too, if we asked him."

"Absolutely not," said Eleanor. The muscles along her jawline tightened. "This is our family home. When we die, it will pass to Frank."

"I don't give a hoot in hell about passing on our childhood home. Besides, the house is half mine. If you and Little Lord Fauntleroy don't want to sell, fine. Buy me out."

"With what money?" asked Iver. "You know that's not possible."

Lena's shrug was almost imperceptible inside the brown cardigan Eleanor had given her one Christmas, many years ago. It fit her well at the time, though she'd grown so thin that she now looked like a child inside her mommy's sweater.

"With the money we could make," continued Lena, "we'd be able to go our separate ways. Wouldn't you like that? I been thinking. I could rent myself a little apartment, employ a college student to take care of my needs. The only reason we've stayed this long was because of what's in the garage. Now that we don't have to protect our secret anymore, I say we get the hell out of Dodge and never look back."

Every single day, Lena came up with some new outrage. "I won't sell, and I won't buy you out."

"Okay, fine. Maybe I'll have to find myself a lawyer."

"And pay him half of what you make if you do find some way to force me to sell?" demanded Eleanor.

"Don't be ridiculous."

"You have a lot of experience with lawyers, do you?"

Lena shot her sister an angry look as she turned her wheelchair around. "Maybe I'll have to figure out another way to convince you to sell."

"Such as?" asked Iver.

"I don't know. Blackmail?" She stopped pushing at her wheels and glanced over her shoulder. "I bet your congregation would love to know you've been banging one of your parishioners in secret all these years."

"Lena!" snapped Eleanor.

"One day you'll go too far," said Iver.

"Yeah. That's what I hear. But still, you gotta agree, it's something to think about."

After she'd rolled out of the room, Eleanor turned to Iver and said, "She's drunk."

"She's lucid enough to know what she's saying."

"Even if she did try to make trouble for you, nobody would believe her."

"On that point, I entirely agree." He leaned in close and gave her a kiss on the cheek. "I better go before I lose control and throttle her. It's been a lifelong ambition of mine."

"Maybe we should do it together."

He smiled. "I'll call you tonight. We'll see this through, Eleanor. We'll be fine."

She'd never understood how, through all of life's twists and turns, he could remain so positive. It was one of the things she counted on most. His love was her fixed point in a spinning universe. His love was, very simply, everything.

After a quick discussion on the porch, Jane asked Britt to meet her at the end of the next block. She didn't want the Skarsvold sisters to realize they knew each other. Britt left first. Jane followed about ten minutes later. Because Britt was determined to talk to the police, Jane drove them to the Griffin Building in Saint Paul, the home of the Saint Paul Police Department. While Britt might have been full of fury at the house, in the car, she didn't say more than a few words. She seemed to be in her own world, perhaps thinking about what she would say.

Accompanying her to the front desk, Jane stood by silently as Britt asked to speak to whoever was conducting the investigation into the bones found in the garage on Cumberland Avenue. She explained to the officer at the desk that she had information the police needed to hear.

Jane thought back to last night, after Sergeant Nesbitt had left. Lena's first comment was, "We're toast." If the truth came out, they—and that meant Eleanor and perhaps even Pastor Iver Dare—might all go to jail. Lena seemed to want to come clean. But then, by today, she and Eleanor had closed ranks, refusing to admit that Lena ever had a son or that the bones in the garage were his. To Jane, it seemed like a pointless lie. DNA could easily reveal Lena's connection to the remains. The only conclusion Jane could come to was that they were stalling for time.

As Jane and Britt sat down to wait, a man in jeans, a blue oxford cloth shirt and gray tie, came up to them, introducing himself as Sergeant Steve Corwin, part of the special investigations unit. He invited them to follow him back to a conference room.

Jane assumed that she'd be asked to wait for Britt in the lobby, that whoever was in charge wouldn't want her to be a part of the discussion, and yet that didn't seem to be the case.

Once they were seated at the conference table, Corwin said, "Now, how can I help you?"

Britt glanced at Jane for support before unloading all the

horror she'd been holding inside. "The bones you found? They belong to my cousin. His name was Timmy." She began her story with the first time she'd met him. Corwin took out a pad and pen and jotted down a few notes. She explained that her aunts had been lying to her, telling her that Timmy never existed, that she was mixing him up with someone else. She explained about the child's drawings she'd found stuffed down into the baseboard in the den, that it was proof that Timmy was real.

"You have these drawings?" asked Corwin.

"Not with me, but yes I have them back at my hotel and I'd be happy to show them to you." She waited while he made a few more notes, and then continued, "I'm in town for a weeklong conference at the U of M."

"What sort of conference?"

"Evolutionary genomics. I'm a professor at Penn State."

He raised an eyebrow.

"I'm not a crank. What I've told you is the truth."

"Tell me how old Timmy was when he went missing."

She slumped in her chair. "That's hard to say. He was six when I met him. We were the same age. I've gone over it again and again in my mind and I've come to the conclusion that he couldn't have lived at that house very long, otherwise people in the neighborhood would remember him. My mom and I came that summer for my grandfather's funeral. Aunt Lena and Timmy were there for the same reason, so it must have happened right around that time. June 1978. We all stayed at the house before the funeral. I'm not saying what occurred was premeditated murder. More likely it was an accident. My aunts must have hidden the body and kept it a secret all these years. I'm told you found a child's bones in that root cellar, right? They have to belong to Timmy."

Corwin tapped his fingers against top of the table. "I'd like to be able to help you with the disappearance of your cousin, but you have to understand, this is an ongoing investigation so I can't really comment. I can tell you that the bones we found have been transferred to the Ramsey County medical examiner's office and I've already received a preliminary report."

"That's all you can say? Nothing else?"

He tossed his pen on the table, sighed. He thought for a moment more, and finally said, "The bones, they're not from a child."

Jane felt her face heat up. "Not . . . a child?"

"That's correct."

She shifted her gaze from the Britt to the police officer. "You're positive?"

"We are."

"An adult then?"

"That's right."

Jane tried to keep her eyes level. "Can you tell us if it was a man or a woman?"

He hesitated. Closing his notebook, he said, "Okay, look. It was a man. Probably middle-aged. And . . ." He paused a second time before saying, "It was a homicide."

Britt just stared straight ahead. "So . . . it's not Timmy."

The officer didn't reply.

"Are you telling me my aunts murdered someone?"

"I'm not saying anything beyond what I just told you. At this point, we're still investigating. We haven't ruled anything in or out."

"But is there any way to narrow down the time of death?" asked Jane. "When the murder happened? Did you dig up any personal information on the victim that could help identify him?"

"All I can say is, we're working on it." He pulled his shirt cuff back and checked his watch. "I'm sorry, but this is about all the time I have right now." He stood, dropping a couple of business cards on the table. "If you come across anything that might help us, you've got my number."

Jane picked one up, pushing the other across to Britt. "Thanks for your time."

"No problem. You two ladies have a good day."

18

"It's hardly your fault," came Julia's voice over the cell phone. "This Britt, she sounds kind of emotionally unstable. She'd already jumped to the conclusion that her aunts had done something nefarious with her cousin. If there even *was* a cousin."

Jane stood by the window in her bedroom at the Skarsvold house, watching the snow drift to the ground in the soft blue twilight, erasing the remains of the burned garage.

"Just stop beating yourself up about it."

Julia was probably right, and yet ever since Britt had exploded at her aunts, Jane felt as if she were holding her breath. She had a strong premonition that something bad was about to happen, though she had no idea what it would be or who might be responsible. "Enough about the trials and tribulations of my day. How was yours?"

"Busy."

"How are you feeling?"

"Not great."

"Listen," said Jane, hoping to inject something more pleasant into the conversation. "There's a vintner in town. Her wines are some of the best wines coming out of the Sonoma Valley right now. She wants to preview a few of her newest at the Lyme House tomorrow night. I was wondering if you'd like to come?"

"Will Cordelia be there?"

"Yes."

"Great. If nothing else, my showing up will ruin her evening. Consider it a date."

Jane heard a noise come from the hallway landing outside her room. Stepping over to the door, she opened it a crack, finding Quentin Henneberry, the young man who'd rented the bedroom next to her, standing very still in the center of the upper landing, his eyes closed. He appeared to be listening to something. Then a familiar voice caught her attention. It drifted up from the downstairs living room. "Oh, lord, no," she whispered, shutting the door.

"What is it?" asked Julia.

"I'm sorry, but I need to go. I'll call you later, okay?" She slipped the phone into her back pocket and left the room.

The tall blond young man seemed to be in another world. Her sudden presence brought him back to earth. "Hi," he said shyly, brushing a lock of hair away from his forehead.

"I'm Jane."

"Right. I met you before." He studied her briefly before turning his attention to the ceiling. Closing his eyes once again, he repeated the words of an old poem. "Yesterday, upon the stair, I met a man who wasn't there. He wasn't there again today.

Oh how I wish he'd go away." And then he turned to Jane and smiled.

Under other circumstances, she might have stayed to pursue the strange recitation, but the voices wafting up from the downstairs living room couldn't be ignored.

Trotting partway down the steps, Jane discovered Cordelia, looking for all the world like the Bette Davis character in the movie, *What Ever Happened to Baby Jane?* sitting on the couch next to Eleanor. Lena was in her wheelchair, roaring with laughter.

As Jane descended into the living room, she cringed at the wig, one with droopy blond ringlets, that Cordelia had donned for the occasion. And as with Davis, she'd applied her red lipstick with a trowel, ignoring the natural lines of her lips, penciled in extra-dark eyebrows, and had lined her eyes, both top and bottom, with thick black eyeliner.

Eleanor glanced up. "Oh, hello, Jane. Looks like we have another renter."

"I'm Olive Hudson," said Cordelia, rising and extending her hand, fingerless glove and all. "My friends call me O."

"O?"

"Or, sometimes Big O. Looks like we're going to be cell mates."

Lena let out another snort. "Give her a good deal," she said to Eleanor. "We need a little levity around this place."

Jane eyed Cordelia's dark peach housedress and clunky black shoes. The white crew socks were, even for Cordelia, too much.

"I'm sorry we only have the small room left to rent," said Eleanor. "It was my mother's sewing room."

"Fine with me," said Cordelia. "As long as I fit."

"If you squeeze in sideways, you'll be fine," said Lena with chuckle, more snide than amused.

Cordelia glowered.

"Why don't I show you the room?" said Eleanor. "And you can decide for yourself."

Jane waited in her bedroom with her door unlocked, knowing Cordelia would eventually appear. She hobbled in a few minutes later, the clunky black shoes clearly too big for her. Flopping backward onto the bed, she said. "I couldn't let you have all the fun. This place is ground zero, the center of the action. You can't solve this case without me, Janey. Admit it. Besides, I had to meet the sisters in person to get a feel for what's going on. Hey, which is the one in the wheelchair? The one with the beaver pelt on her head."

"Lena. The younger sister. Eleanor is older by ten years."

"Older and nicer. She's the murderer."

Jane did a double take. "Excuse me?"

"It's called casting against type. The murderer is always the nice one. Secretly, she probably eats children for lunch. I know, I know. Lena seems far more homicidal."

"I don't think either one of them seems homicidal."

"Well, now that Olive Hudson—aka Cordelia M. Thorn—is here, we'll get to the bottom of it. One of them murdered Tiny Tim and hid his remains in the garage."

Jane figured it was time to fill her in on her aborted lunch with Britt, Britt's visit to the house, and her screaming match with Lena. She finished by telling Cordelia what she'd learned from talking to a Saint Paul police investigator earlier in the afternoon.

"Are you kidding me? Those bones didn't belong to Tiny Tim?"

"It was a middle-aged man."

"Oh my stars and garters," she said, waving air into her face.

Jane asked her if she'd had a chance to study the pictures she'd surreptitiously snapped of the two small bones and the piece of metal. She'd sent copies to both Cordelia and Britt.

"Yeah, I looked at them. Didn't tell me much."

Jane had to agree, though she continued to think they might be important. She wished she'd been able to get a readout of everything the crime scene unit had collected from the root cellar. Even many years after the fact, there still had to be evidence.

"So, if the bones belonged to a grown man," said Cordelia, sitting up and adjusting her wig, "I wonder who he was? A neighbor maybe? Someone Eleanor and Lena didn't like?"

Jane's cell phone rang. Checking the screen, she saw that it was Britt. "I better get that."

"I need to talk to you," came Britt's breathless voice. "Right away. I'm at the hotel. The Marriott Courtyard over by the U. Room three twenty-eight. Can you come? Now?"

"Are you okay?"

"No. There's something you've got to see."

"Can't you tell me over the phone?"

"Please. Just come. It's important." The line disconnected.

The last thing Jane wanted to do was drive around in a snowstorm. "Are you up for a visit to Britt's hotel?" she asked, glancing sideways at Cordelia.

"I'll get my coat."

"Aren't you going to change clothes?"

"Why?"

"Oh, I don't know. Just a random thought."

"I conceived this outfit as part of Olive's idiom. She was a child star, Janey. Has a decidedly thrift-store sensibility. Think about it. The poor dear can only afford a room the size of a deck of cards."

"Am I supposed to feel sorry for you?"

"Possibly. But come on, we're wasting precious time. Olive will leave first. You will follow a few minutes later. We have to be stealthy." She put a finger to her lips.

"Stealthy," repeated Jane with a weak smile.

The problem was, if anybody in the Skarsvold house looked outside and saw Cordelia brushing snow off her gleaming new Subaru, her "idiom" wouldn't make sense. Then again, that sort of logic would hardly deter Cordelia.

"Just act like you don't know me." She gave a broad wink.

"When I get into your car?"

"Exactly. Now, chop chop, Jane. The game's afoot."

19

Driving across town during the first heavy snow of the year was a slow process. Even with Cordelia's lead foot, it took them nearly an hour. The plows were out, but because it was snowing so heavily, they weren't making much headway. As soon as the snow was pushed aside by the mighty snowplow blades and a mixture of salt and sand was sprayed on the road, more snow covered it up. They eventually fishtailed into the lot next to the hotel, grabbed for a ticket as they slid by, and found a place to park. Taking the elevator up to the third floor, they hustled toward the room. Britt was out in the hallway, pacing. She seemed relieved to see them, motioning them inside.

"I don't suppose the Marriott is classy enough to furnish a roaring fire in their guest rooms," said Cordelia, dumping herself into one of the two chairs in the small living room.

Britt tried but failed not to stare. "You look—"

"Marvelous?" said Cordelia. "Mysterious?"

"I was going to say . . . strange."

Cordelia glanced down at the housedress and smiled. "When

one goes undercover, one has to take fashion seriously. In other words, sometimes you've got to stand out to blend in. You feel me? It's PI 101."

Jane took off her coat and stepped out of her wet boots. "You sounded upset on the phone. What's going on?"

"Come here," said Britt. She sat at the desk next to the TV and opened her laptop. "You sent me two pictures this afternoon. I didn't get a chance to really look at them until a few minutes before I called you."

Jane stood behind her as she pulled up the two shots.

"It's that piece of metal. Look at it closely."

Jane already had, multiple times. Under the rust she thought she could see indistinct letters, though it was hard to be sure. It could have simply been the way the rust had formed.

"It's a belt buckle," said Britt, enlarging the picture.

"How do you know that?" asked Cordelia, fingering her blond ringlets.

"Because I've seen it before." She opened the desk drawer and took out a photo, an old snapshot. "Look." She handed it to Jane.

Cordelia was up in a flash, bending over Jane's shoulder. "Who's the guy?"

"My father."

"And the little girl?" asked Jane.

"That's me. I was six. It was the last photo taken of me and my dad before he left. I've carried it in my wallet for years."

"Where'd he go?" asked Cordelia.

"I don't know. We never found out. He and Mom were in the midst of a divorce, so I hadn't seen him for a while. Actually, he'd always been around pretty erratically. He'd be gone for weeks and then he'd be sitting in the living room when I came home from school. Mom never knew his schedule. He was an over-the-road trucker. Gone for long periods."

The stocky, sandy-haired man and the somber little girl were standing in front of an old locomotive.

"We were at a train museum. My dad loved trains." She hesitated, returning to the photo on her laptop. "Look at his belt buckle and then compare it to this rusted piece of metal."

Jane held the snapshot next to the screen. The rust had changed the shape a little, but it seemed pretty clear that they were identical.

"S-I-N," read Cordelia. "He had the word '*sin*' on his belt?"

"They were his initials. His first name was Stew. Stewart Neil Ickles. He asked a guy, a friend of his, to make a belt buckle for him. Monograms often have the last name in the middle, sometimes larger. That's what my dad asked for. He loved that buckle. Always wore it. He wasn't," she added, somewhat wistfully, "a very good man." She continued, "He was nice enough to me, when he was around. Back then, we lived in a small town just north of Milwaukee. Mom had a degree in library science, so she worked in the town library. I grew up there until I was twelve, when we moved down to Chicago. Mom had been offered a better job. That's when she met Alan Kershaw and everything changed, for both of us. Alan was an environmental scientist, worked for the state of Washington. Mom and I moved out there to live with him when I was fifteen. He had a home right on Puget Sound. I thought I'd died and gone to heaven. He was a wonderful person, the one who got me interested in science."

"So your mom married him?" asked Jane.

"Not right away. She had to wait seven years before she could petition to have my father declared dead in absentia. She actually waited much longer."

"So, let me get this straight," said Jane. "Nobody ever saw your dad again after that photo was taken?"

"No," she said, biting at her lower lip.

"I'm sorry," said Jane. "This must be hard for you."

Britt gave a tight nod.

"Did your mom ever try to find him?" asked Cordelia.

"Sure. When he didn't sign the divorce agreement, as he said he would, she called the apartment he'd rented after they'd separated. It was in Milwaukee. She left messages, but he never called her back. Next, she phoned the trucking company he worked for. They told her he'd stopped coming to work in mid August. She called a couple of his friends, but nobody had seen him. It took her almost a year, but she eventually gave up. Then years later, when she and Alan started talking about getting married, they knew they'd have to petition the court for a legal finding about my dad, so they hired an investigator to look for him. The guy tried, but never had any luck. Dad had a younger brother living in Boston—Matt Ickles—but he hadn't seen or heard from my father in years. No other living family as far as we knew. It was all a dead end."

"Refresh my memory," said Jane. "When exactly did you and your mother visit your aunts—when you met Timmy?"

"It was June 1978. We could probably find the exact date if we searched for Minnesota State death records."

"And tell me again. You were how old?"

"I'd just turned six. Timmy was six, too. And Frank was maybe thirteen."

Cordelia seemed to have tuned them out. She was clomping to and fro in front of the couch, hands on her hips. "Let's cut to the chase, shall we? Stew's belt buckle was found in the root cellar, ergo, he must be the man buried there. I mean, it's axiomatic, right?" She whirled around and spread her arms wide. "I've solved the crime."

"But I've still got so many questions," said Britt.

"It would be easy enough for you to give the Saint Paul PD a DNA sample," said Jane. She sat down on one of the living room chairs. "You could go by tomorrow and show them the photo."

"Back up a minute," said Cordelia, collapsing onto the couch. "Let's talk about this a little more. To your knowledge, did your father ever visit your aunts in Saint Paul? Were they close? Maybe he was trying to find dirt on your mother because of the impending divorce."

"That's what I've been trying to figure out," said Britt, slumping against the back of her chair. "As far as I know, he'd only met my aunts once—when he and Mom were married. I have an old family album back home with pictures of their wedding. I haven't looked at it in years."

"Is it possible that there was bad blood between your aunts and your father?" asked Jane.

"Not that I ever knew about. He wasn't a real friendly guy. He never liked people coming to the house. He didn't even want Mom and me going back for the funeral. I remember that clearly. They had a big argument about it. It was the one time I remember Mom absolutely defying him. And then, shortly after we got back, she must have told him she wanted a divorce."

"Do you remember how he took it?" asked Jane.

Britt tilted her head back and closed her eyes. "I just remember that it was a very tense time. A lot of fights. A lot of shouting. I hid under the bed when they'd go at it, cover my ears. And then he was gone. Poof. And I never saw him again."

Jane spent a few moments digesting the information.

"Here's one question," said Britt. "If those are my dad's remains, do I talk to my aunts, demand that they tell me the truth about what happened, or do I simply talk to the police and let them figure it out?"

"You think your aunts would tell you the truth?" asked Cordelia. "Or even talk to you again?"

"I'd like think they would, given what I know."

"You want my advice?" asked Jane.

"I do," said Britt.

"Give the police your DNA and tell them what you know. Assuming you're right about the belt buckle, and I believe you are, they'll nail it down. Once you have the facts—not just your word against theirs—then you can talk to them."

"But by the time the police get the DNA results, I'll be back home."

"It's better to take it slow and do it right than to go off half-cocked, accuse them of something you can't prove."

Britt groaned. She didn't say anything for almost a minute. "You're right," she agreed. "I'll head over to the police station again tomorrow morning."

"But," said Cordelia, her finger rising into the air, "we can't forget that we still don't know the whereabouts of Tiny Tim."

"You want me to keep working on it?" asked Jane.

"Absolutely," replied Britt.

"I don't suppose anyone's interested in ordering up some dinner?" said Cordelia. "All this cerebration is making me ravenous. Besides, it must be dinnertime somewhere." She glanced at her watch. Pointing to it, she said, "Look! It's almost seven."

"Dinner is the least I can do," said Britt. "You two are saving my life."

"Of course we are," said Cordelia, kicking off her clunky shoes and stretching out across the couch. "We're the kickass sisters. The complete bag of Fritos. No worries. We'll figure this all out or my name isn't Olive Hudson."

Britt appeared confused. "Who?"

"Don't ask," said Jane.

20

Frank was supremely annoyed by reality TV and yet he couldn't seem to stop watching it. He bounced a beer bottle on his knee, full of disgust, but still pulled in by the sight of Tia Torres rescuing another dog. *Pitt Bulls & Parolees* was his current favorite. This wasn't a particularly good episode, which was disappointing. He thought about switching to Fox News for a few laughs.

"Nah," he whispered. Fake reality TV was bad enough. The real thing was too much to take tonight. When his stomach growled, he drank more beer.

Wendy had called around five to say that she'd be late getting home. He asked her to stop by the Chinese restaurant near their house to pick up their usual—two double orders of egg rolls, one of fried dumplings, an order of sweet and sour chicken, and an order of moo shoo pork, her favorite, with extra pancakes. He didn't want to tell her his good news—as well as the not so good news—on the phone.

Wendy explained that she'd promised her parents that she'd swing by their place after work to look at some of the years of collected crap they were planning to donate to charity. They were downsizing so they could move into an assisted living facility in the spring. Frank assumed Wendy's visit would mean that she'd stuff the car with a bunch of useless junk, destined, as usual, for their basement.

Hearing the back door open, he pushed out of the chair, feeling a pleasant buzz. He was on his third beer and hoped it wouldn't be his last of the evening.

Wendy lumbered into the kitchen carrying the sacks of food. "I parked in the garage. We could have seven inches by morning." She set everything on the kitchen island and then removed her coat. "When did you get home?"

"Around four."

She glanced at the kitchen sink, still filled with dishes.

"I'll load the dishwasher after dinner, hon," he said, pulling out a stool and sitting down.

Wendy grabbed herself a beer from the refrigerator and sat down next to him, opening the packages and removing the white containers.

"Did you bring home a lot of junk?" he asked, yanking the paper off the chopsticks. They usually ate straight from the cartons, thus creating fewer dishes. Neither one of them liked to cook or clean.

"Not so much," she said, taking a bite of egg roll.

They talked amiably about nothing in particular while they ate. Frank could hear barking coming from the TV in the family room, but figured the pit bull's fate would remain forever a mystery, unless he caught a rerun.

As he was polishing off his fourth beer, feeling utterly stuffed and deeply mellow, he asked Wendy a question. "I have good news and bad news. Which do you want to hear first?"

She stopped chewing and turned to face him. "Is that a trick question?"

"Don't overanalyze. Good or bad first."

"Good."

He told her about the meeting he'd had with Walter Mann. He'd been practicing what he would tell her all afternoon. He wanted to relish the moment, to enjoy the surprise and delight in her eyes, but instead of taking his time, the words tumbled out too fast. Still, she did seem pleased, if a little bewildered.

"Does that mean you're quitting your tax preparation job?"

"I don't know yet. Yeah, I hope so. Wouldn't it be incredibly cool if it all worked out? Which it will. For the first time in forever, I see a way out of my daily grind."

"You hate your job that much?"

"Of course I hate it."

"So," she said, wiping her mouth on a napkin, keeping her eyes averted, "what's the bad news?"

"Well, ah—" He pushed the empty beer bottle away. "See, here's the deal. I told you that my mother's garage burned down, right?"

"Yeah."

"When the arson investigator was looking through the rubble, she found some bones."

Wendy straightened up. "Yeah?"

"Yeah."

"Animal bones?"

"Human."

"Whose bones?"

"They don't know. I shoulda called my mom when I got home to get more details, but I was in such a good mood because of the meeting with Mr. Mann that I couldn't. I'll call tomorrow."

"You have absolutely no idea who the bones belong to?"

Of course he knew. He got up to find another beer. "Nope. Sorry, hon. It's probably nothing to worry about."

She pushed back from the island. "The police find human bones in your mother's garage and you think it's nothing to worry about?"

The food he'd just eaten felt like an anvil inside his stomach. Thank God it was Chinese food. He'd be hungry again in an hour. "Please, don't get upset. Whoever the bones belong to—and however they got there—it has nothing to do with me."

She didn't respond. Instead, she stared at him. Looked right through him.

"Hey, why don't I go unload some of the stuff you brought home."

"What aren't you telling me?"

"Nothing," he said, giving her a peck on the cheek. On his way to the back door that lead out to the garage, he grabbed her keys. "Anything you'd like me to bring in first?"

She was already clearing the cartons from the island. "I thought you might like some of my dad's tools. They're in the trunk."

"Oh, sure. That sounds good."

"Don't try to carry in too much at one time. You'll hurt your back."

He chuckled, opening the door and flipping on the overhead light. The car sat next to his Suburban, still covered with snow, dripping water all over the concrete floor. He wasn't the least bit interested in his father-in-law's tools. He merely wanted to get away from his wife. To flee.

As he descended the steps, he used the remote to open the trunk. Sure enough, when he looked inside, he found a bucket load of old stuff. He picked up a cordless leaf blower that looked like it had seen better days. Next to a set of gear wrenches were a couple of metal measuring tapes and a circular saw blade. There was an oil filter wrench, a socket set, several shovels, and a plastic partitioned box filled with various screws, bolts, and nails. Toward the back of the trunk was a roll of wire mesh. When he pulled it out, the sight that caught his eyes caused him to gasp.

Feeling all the blood drain from his face, he reached for the ax. Staring dumbly at the blade, he swallowed. Then swallowed again. The ax felt heavy in his hand. Heavy and cold and dangerous. He needed to put it down, to get rid of it, and yet something stopped him. What the hell was he doing? Just drop it, he ordered himself. Back away.

From the kitchen doorway, his wife called, "Did you find something you like?"

He raised his eyes to hers, felt himself break into a cold sweat.

"Frank? Is something wrong?"

"No, no. Everything's fine."

"It's cold out there. You can do that later. Come inside."

He shut the trunk. The ax was still in his hand.

"Come on. I made us some decaf."

"Sure, hon. Sounds good." Holding the ax at his side, he went back into the house, shutting the door quietly behind him.

21

Eleanor had just finished getting a fire going in the fireplace when Lena rolled herself into the living room. By the smell of her, Eleanor could tell she'd been at the bottle again. Lena had taken to smoking in her room, thus containing the reek of her menthol cigarettes to a small part of the house. Even so, wherever she went, she carried the stink of her various vices with her.

"It's really coming down out there," said Eleanor.

Lena's lap was covered with a blanket. She wore two sweaters over her bony shoulders. "We better call that kid who shoveled for us last year, see if he's up for doing it again this winter."

"Already did," said Eleanor, closing the top of the kindling box and then sitting down on top of it, warming her hands near the flames. "I spoke to his mother. The snow's supposed to taper off midmorning. She said she'd send him over after he gets home from school."

"If there is school tomorrow. They may cancel it." She cackled. "Do you ever remember our school being canceled because of seven inches when we were kids?"

"No," said Eleanor, thinking back. "Only for a blizzard."

"I used to love going for walks when it was snowing out. Nothing like it. A real wonderland."

"I remember that, too," said Eleanor. She twisted around when she heard the TV snap off. The tall blond renter emerged from the den carrying a sack of pretzels and immediately headed up the stairs, taking the steps them two at a time. Once she figured he'd gone into his bedroom, she looked back at Lena and was about to comment on him when she saw that her sister was still staring at the empty stairway, seemingly deep in thought.

"He remind you of anyone?" asked Lena.

"Not really. Should he?"

"If Timmy'd had a son, he'd look just like that kid. He'd be the right age, too."

"Timmy didn't have a son. You know that. He died when he was a boy." She decided to get something off her chest. "Speaking of Tim, why on earth did you have to tell Britt that he was a figment of her imagination?" She'd been upstairs at the time getting her purse. When she came back down into the living room, she had to scramble to figure out what Lena had told Britt.

"I didn't want to bare my soul to the likes of her. It was none of her goddamn business. All I wanted was for her to leave and never come back. But no, oh no. You had to invite her to dinner."

"You put me in a terrible position. You made me lie to her to back up some ridiculous story that Tim never existed. I'll never, to my dying day, understand you."

"You're always talking about family solidarity. That's all I was asking."

Eleanor looked into the fire, deciding to take a more gentle tone. "Tim died in a car accident, Lena. It wasn't your fault. His death doesn't make you a bad mother."

Lena rolled her wheelchair closer to the fire—closer to her sister. She pulled a flask from inside her sweater, unscrewed the cap, and took a several swallows. "Our family secrets seem to be unraveling. I might as well toss another one on the pile."

Eleanor sensed the old house breathing around her. She loved the feeling of being cocooned, cradled, safe. "What are you talking about?"

"Timmy."

"What about him?"

"You're going to hate me."

"I already hate you."

She smiled. "I lied to you."

Eleanor closed her eyes and groaned. "Might as well say it, whatever it is."

"I'm an old woman," said Lena. "I need absolution."

"And you think I can provide it?"

"I didn't say I was crazy," she said with a wry smile.

"Just tell me," said Eleanor. She was tired and ready for bed.

"The fact is, when Timmy and I left after . . . after we buried the body in the garage, I drove back to a commune in upper New York State, where we'd been living for several years. Don't give me that look. It was the seventies. Seemed like the thing to do. I'd been with a guy there. Timmy loved him and he loved Tim. And, well, you know me. I wasn't a very good mother, or partner. I cheated on this guy. I'd go into town, have a few drinks at the local bar. Some nights I didn't come home. It got pretty bad between us. He finally kicked me out, told me I couldn't stay at the farm anymore. I wasn't pulling my weight. He said that

160

Tim would be better off with him. He figured he was Tim's father, so he had rights. I disabused him of that idea, which only made him angrier. He told me he didn't care. He loved Tim."

Eleanor had lived with her sister for a large part of her life. She didn't think Lena had the capacity to surprise her anymore, and yet now she had.

"I left Timmy there. With him."

Eleanor was stunned. "You're telling me you left your son with some hippie on a commune and just took off?"

"Yes."

"You mean, Timmy didn't die in a car accident like you said when you came back home?"

"He's alive. Somewhere. He probably hates me. He has every right to."

Eleanor wasn't just stunned, she was outraged. "You abandoned him? Your own son? How do you think that made him feel?"

Lena fortified herself with another swallow from the flask. "The guy I'd been with told me to leave, go off at night like I often did. We agreed that he'd wait a few days and then tell Timmy that I'd . . . you know, died. Gone to heaven. That I was in a better place and all that crap."

Revulsion rose up inside Eleanor, nearly cutting off her breath. She couldn't believe her sister could be that cold, that irresponsible. "Did you *ever* love your son?"

Lena leaned forward in her wheelchair, wiped the cuff of her sweater across one eye. "Of course I loved him. I regretted what I'd done almost immediately. But what could I do? Go back and make my boyfriend look like a liar? Confuse Timmy even more? What could I give him? I had no money, no prospects. I saw myself the same way you did—a loser. A screwup. Cheap. Genetically deficient. You can't call me a name I haven't called myself."

As always, Lena was making the story, this sepia-stained semireality, all about herself. Poor Lena, Eleanor wanted to say, but instead, said, "You never tried to find Timmy?"

"It was years before I did. But yeah, I tried. By the time I took a motorcycle trip back to the farm, it wasn't there anymore. Nobody knew where any of the people who lived there had gone. It was a dead end. I stayed in the town where I used to go drinking at night, spent some time at the bar. I walked around berating myself. I felt close to Timmy for the first time in forever. I guess I'm glad he doesn't know I'm still alive. If he did, and he had any balls at all, he'd find me and take revenge. I used to be afraid of that—of him finding his contemptible mother. Of course, other times I prayed that he would find me, no matter what the outcome, just so I could see him again."

Eleanor was rarely so angry that she contemplated violence, and yet what she felt toward her sister at this moment wasn't anger, it was pure rage.

"Where are you going?" asked Lena, rolling her wheelchair back as Eleanor got up.

"My room."

"Do you hate me?"

Eleanor felt nothing but wreckage in her stomach. She'd always felt guilty for judging her sister so harshly. She no longer did. Lena was the black hole who'd dragged everyone down into the abyss with her. "What do you think?"

Looking up, her eyes wet, she held Eleanor's gaze. "It's like I've spent my entire life suspended over this terrible, brutal darkness."

All Eleanor could force out in response was, "Poor Lena. Poor, sad, put-upon Lena. It's always about you, isn't it. Your pain. Your problems."

Lena stared at her for a long moment, then, with her lips pressed into a thin, determined line, she returned her attention to the fire. "I knew you'd understand. You're always so kind. Such a fine, generous woman. People love you because you're sugar sweet." She took another gulp from the flask. "I may be a mess, but I don't hide behind a bunch of empty platitudes."

"Goodnight, Lena."

"Yeah. Whatever you say, Eleanor. You always know best."

22

When Butch was in high school, his best friend, Corey Miller, would sneak out of his house, almost always during a winter storm, borrow his dad's car, a sweet BMW E30 325iX with all-wheel drive, and come by Butch's place. He'd wait at the end of the drive with the lights off until Butch climbed out of his bedroom window, and then the two of them would drive around town, reveling in the empty streets. On those nights, they rarely saw a cop car. If they came upon someone in the ditch, they'd help out, but mostly they kept to themselves, smoking cigarettes and turning the radio up loud. Driving in winter storms was not only something Butch was accustomed to, it was, strange as it might sound to people born and raised in Arizona or Florida, something he craved.

Tonight, though many people in the Twin Cities were heading home early, he was sitting in a quiet, residential part of Bloomington, watching a house across the street. He had yet another Jenny in his sights and the weather only added to his excitement.

Butch had always found Jenny a beautiful name. He'd known

a couple girls named Jenny in high school. Both were friendly, easy to talk to. He was beginning to think of his time in Minnesota as an odyssey, a quest. He wasn't a warrior returning home, as Odysseus had been, though he was seeking something to soothe— and perhaps end—the aching inside him. A confusing romantic breakup in the fall had left him reeling. He'd managed to work his way through four of the seven stages of grief, but seemed to be stuck most days on the anger part. If he didn't find some way to relieve the pressure building inside him, he feared he'd never get to the acceptance stage, that he would forever be locked in a battle between loneliness and despair.

The snow seemed to come in waves—sometimes heavy, though periodically it would let up long enough for him to snap a few shots of the living room. It was Christmastime. The tree in the picture window was covered in twinkling lights. He wanted a close-up of Jenny, of course, but the people around her were every bit as important. He could see a couple of men, neither of them old, both with big guts spilling over their belts as they sat on the couch watching TV. No children were visible. No toys. Nothing that would indicate that children lived in the house. There'd been a couple of times when he'd knocked on a door, asking for this or that, hoping to be invited in. Tonight's storm gave him a perfect excuse. He could say his car was stuck in the snow, that his cell phone was out of juice, and that he needed to use her phone to call a tow truck. Alas, he could tell by the people sur- rounding her that he'd barked up another fruitless tree. He'd been so confident this time. This Jenny fit the bill in so many important ways.

Feeling disappointed, he was about to pull away from the curb when his cell phone rang.

"This Butch?" came a familiar voice.

"Sure is. Hi, Lena. What's up?"

"Are you home?"

"Um, no. Just came out of a movie. It's really snowing hard. Have you looked outside?"

"Yeah, yeah. Listen up. I'm just about out of booze. I was wondering if you could swing by a liquor store on your way back and buy me another bottle of Old Crow. The bigger one this time— the one in the plastic bottle."

"I can try," said Butch. "It looks to me like everything is closing early. I've got a bottle of Canadian Club back at my house. It should tide you over until I can get to a store. That work for you?"

"I suppose. I used to like CC and Coke. Yeah, sounds good. Look, don't knock on the door when you come. There's a key hidden outside. You remember that old concrete birdbath that's filled with rocks? Sits on far end of the porch? Just dig around in the rocks and you'll find it. Be sure to put it back before you leave."

"Will do," said Butch.

"Good man. Drive safe."

Even with four-wheel drive, it took Butch almost forty-five minutes to cross the city. When he entered his house, he was overwhelmed by everything that still needed to be done. Hammond had dropped off the linoleum he wanted installed in the kitchen. He'd also left a note on the kitchen table, telling Butch that he'd decided the wallpaper in one of the bedrooms needed to come off. Butch felt like a slave. The money he was saving by agreeing to such cheap rent in return for his work in the house hardly covered his time. But it was the price he had to pay. He set his camera on the futon in the front room. He wanted to download the photos he'd taken right away, take a closer look at his new Jenny, but he also needed to deliver the booze to Lena.

Finding the key where she said it would be, he opened the front door, then returned the key to the birdbath. The interior of the house felt deliciously warm. Lena was staring into the fire in the living room when he came in and didn't seem to hear him. As he kicked the snow from his boots on the rug by the front door, Novak sailed into the room from the dining room, his arms cupped under a heavy load of firewood. He dumped it next to the fireplace and then turned to Butch.

"Averil," he said. "You made it."

Butch found himself wondering why Novak spent so much time at the Skarsvold place.

Backing her wheelchair up, Lena turned around. "Welcome to the party."

Butch handed her the bottle.

"Can't stay," said Novak. "Gotta get home to the ball and chain."

"Don't call her that," said Lena. "It's disgusting. Unless you hate her."

"Sorry," said Novak, looking both surprised and a little put out. "I just wanted to find out if you'd made any decision about selling your house."

"Eleanor's having none of it."

"Yeah, but you own half of it. Make her buy you out."

"With what? Tea bags?"

"You got rights, Lena. Ain't good to let her walk all over you."

She considered it. "If you did help us do some painting, some repairs, we couldn't pay you."

"Just cover the cost of the materials. If you wanna give me something more when you sell the place, that's cool."

"We can't even afford the materials."

Butch pulled the piano bench out and sat down.

"Yeah, but you're gonna get a settlement from your insurance company to rebuild the garage, remember? Just have the rubble removed and use the rest for repairs. Far as I can see, it's win-win. Just think what you could do with the money you'd make from the sale."

"I have thought about it," said Lena. "The only way I can figure to make Eleanor sell the house is blackmail."

"Hilarious," said Novak. "No, I'm serious."

"You don't think old people have secrets they might want to protect?"

"We'll figure a legal way out," said Novak. "Prison ain't really an option."

Watching Lena and Novak go back and forth, Butch couldn't help but wonder why Novak was pushing her so hard to sell.

"Well, better head home to the . . . my lovely, smart, super-sexy wife," said Novak He eyed Lena. "That better?"

"Much."

He grabbed his coat, calling "Later" as he drifted out the front door.

When Butch looked at Lena, he could tell she was deep in thought. "I should probably let you have some peace and quiet."

"I'll have plenty of peace and quiet when I'm six feet under. Toss another log on that fire, will you?" She wheeled herself over to the recliner by the couch.

After stoking the embers and tossing on a couple chunks of

birch, Butch turned around, seeing that Lena was struggling to get up.

"Let me help you."

"No, I can do it myself." With a lot of grimacing, she stood and moved over to the chair. "I need to get my feet up. Puts less pressure on my knees."

He'd never seen her out of the chair before and was glad to know that she had some ability to maneuver.

"Come sit down on the couch. I have a question for you."

He brushed the wood dust off his sweater. "Sure." As he sat down next to her, he said, "Shoot."

"You ever get a tattoo?"

He blinked. "Tattoos? Yeah, I've got a couple."

"Let me see."

"Seriously?"

"Come on. Don't be shy. Where are they?"

He was appalled and enchanted in equal measure. She never failed to surprise him. "I've got one on my chest that runs down my arm."

"Great. Take off your sweater."

Again, he laughed. "Okay. You asked for it." He removed it and then the black T-shirt he wore under it.

She reached behind her and turned on a lamp. "Come closer."

He bent down next to her.

"It's beautiful. What's it mean?"

"Well . . . it's all kind of personal stuff."

"Did it hurt? The needle? When they were doing it?"

"Yeah. Sometimes."

"But it was worth it?"

He shrugged. "I thought so."

"Okay, put your shirt back on. And, may I add, you have a nice body."

He blushed. Sitting back down on the couch, he wondered where she'd take the conversation next.

"Christmas is coming," she said.

"Don't I know it."

"I want a tattoo for Christmas. Been thinking about it for months. I even designed one. You know any tattoo artists here in town who wouldn't mind working on an ancient old lady?"

He was amazed at how alive she was. She was confined to the house, living in a chair, always in pain, and yet she still had a sense of humor and . . . a spark. A deeply human spark. "I'm sure I could find one for you."

"Would you take me? You'd have to carry me out to the car. I'm not heavy."

He said the first thing that came into his head. "I'd be honored."

"Oh, come on," she said, rolling her eyes, "you don't have to go that far."

"Let me check it out. I'll get back to you."

"Perfect. Also, if you don't have anywhere to go on Christmas, you can always join us here. Except?" She looked over at the fireplace. "We need to bring the Christmas decorations up from the basement."

"And you should have a tree. A nice big one for that corner over there." He pointed.

She sighed. "Sometimes we can get Frank to buy one for us, but he's got a bad back. It's always something with that man."

"Not a problem. I'll bring one by in the next couple of days."

"Really?" Her face brightened. "A white spruce. They're my favorite."

"My gift to you."

"You're a good kid, you know that? You and Rich. He irritates the hell out of me sometimes, but you've both become my friends. Warms an old lady's evil heart."

"Don't say that. You're not evil."

She struggled to pull the lever on the side of the recliner, to raise her feet.

Butch wanted to help, but remained in his seat, assuming she wanted to do it herself.

"I am what I am," she said, stretching out. "Whatever the hell that is. It's too late to change now. Hey, be a good lad and run get the bottle of Old Crow in my room. I'll finish it and then start in on the CC tomorrow. And then," she said as he rose from the couch, "you are officially dismissed." Reaching for his hand as he moved past her chair, she said, more softly this time, "Thank you, Butch. I mean it."

23

The heavy snow had stopped around two in the morning, leaving a quiet, crystalline world in its wake. Jane had wanted to be home to see the dogs' excitement at the first snow of the year. Watching them play in the backyard, tunneling, leaping, eating the flakes was a moment of pure joy for her. But, alas, after she and Cordelia had finished their dinner with Britt, they'd returned to the Skarsvold house.

Jane made it in to work by nine, late for her. She'd slept in because, in the middle of the night, Cordelia had appeared at her bedside saying that she'd heard a funny noise. She was sure it was a ghost, the soul of the malevolent Stew Ickles, unleashed by the bones discovered in the garage. Jane let her crawl in, but once she was asleep, she moved across the hall to Cordelia's tiny bedroom. She kept the door open a crack, wondering if Cordelia really had heard something strange. The door to Eleanor's bedroom was closed, as usual, as was the door to Quentin Henneberry's room. She listened for the "funny noises," but eventually fell asleep.

Sitting behind her desk at the restaurant, she checked her stack of messages, then, pushing them aside, took out the folder of notes she'd made on Britt's case. Beginning a new page, she quickly detailed what Britt had explained last night. The private investigator Britt's mother had hired to track down information on Stew Ickles likely did a reasonable job, though Jane wanted to follow up on a few things to see if she could shake more information loose. She transferred the photos she'd taken during the last few days from her phone to her laptop, hoping that enlarging them might prove useful.

Coming across the shots she'd taken of the interior of the garage, she was once again intrigued by the mural painted on the rear wall. It seemed a shame that so much junk covered it. A series of license plates had been tacked up somewhat haphazardly around the top. One, orange with a black boarder, went all the way back to 1953. Most were from the seventies and eighties with a few from the nineties. Not every year was represented, but there had to be several dozen. All were Minnesota plates except for one that stood out because the lettering was green. Squinting at the photo, Jane struggled to read the date.

"Nineteen seventy-eight," she whispered. That was the year Britt's grandfather had died and the same year Stew Ickles had gone missing. It was a North Carolina plate, which didn't make much sense. It was possible, she supposed, that someone in the family had bought a used car that year, replacing the NC plate with one from Minnesota. As Jane sat back, wondering how she could check it out, her cell phone trilled. It was a text from Britt:

Talked to cops. Told them my story.
Hard to tell what they thought. I gave
DNA sample. Now we wait.

Drawing a circle around the name Matt Ickles, Jane brought up the online version of the Boston White Pages. Sure enough, his name was there. Only one Matt Ickles listed. She punched in the number, noting that it was an hour later on the East Coast.

A woman's voice said, "Hello?"

"Is Matt there?"

"Who's calling?"

"My name's Jane Lawless. I'm a private investigator."

A pause. "What's this about?"

"I'm working for Britt Ickles, Matt's niece. She's trying to find information about her father's disappearance back in 1978."

Another pause. "I believe my husband already talked to someone about that. I doubt he has more to offer."

"I just have a couple of questions," said Jane. "It won't take long."

"Oh, all right," the woman said with an exaggerated sigh. "Let me see if he'll talk to you."

A few seconds later, a man's voice came on the line.

"This is Matt. Not sure what I can say to help. I haven't seen or heard from my brother in forty years."

"I appreciate that," said Jane. She had a theory about the plate and hoped he could confirm or deny it. "Do you remember if your brother ever traveled to North Carolina—or knew anyone there."

"Oh, gosh," he said. "Let me think. Yeah, I believe he had a girlfriend who lived near Raleigh. He was married, but, you know, my brother didn't really believe in monogamy."

"Do you remember her name?"

"Just a sec." He called to his wife. "Connie, bring me our old address book. The red one. I think it's in the hall closet in that white storage box. Probably the one on the bottom."

Jane waited, tapping a pen impatiently against a mug of cold coffee.

"Yeah, here it is," said Matt. "He called me once from her place. It was on his truck route. I thought it was Raleigh, but I made a note that it was Charlotte. I've got a phone number, but no name. Do you want it?"

"Please," said Jane. She wrote it down and then repeated it back to him.

"Yup, that's it. You know, as I think about it, I believe her name was Dixie. I remember now because I thought it was funny. A woman from the South named Dixie."

"You've been very helpful," said Jane.

"I don't know what happened to Stewart. Probably something bad. If he was still alive, I'm sure I would have heard from him. If nothing else, he would have hit me up for a loan. You have any idea about what happened?"

"Possibly," said Jane. "Nothing for certain. But I'd be happy to let you know when I find out something definitive."

"Great. Well. You've got my number. It's hard, you know? Losing a brother like that."

Jane thought of her own brother, now working as a documentary artist in England. She hadn't seen him or his wife and daughter for several years. Something had been amiss with Peter before he and his family had left for South America to shoot a documentary on the Latin American Spring in 2013. She could never quite put her finger on what it was. He emailed occasionally—a few times a year. It was never enough. "I'm sorry," said Jane.

"Yeah, thanks."

They spoke for another few seconds and then said goodbye.

Immediately punching in the number he'd given her, Jane pulled the notebook in front of her and began doodling. After four rings, the call went to a voice mail box. "This is Dix," came a high voice with a heavy southern accent. "Keep it short and I'll get back to you." Jane left a brief message, saying that she was a private investigator looking into the disappearance of Stew Ickles. She left her cell phone number and asked Dixie to give her a call. If Matt was right and she had been Stew's girlfriend, Jane hoped her curiosity would cause her to reply.

A few months back, Jane had hired an ex-cop, Nicole Gunness, to do background checks for her. She'd forwarded the names Britt had given her to Nicole and, yesterday morning, the faxed response had landed on her desk. She'd already read through most of the information. Nothing had stood out. Now she emailed Nicole Stew Ickles's name and what little she knew about him and asked her to get the info to her ASAP. She also wanted information on Frank Devine and Richard Novak, the block captain on Cumberland Avenue. She'd seen him talking to Lena more than once. She'd also watched him outside one evening just before dark, staring into the remains of the burned garage. Perhaps he was nothing more than a neighbor, a friend of Lena's. Whatever he turned out to be, she had to do a little due diligence to figure it out.

Jane was about to run upstairs to go check on the food for the wine tasting when her cell phone rang. Seeing that it was Julia, she scooped it up. "Hey, hi."

"Hey, yourself."

"Are we still on for the wine tasting tonight?"

"I'm looking forward to it. Have you been outside? How are the roads?"

"The main routes are fine. The side streets are a mess."

"Yeah, figured as much. Carol and I are planning to work from the house this morning. I've got a doctor's appointment at two. Hopefully, the roads will be okay by then. By the way, your snow removal guys are here at the house right now."

"How are you feeling?"

"Better. That headache that's been dogging me for the last couple of weeks is pretty much gone this morning. Anyway, tell me what time I need to be at the restaurant."

"Eight. I'm setting it up in the Fireside Room." There were two banquet spaces at the Lyme House. The larger of the two, the Lakeside Room, was upstairs, across from the main dining room, and could comfortably seat fifty. The Fireside Room was smaller, on the lower level across from the pub. As the name implied, it contained a large handmade fieldstone fireplace, something that Jane considered a work of art. "Do you need me to pick you up?"

"No, Carol can drop me off."

"Great. See you tonight."

Jane sent up a silent prayer that Julia and Cordelia could keep a lid on their animosity for a few hours. As much as Jane loved Cordelia and cared about Julia, she was sick to death of the personal melodrama they both lived to stoke. After texting Cordelia the time of the event, she headed up the back stairs to the kitchen.

24

Frank sat in his therapist's office, watching the snow melt off the soles of his Maine hunting boots and drip onto the carpet. He had little idea of what to say, even though he'd been the one to call Dr. Bachelder last night in a panic, pleading for another session.

"So," said Bachelder in his typically calm voice, a voice that, during the last couple of weeks, had come to sound just like nails on a blackboard to Frank. "You were upset last night. What's going on?"

With his eyes still on his boots, Frank shrugged.

"Did you have another fight with your wife?"

"No."

"I'm here for you, but I can't help if you won't talk to me."

Frank flicked his eyes to the doctor. Bowing his head, he said, "Well, the fact is . . . I'm scared."

"Scared of what?"

He cleared his throat. "Me."

"You're scared of yourself?"

"Yeah."

The doctor shifted in his chair. "Can you give me more? For instance, are you afraid you'll do something to hurt yourself?"

"No."

"But something . . . you'll regret?"

"Yeah." He felt all itchy inside. He shouldn't have come.

"Like . . . hurt someone else?"

"Maybe."

Bachelder leaned forward in his chair. "The last time you were here, we talked about your anger. You said you'd never hurt Wendy. Is that still true?"

"This has nothing to do with my wife."

Bachelder hesitated. "Okay, then does it have something to do with that time in your life you don't want to talk about? When you were thirteen?"

Frank looked out the window, then up at the ceiling, anywhere but at Bachelder. "Sometimes . . . you know . . . when you can't control your feelings? Does that ever happen to you? When they get ahead of your better judgment and you just . . . you react?"

"Go on."

"How do I stop that?"

Bachelder frowned, pausing before he spoke. "I'm not going to sugarcoat this, Frank. What you're telling me is serious. If you won't face what happened when you were young, if you continue to push it away, there will be consequences. Not just for you, but for the people you love. I'm assuming you don't want that."

What Frank wanted was to move to Neptune and set up housekeeping with an alien life-form. He was sure he'd feel more at home with an arrangement like that. "No, that's not what I want."

"Then talk to me. Let it out. I'm not going to judge you."

Frank felt himself beginning to crack. He wanted to tell someone. He ached to tell the truth, let it all hang out there. He took a few breaths. Squared his shoulders. Then lost his nerve.

"Tell me what you're thinking. It will help. I promise you that."

"I'm thinking," said Frank, his eyes bouncing around the room, "that this was a mistake." He pushed off his chair and made for the door. "I'm fine," he said as he negotiated a swift but awkward exit. He would deal with it the way he always had. So what if that ax had frightened him last night? An ax was just an ax. A simple tool. Nothing to worry about. Of course, there were other ways to take care of business. Pills. A gun. A knife. A garrote.

"Dream away," he whispered, jamming his key into the lock on his car. At times like this, being a gutless wonder might be the better part of valor.

Eleanor poured more coffee into Iver's mug. Setting the carafe back in its holder, she joined him at the table.

"Marge is really failing," he said, toying with the half-eaten tuna sandwich on his plate.

"I'm so sorry," said Eleanor, covering his hand with her own.

"It's funny. It's been devastating to watch her succumb to Alzheimer's, but at the same time, you kind of get used to the status quo. I can't imagine losing—" He swallowed back the words, unable to complete the sentence.

In her younger, more romantic days, Eleanor would never have accepted the notion that a person could love two people simultaneously. She believed in one true love. A soul mate. Loving two women and refusing to give either up went against all the rules, whether religious or cultural. Once upon a time she'd been terribly jealous of Marge. As Iver's wife, she had the status and social position that Eleanor never would. She also had a physical relationship with him, one Eleanor could only dream about. And yet, as time went on, Eleanor began to see that she had a kind of freedom Marge's life completely lacked.

Iver shot up from his chair to give a hard rap on the window overlooking the backyard. "Frank's out there. He's ripping down the yellow crime scene tape."

"Goodness," said Eleanor, covering her mouth. "They told us not to touch it."

"That man has no sense." He kept rapping until Frank turned around. "Come inside," he mouthed, pointing to the side door.

Slogging through the snow, Frank came back toward the house.

"If there was ever a time we need to be careful not to call attention to ourselves," said Iver, "it's now."

"He'll want coffee," said Eleanor, rising from the table. "And maybe a sandwich."

"Where's Lena today?" asked Iver.

"Asleep. Now that she's drinking again, I never know when I'll see her." She glanced at her watch. "I believe she has a piano lesson at four."

Frank trudged up the stairs into the kitchen. He stood next to the refrigerator and struggled out of his boots. "Crap, now my socks are wet."

"You should have left that tape alone," said Iver, sitting back down at the table.

"What are the cops gonna do? Arrest me for felony destruction of plastic?"

Eleanor and Iver exchanged glances.

"Are you hungry?" asked Eleanor. It was a moot question. She'd already begun making a sandwich.

"I could eat." He moved over to the table and squeezed into the chair nearest the wall, still wearing his puffy fleece-lined parka. He unzipped it, watching Eleanor work at the counter. "I come bearing good news. It's about that guy you turned me on to," he said, turning to Iver. "Walter Mann. He wants me to illustrate a children's book. In fact," he added, moving back as Eleanor set the plate in front of him, "I just talked to the art director at the publishing house. If everything works out, he said he has two or three more books he'd like me to think about illustrating. I can hardly believe my good luck." He tucked into the sandwich, chewing hungrily, pushing a straggly piece of lettuce into his mouth. He stopped for a second to grin.

"That's marvelous news," said Eleanor. "I'm proud of you."

"Yeah, might be a new career path for me. Wendy's over the moon."

As Eleanor cleaned up the counter, putting the mayonnaise and the bowl of tuna salad away, the phone rang. "I'll get it," she said, grabbing the cordless hanging on the wall. "Hello?"

"This is Patrolman Applewhite, Saint Paul PD. Who am I talking to?"

"Eleanor Devine."

"We need to get samples of DNA from you and your sister. I could send someone out tomorrow. Would the two of you be home around one?"

"Is this about the bones found in the garage?"

"Yes, ma'am."

Eleanor was glad that she'd had a chance to talk it over with Iver. Giving their DNA would tell the police absolutely nothing about who was buried in the garage. Still, she had to ask, if not for herself, then for Lena. "Does it hurt?"

"No, no," said Applewhite. "If you're concerned, you can ask your niece, Britt Ickles, about it. She gave us a sample this morning. The tech just does a swab of your mouth. Very simple and easy."

"You say——" She put a hand on the wall to steady herself. "Britt gave a DNA sample?"

"That's right."

His words felt like darts hitting her bare skin. "Of course," she said, working to keep her voice even. He spoke for a few more seconds, but Eleanor had stopped listening. "Fine, fine," she said. "We should be home all day tomorrow."

Lena rolled into the room, still in her pajamas. She spent a moment assaying what had just happened. "Was that the police?" she asked.

Eleanor nodded.

"Britt gave her DNA?"

Another nod.

Lena rested her fingers against her temples, mulling over the news. Then, crossing her arms defiantly, she said, "I will not take the fall for what happened. I had nothing to do with it."

"*Nothing* to do with it," repeated Eleanor, a deep shiver settling down inside her. "You're the whole reason it happened."

"Oh, no. You can't pin it on me. I never touched that man."

"Stop it," demanded Iver. "Come on now, everybody. Let's slow this down. This isn't the time to fall apart and turn on each other."

"No?" said Lena. "If this isn't the time, when is?"

"Shut up, you pathetic hag," said Frank. "Keep the threats coming and see what happens."

"Like I'm scared of you. Poor put-upon Frankie."

"Please," pleaded Iver, standing up and tossing down his napkin. "Let's just give ourselves a little breathing room. DNA can take months, sometimes years, to be processed. And then what? If we stick together, if none of us talks, the police can only surmise. I say we table the discussion and spend the evening praying about it. We can come together tomorrow and, hopefully, with cooler heads, come up with a plan."

"You really think prayer will solve our problems?" asked Lena, lips curled in distain.

"I really do," said Iver, holding her gaze.

It was at that moment when the truth revealed itself to Eleanor. Until now, even with everything that had happened between them, she'd never truly hated her sister. Clenching her shoulders, bracing herself against the judgment welling up side her, she said, "Iver's right. We need to step back and think it through before one of us does something that can't be taken back."

"You mean me," said Lena.

"Get out of here you wretched old skank," said Frank, "before I—"

"Enough," snapped Eleanor, cutting him off midsentence. Frank appeared stricken by the rebuke, but Eleanor was past caring about his hurt feelings. She needed to buy time. "Let's agree to a meeting tomorrow morning and see where we are." She paused. "Lena?" she said, looking down at her sister. "Are we agreed?"

"Oh, hell," said Lena. "I'm not gonna pray, but I will drink on it. That good enough?"

25

"This looks wonderful," said Jane, standing next to the chef who'd set up the table for the wine tasting in the Fireside Room. Dozens of wineglasses had been arranged, along with palate cleansers such as rare roast beef, thin-sliced French bread, crackers, and small slices of barely ripe pineapple. "And thanks, Henry, for getting the fire going," she added, turning and smiling as guests began to arrive. Not only had Cordelia and Julia been invited, but Jane had asked both of her sommeliers, her general manager, her executive chef, two sous chefs, her headwaiter, and three of the bartenders to attend.

Berengaria's assistant, a furtive bald man who never made eye contact, had set up several bottles each of seven wines: three reds, three whites, and a rosé. Cordelia, dressed to the nines in all black—a sequined black satin gown with a deeply plunging neckline—towered over the round, red-haired vintner as they stood by the fire talking and laughing. Jane could tell by Cordelia's rapt expression that she continued to be smitten. But because Jane wasn't getting a lesbian vibe from Berengaria, she hoped that her friend wasn't setting herself up for a fall. Nevertheless, Cordelia's charm offensive was in full swing as people began to gather around them.

When Julia walked in, ten minutes late, Jane finally relaxed. Oddly, the mere sight of her caused Jane's breath to catch in her throat. She hadn't seen Julia in almost two days and was more than a little surprised by the intensity of her reaction. Brushing her feelings away, she walked over and gave Julia a quick kiss. "Glad you could make it. You're not wearing your dark glasses."

Julia surveyed the room. "I don't know why, but I don't seem to need them. Maybe it's the new drug I started taking a few weeks ago." Her cheeks were flushed, probably from the cold. "I'm famished. Are we having anything to eat? I hope?"

"Not during the wine tasting," said Jane, delighted to hear that Julia's appetite had returned. "When we're done, the kitchen will set up small a buffet." Jane had ordered several pork pies, a corned beef panackelty, sautéed greens and, of course, an English trifle.

"Cordelia looks . . . intent," said Julia, walking over to the table and picking up one of the wine bottles to examine the label. "She hasn't even looked at me. I'm wounded."

Jane was thrilled that Cordelia's usual snarky antagonism had been short-circuited by Berengaria's presence. She hoped it would stay that way.

Everyone moved in close as Berengaria raised her voice and began to talk about her winery, what she was trying to accomplish, some of the hurdles her team had overcome, the methods she used for growth and fermentation, and finally detailing some of the awards her wines had received in the last five years. She quickly moved on to the wines on offer, her newest, something she audaciously referred to as a Grand Cru—quality Pinot Noir. The woman had confidence to burn, thought Jane, noting the less-than-positive reaction her two sommeliers gave the comment.

As everyone began to sample the first white, Jane felt Julia grip her arm. "Are you all right?" she whispered, turning toward her. Julia's face had gone deathly pale.

"I feel dizzy," she said, staggering slightly. "I think . . . I'm going to be sick."

"Let me help you."

When Julia drooped and began to fall, Jane caught her and eased her to the carpet.

"Is she okay?" asked one of the sommeliers.

Jane crouched down next to her as everyone gathered around. "Julia? Can you tell me what's wrong?"

Julia just kept groaning and holding her head.

Pulling her cell phone out, Jane tapped in 911. She gave the woman on the other end of the line the information she asked for, punctuating each answer with a request for them to hurry.

As Jane held Julia's hand, Cordelia bent down next to her. "She's made of steel. She'll be okay. Just tell me if there's anything I can do."

"Stay with me," said Jane, pressing a hand to Julia's forehead to see if she had a fever. "Would you like some water? Is there anything we can get for you?" When Julia didn't respond, she asked, "Are you in pain?"

It took a several seconds, but Julia finally said, "Yeah. My head."

For the next few minutes, Jane allowed the rest of the room to fade around her. When the paramedics arrived and went to work, she stood next to Cordelia as they asked Julia questions, took a blood pressure reading, and generally tried to make sense of what was going on. Jane asked her own questions but didn't get any answers, at least none that satisfied her. The two men loaded Julia onto a gurney so they could transfer her to HCMC in downtown Minneapolis.

"Let me drive you to the hospital," said Cordelia. "You're in no shape to drive yourself."

"I'm fine."

"No, you're not. This is no time for stubbornness."

Jane apologized briefly to Berengaria. She asked her to continue with the wine tasting, saying that her staff would benefit from the opportunity if she was willing to stay, adding that she would taste the wines herself later and they could meet to discuss them or, if Berengaria was leaving soon, on the phone. She noticed the vintner and Cordelia exchange looks. Whatever it meant, she had no doubt that Cordelia would explain it later in great detail.

Jane spent the next couple of hours in the emergency waiting room sitting next to a nervous Cordelia who chewed gum at warp speed. Jane had initially asked to be allowed into Julia's room to sit with her, but the nurse at the front desk said she was being taken to another part of the hospital for tests.

"Want some candy corn?" asked Cordelia, digging through her sequined purse.

"You actually eat that stuff?"

She cocked her head. "Some reason I shouldn't?"

"Why do you have candy corn in your evening bag?"

"Hattie borrowed it as part of her Halloween costume."

"Which was?"

"She went as a flaming carrot this year. She thinks the purse is hilarious. I told her to take it, that it would give the carrot a little fashionista attitude."

Jane had no idea how to respond.

"This place makes me feel crawly," said Cordelia between chews, adjusting her plunging neckline while starring daggers at an old guy ogling her from across the room.

"You could catch the plague just breathing the air," said Jane absently, pretty much tuning her out.

"You really think so? Which plague?"

"Bubonic," said Jane, staring at the doorway, willing someone—anyone—to come and tell her how Julia was doing.

"Seriously?" She dug through the evening bag again and came up with a tissue, quickly covering her nose.

"I'm kidding," said Jane.

"You can't be too careful. You know," she added, musing out loud. "I thought Julia looked pretty good tonight. Healthier than the last time I saw her."

"I didn't notice you noticing her at all."

"Oh, you mean Berengaria?" She chuckled. Checking her phone, she added, "I've got a couple of texts from her. She wants to know how Julia is doing."

"That's nice of her."

"Yeah, she's a stunner, isn't she? We made a date."

"For what?"

"Dinner. At Thornfield."

"You mean Thorn Hall?"

Cordelia lived in a Kenwood mansion purchased by her rich sister, Octavia Thorn Lester, though the sister was rarely in the country these days. Since Cordelia and Octavia didn't get along, it was a perfect arrangement. "Why the name change?"

"Oh, well," she said, waving the question away. "I was already halfway to Thornfield Hall when I named it Thorn Hall. Might as well do the full Charlotte Brontë."

"Sure. Why not?" Jane assumed it all made perfect sense to Cordelia. "When you and Berengaria have dinner together, you should wear your Olive Hudson duds."

"Funny." She chewed a couple of times. "Berengaria's a keeper."

"You think she's a member of the tribe?"

"I don't just think, I know." After a pregnant pause, she winked.

"You up for a long-distance romance? I mean, she lives in California."

Before Cordelia could answer, a man in a white coat came through the door and called Jane's name. She shot to her feet and raised her hand. "How is she?" she asked as the doctor sat down next to her.

"I'm Dr. Reid. I've been working with Julia for the last month. She's told me a lot about you, so I'm sure you've heard all about the clinical trial she's taking part in. We're in the first phase, so there's much we don't know about this new drug."

Julia hadn't said word one about any of it. "I don't have a lot of information."

"Well, we can go into more detail later, if you want. As for now, Julia presented tonight with vertigo. We've determined that she's had a small stroke."

"A stroke," repeated Jane.

"What do you mean by 'small'?" asked Cordelia.

He turned to her. "I'm sorry. You are?"

"Cordelia M. Thorn, dear old friend of Dr. Martinsen."

He took in her gown, the jewels around her neck, his gaze

coming to rest on the tissue she held over her nose. "The flu's going around. Good to get your flu shot early."

"Bubonic plague," Cordelia corrected him.

"Excuse me?"

"Back to Julia?" said Jane.

He drew his eyes away, gave himself a moment to process the comment, and finally continued. "Um, yes, we need do more tests to determine what's going on. I'm admitting her to the ICU."

Jane gave a start. "You think she's that sick?"

"We need to monitor her closely. I'm sure you understand."

"But . . . will the stroke have any lasting effects?"

"I can't give you anything definitive. Let's hope not."

"Can she talk?"

"Yes, there's no problem with her speech. I've started her on a medication that should help with the dizziness. Also given her something for nausea. She's feeling a bit better, although she's still weak. I have to be honest. The weakness worries me."

"Can I see her?" asked Jane.

"Once she's in her room, then yes. She's been asking for you. I'm sure I must have your phone number in my records, but if you'd give it to the reception nurse, I'll make sure you get updates on her condition." He gave Cordelia a sidelong glance. "I'll be in touch."

After he was gone, Jane sat in stunned silence, staring into space. Of all the scenarios she'd anticipated, a stroke wasn't one of them.

"Are you okay?" asked Cordelia, gently touching Jane's arm.

"Yeah. It's just a lot to take in."

"Don't worry. I'm on the case. I'll go home and do a tarot reading. That should give us a better sense of where we're at."

Tarot readings had no meaning to Jane, and yet, because they were a centerpiece of Cordelia's spiritual life, she figured it would probably make her feel better, as if she was actually doing something to help. "Thank you."

"I'll stay until you head up to Julia's room."

"Would you do me a huge favor?"

"Anything."

"I called Evelyn Bratrude before we left the restaurant, asked her to let the dogs out. She has family visiting right now, so I didn't want to ask her to do more. Could you stop by my place and make sure they're okay? Give them their evening kibble and rub their tummies for a few minutes. Make sure they have some time outside in the backyard."

"I'll do more than that. I'll take them home with me. Hattie will be thrilled. Except—" She removed the tissue from her nose. "What about the Skarsvold place? Maybe Olive Hudson should put in another appearance tonight. I could ask Bolger to drive over and take care of the pups."

Bolger Aspinwall III was Hattie's part-time nanny. He'd completed film school several years back and was currently living with Cordelia at the mansion, working on a screenplay. "Honestly, it's up to you. I'll probably spend the rest of the night here."

She patted Jane's hand. "No problemo." Glancing at her phone as another text came in, she read it silently and then added, "Berengaria wants to come by Thornfield."

"Let's put the investigation on hold for the rest of the night."

"She's dying to meet Hatts. She adores kids."

Maybe the vintner actually was a keeper after all, thought Jane. "You don't need to stick around. I'll be fine."

"You'll call me with updates, yes?"

"If you want."

"Look, Janey. I care about you and you care about Julia. Axiomatically, that means I care about her. That is," she added, standing and shrugging into her coat, "until she pulls through and goes back to being Julia Martinsen, Dr. Mega Bitch. When she's home and reasonably well, I can go back to loathing her and all will be right with the world."

26

One of the nurses in the ICU brought in a recliner for Jane, telling her that the doctor had given Julia a sedative and that she would likely sleep for the next few hours. As Jane sat in the dimly lit room, her eyes fixed on the thin, pale woman in the hospital bed, it hurt her to see how many medical devices had been set up to monitor Julia's condition. Nurses and staff were in and out, checking on her. Jane was grateful for the constant attention. Since she had nothing to do but wait and watch, the quiet gave her time to reflect on the last few weeks.

If Julia had agreed to become part of a clinical trial, something that carried with it a certain amount of risk, perhaps that was the reason she'd kept the details to herself. Jane ached for Julia to wake up. She wanted to talk to her, to understand what she was thinking and feeling, although Jane knew that sleeping through the worst of the vertigo was a mercy. Eventually, she fell asleep herself. She woke to the sound of a gurney being rolled past the door. Sitting up, she saw that Julia's eyes were open.

"You're awake," said Jane, moving to the bed. "How are you feeling?"

"Better," said Julia. "I'm sorry I gave you such a scare."

"Don't worry about me. Do you remember what happened?"

With a thin, tired smile Julia said, "I do. When I saw Cordelia looking down at me with such concern on her face, not the usual hostility, I thought, for just a moment, that I'd died and gone to heaven."

"You're safe now. Lots of people looking after you."

"Thanks for staying."

"Where else would I be? Did the doctor talk to you? Do you know what's going on?"

"You mean Reid? I've got so many doctors these days, it's hard to keep track of them. Yeah, he said he thought I'd had a stroke. I guess my blood pressure was through the roof. I should have taken a reading myself before Carol drove me over to your restaurant. Sometimes it all gets to be too much." She lifted her arm, but seeing that she was hooked up to an IV, she gave up. "Speaking of Carol, will you call her? Tell her I need to see her in the morning."

"I don't think they'll let her into the ICU. And even if they did, you need to relax for the next few days, see what the doctors have to say."

"Oh, all right. What time is it?"

Jane checked her watch. "Going on five in the morning." It was still pitch dark outside. The sun wouldn't be up for another couple of hours. "I'm so glad to see you awake. How's the headache?"

"Not bad. I had a bunch of tests a few days ago. The results should be back soon."

"Julia?" Jane bent close and spoke more softly. "Why do you

keep me in the dark about your health? I only get a few comments here and there. Never the full story."

"How much do you want to know? I mean, really."

Jane was taken aback. "I want to know everything."

"Do you? I love you, Jane. So much. I can't tell you how grateful I am that you'd invite me into your home so I wouldn't have to go through this alone. But—" She turned her face away. "I have to stay realistic. Otherwise it hurts too much."

Two nurses and a woman in a white lab coat came into the room. "Julia Martinsen?" said one of the nurses. "We're here to take you down for tests."

"This early?" said Jane.

"We start early around here," said the other nurse, unhooking the monitors and preparing Julia's bed for the transfer.

"How long will it take?" asked Jane, stepping back as the first nurse bent over to release the breaks on the wheels.

"Hard to say," said the woman in the white coat. "At least a few hours."

"You go," said Julia.

"No, I'm staying."

"Go home. Take a shower. Get some rest. Come back later if you want."

"Are you sure?"

"I'm going to be busy. No use hanging out in an empty room."

Jane was deeply conflicted. If there ever was a time when saying "I love you," seemed important, it was now. And yet she resisted. She knew very well what Julia wanted, and yet she also knew that she wasn't able to give it. She'd set some important boundaries for herself before Julia had moved in, rules she was determined to keep. Their difficult history together made it impossible for Jane to act in any other way. Even so, the emotion of the moment threatened to overwhelm her.

Moving up to the bed, she bent to give Julia a kiss. "Good luck with the tests. I'll see you soon."

Julia kept her gaze on Jane as she was wheeled out, her beautiful blue eyes big and sad and serious. For someone so fearsomely contained, it was an admission of sorts, as clear as it would ever be, of need.

Because she didn't have to take care of her dogs, Jane decided to return to the Skarsvold place. Exhaustion was beginning to overtake her as she pulled her Mini up to the curb, hoping to find a spot that was fairly clear of snow. The plows had been through, although, because a few cars hadn't been moved along Cumberland Avenue, they hadn't been able to clear the street curb to curb. As the winter progressed, and the police got their act together, those cars would be ticketed and towed to impound lots.

Climbing up a mound of snow on the boulevard, Jane slid down the other side and headed for the front walk. She was startled when she noticed Lena's wheelchair on the front porch. As she came closer, she saw a body lying facedown in the snow.

Rushing now, Jane skidded to a stop next to Lena, feeling for a pulse. "Can you hear me? Lena?" She was alive, though only barely. The smell of alcohol wafting off her body was so strong, it was almost as if she'd bathed in a tub of bourbon.

Jane fumbled for her cell phone and called 911. As she spoke, she took in the scene, noticing that the snow around her had been disturbed. Was it possible that Lena had somehow fallen off the porch and crawled around, trying to get back up?

"Yes, she's breathing," said Jane, responding to the 911 operator's question. She bent closer. "Her skin is ice cold."

Jane had no idea how long Lena had been lying in the snow and feared that hypothermia had set in. "She's not wearing a coat or gloves. Just a thin sweater, jeans, and bedroom slippers. No socks. And it smells like she's been drinking."

The 911 operator said she was sending an ambulance. "Does she seem injured?"

"I don't know. It's hard to tell."

The operator said not to move her, just in case she'd injured her spine, but to cover her with something warm.

As soon as she was done talking, Jane scrambled to her feet and raced back to her car. She found the heavy wool blanket she kept in the trunk as part of a winter survival kit. Returning to Lena, she covered her up, tucking the folds under her torso, the most critical part of her body to rewarm. Next, she took off her wool peacoat and placed it over Lena's upper back and head.

And then she waited. It didn't take long for the ambulance to arrive.

"Be real gentle with her," said one of the paramedics as they began checking her vitals.

As soon as Jane was sure the two men had the situation well in hand, she rushed up the steps to the front door, letting herself in with her key. The smell of the evening's wood fire still lingered in the air. Charging up the stairs, she knocked on Eleanor's door. Because Eleanor was hard of hearing Jane figured she might actually have to go into the room to wake her. Another few seconds went by before the door was finally drawn back.

Tying her bathrobe, Eleanor peered quizzically at Jane. "It's awfully early. Is something wrong?"

Without her glasses, Eleanor seemed older and more vulnerable. "It's Lena. I just got home. When I came up the walk, I found her in the front yard, facedown in the snow."

She appeared confused. "Lena, you say? Wait, let me get my hearing aids." She crossed to her nightstand, sat down on the bed and spent a few seconds fitting one in each ear. "Now," she said, "say that again." Hearing Jane's words more clearly this time, her face lost all expression. Standing up, she said, "I suppose I should go make something hot for her to drink. Do you think you can help her into the house?"

"She's unconscious," said Jane. "I called 911. The ambulance just arrived."

Looking dazed, Eleanor sat back down on the bed. "Oh my," she whispered. "I need to call Iver. He should be here." Glancing up, she asked, "Was she still . . . breathing?"

"Yes," said Jane. "Do you have any idea how long she might have been out there?"

Eleanor's eyes roamed the room. "I go to bed early. Usually by ten. I came up to read last night around eight, so I have no idea. She's back to drinking again. She stopped for many years. I know this may sound cold, but . . . watching her kill herself with booze . . . it repulses me." Folding her hands together in her lap, she said, "I'll go down and talk to the paramedics. Are the police here, too?"

"Not yet."

"I wonder . . . could you make a pot of coffee? Everyone will be chilled to the bone."

"Of course."

"Will this nightmare never end?" she asked, searching Jane's face as if she might find an answer there. Slipping on her glasses, she hesitated for another moment, perhaps steeling herself for what was to come, then rose. She paused as she passed Jane. "Finding Lena couldn't have been easy for you. If you want, I'll gladly give you back the rent you paid for the week."

"Go take care of your sister," said Jane, squeezing Eleanor's hand. "I'll get that coffee going."

After watching Eleanor disappear down stairs, Jane took a moment to survey the bedroom. Nothing stood out or seemed to indicate anything untoward. On the nightstand by the bed lay an open copy of Boswell's *The Life of Samuel Johnson*. Next to that was an empty coffee mug. Everything looked neat. The curtains were pulled. Was it possible that Lena had fallen off the porch? Or was it an attempted suicide? After what Jane had heard pass between the two sisters about the bones in the garage, she would've been naïve to think that suicide was a foregone conclusion. Depending on what that truth was, Lena's desire, or perhaps even her determination, to come clean to the police might have presented Eleanor with a difficult choice. Eleanor or Iver. Or even Frank. But Jane was getting ahead of herself. Hopefully, it was nothing more than a bad accident and Lena would recover.

On her way back downstairs to make the coffee, Jane decided to take a detour into Lena's bedroom. Still wearing her leather gloves, she moved silently through the dining room and drew back the French doors to the sunroom. She used the flashlight app on her phone to illuminate the darkness.

The room was larger than she'd expected, with a twin bed in one corner, and a recliner next to a table with a lamp, some pills bottles, an ashtray, and an open package of cigarettes, as well as a bunch of dirty dishes. On the floor in front of the recliner was an empty bottle of Canadian Club resting on its side. Books and magazines were scattered here and there. A cheap stereo system with bookshelf speakers took up the entire top of an old dresser. The top drawer was open, revealing dozens and dozens of music CDs. Ancient rock band posters filled the walls. Across from the bed was a bookcase and a black Ikea wardrobe.

Jane was most interested in Lena's laptop, which was propped against the recliner. Lifting it up onto the table, she opened the cover. Lena's Facebook homepage popped up. Jane had already tried to view it from her own computer, but Lena didn't allow just anyone to see her posts. Because Jane wanted to maintain her anonymity while staying at the house, she hadn't sent a friend request.

Scrolling down the page, she saw that Lena's posts were mostly about music, haunted houses, and politics, with an occasional "share" of something raunchy or snidely humorous. She appeared to be big on attitude, but short on personal disclosures, anything that might indicate her state of mind.

Lena had 154 friends. No photos of herself, not even the profile picture. One woman in particular seemed to post more than anyone else. Karen Ritter. The photo was of a middle-aged woman with straight, dark shoulder-length hair and squarish dark-rimmed glasses. Jane snapped a photo of the page, then turned around and began to take pictures of the room. She was about to examine the contents of the closet when she heard the floor outside the sunroom give an ominous creak.

Quentin Henneberry stood in the doorway, watching her. "What are you doing?" he asked mildly.

Jane was flooded with panic. She had no good reason for taking pictures of Lena's room. As she thrashed around in her mind for something to say, it struck her that it was odd that he was up and fully dressed as such an early hour.

"Didn't you hear the siren?" she asked.

"What siren? I just came up from the basement."

Outside, the sound of another siren approached the house. "You're up awfully early," she said.

"The hours before sunrise are always the most interesting, don't you agree?" He turned as the siren grew louder. "What's going on?"

"It's Lena," said Jane. "She's outside in the snow, unconscious."

He didn't move or respond in any way.

"Look, Eleanor asked me to make coffee." As she crossed the space between them, he stepped out of her way, but only at the last second.

Odd guy, she mused as she entered the kitchen and switched on the light. With so much already on her mind, she let the thought pass.

27

The TV across from the kitchen island droned on. Frank tuned it out as he sat staring into his cup of coffee. He had no interest in what passed for entertainment at such an early hour. If pressed on why he always kept the TV on when he was home, he would have refused to explain it. The truth, however, was simple. Silence oppressed him, even frightened him a little. He wasn't stupid. He knew it was just a soulless box of electronics buzzing away, and yet without the company it provided, he would have felt profoundly alone. The TV distracted him from himself. It was a crutch and Frank was all for crutches.

He was so lost in thought that when Wendy came in, he didn't hear her at first. Only when she stepped to the opposite side of the island and waved a hand in front of his face did he look up. "Oh. Um, hi."

"Hi."

"There's a pot of fresh coffee."

"I can see that." She settled her elbows on the counter, rested her head in her hands, and continued to stare at him.

"What?"

"Where were you in the middle of the night?"

"Huh?"

"I woke up. You weren't in bed."

"I was probably in the bathroom."

"Nope. I checked that. And I checked the garage. Your car was gone."

Wendy's wiry brown hair was matted and tangled from sleep. And she hadn't brushed her teeth. Frank was disgusted by unbrushed teeth. "I needed some air."

"Why not simply stand on the front steps and breathe deeply?"

"What is this? A CIA interrogation?"

"It just seems kind of weird for you to take off in the middle of the night. You've never done it before."

"Are you trying to make me mad, Wendy? Do you want a repeat of the other night?"

She straightened up. "What's *wrong* with you? What happened to the man I married?"

He shoved his coffee away. "He's right here. I'm the same guy. You just know me better now."

She poured herself a cup, never turning her back on him. She was right to be afraid. He wasn't safe to be around.

"Honey, you're scaring me," she said.

"I'm sorry."

She took a sip, studying him over the rim of the cup. After a few seconds, her eyes softened and she said, "I love you, Frank. You mean everything to me. Don't you know you're my hero?"

In one lightning-swift movement, he shot to his feet and hurled his stool across the room. "Don't you ever say that word again,

Wendy. I'm nobody's hero. I hate that word," he screamed, feeling his face flush.

She backed away, letting the mug crash to the floor, protecting her head with her forearms.

"Goddamnit," he yelled. "Why do you always antagonize me? Is it your mission in life to piss me off?" He stood next to the island, clenching and unclenching his fists.

This time, she rushed to the bedroom and locked the door.

"Shit, shit shit," he shouted. Grabbing his car keys and his coat, he headed out the kitchen door into the garage. If he stayed another second, he was afraid he'd do something he couldn't take back.

Butch paused on the sidewalk and watched the paramedics work on Lena. He'd been asleep on the futon couch in his living room when the sound of a siren woke him. Strobe lights flashed through the picture window, throwing bursts of red and blue light against the walls. Novak was already outside when Butch approached him and nodded to the ambulance.

"Yo," said Novak. "It's Lena. Someone found her unconscious in the snow."

"Jesus," whispered Butch. "Is she—"

"She's alive. I got a friend who works as a paramedic in Fargo." He stamped his feet to keep them warm. "Nobody's ever considered dead until they're *warm* and dead."

One of the police officers ambled toward them. "Morning, gentlemen."

"Morning," said Novak.

"You guys live around here?"

"Me, I live over there." Novak pointed to his house across the street. "I'm the block captain. If I can do anything to assist, just let me know."

"I live next door," said Butch.

The officer took in the comments. "You know the lady?"

"We both do," said Novak. "Not well, but . . . like good neighbors. I'll say this much. She was a drinker. Always seemed kind of depressed to me."

"You agree?" asked the cop, switching his gaze to Butch.

"I don't know. No more depressed than me." It wasn't saying much, since he alternated between excitement and a feeling that what he wanted most in life would be forever out of reach.

When Eleanor appeared on the front porch, the officer excused himself.

"Poor old woman," said Novak. "It's been one damn thing after another with that family. Makes you think they got bad karma." His eyes slid toward Butch. "Hey?" He turned to face him. "You crying?"

Butch scraped at his cheeks. "Life's a bitch sometimes."

"Oh, don't I know it," agreed Novak. "But then, what goes around comes around."

"Meaning what?"

"Oh, don't mind me. I get philosophical at the weirdest times. Anyway, I better get back to the wife before she files for divorce. She don't much like my block-captain status."

Butch spent the next few minutes standing with a group of on-lookers, neighbors who'd come out of their houses to see what all the flashing lights and sirens were about. Nobody said much, which was fine with him. He wasn't interested in conversation.

Lena's face looked pale and waxy when she was finally rolled past him. Once she was loaded into the back of the van, people began to drift back to their houses, leaving Butch alone on the street. Eleanor had gone inside, but one of the renters, the one named Jane, stood on the sidewalk by the front steps talking to one of the cops. Butch ambled up to them to see if he could find out more information on Lena's condition. He nodded to the guy, but didn't interrupt.

"You found the woman?" asked the officer.

"That's right," said Jane. "A friend ended up in the hospital last night, so I didn't get home until around five thirty. That's when I found Lena outside in the snow and called 911."

Butch didn't remember her all that well from the first few times they'd met. He recalled nothing more than an ordinary looking middle-aged woman. Standing next to her now, her face lit by the soft porch light, she seemed far more attractive. Her hair was dark and shiny and her eyes were large, intense and pretty. Her best feature by far was her smile.

"Name?" said the cop, removing a notebook from his back pocket.

"Jane."

He shot her an annoyed look. "Last name."

"Lawless."

"How long have you lived here, Ms. Lawless?"

"Less than a week."

"Where'd you live before you moved here?"

"Well, ah—" She glanced at Butch, smiled. "In Linden Hills."

"Minneapolis?"

"That's right."

"Another rented room?"

"Actually . . . I have a home there."

207

The officer stopped writing. "You own a home in Linden Hills and you're also renting a room in that house? Care to explain?"

She removed a billfold from the back pocket of her jeans and took out a business card. "I'm a PI."

The officer took the card and examined it, moving backward, closer to the porch light.

Butch hadn't expected that. By the startled look on the cop's face, neither had he.

"You working on something?" asked the cop.

"Yes."

"Look, you're gonna have to give me more. I'm not sure what we have here, but if it turns out not to be an accident, you're going to have to answer questions down at the station. You might as well give me the details now."

Butch watched the woman process the request. She seemed hesitant. Finally, she said, "Lena——"

"Lena Skarsvold," said the cop, paging back through his notes. "The woman we just took to the hospital."

"She has a niece. That's who I'm working for."

Butch recalled being introduced to her last Sunday night, when she'd been having dinner at the house. He remembered her saying that she was staying at the Marriott Courtyard on the West Bank. He had no idea what "the west bank" meant, but assumed it was close to the university, where she was attending a conference.

"And?" said the cop.

"Well, the niece, she remembers meeting a cousin here when she was younger. A boy named Timmy. Lena's son. She even has proof that he existed. The Skarsvold sisters—Lena and Eleanor—insist that she's got him mixed up with someone else. That there never was a Timmy. She hired me to find out the truth."

"Have you?"

"I'm working on it."

Paging farther back in his notes, he said, "There was a fire in the garage at this property a few days ago. Human bones were found, if I'm not mistaken. You think your investigation might touch on that?"

"It's possible," said Jane. "The niece, Britt Ickles, and I talked to a Sergeant Corwin of the PPD on Wednesday. Yesterday, she gave a sample of her DNA. Corwin could probably fill you in on details I don't have."

He nodded. "The Skarsvold sisters know you're a PI?"

"No," said Jane.

"It's probably gonna come out." Turning to Butch he said, "And you are?"

"A neighbor." He pointed to his house. "Butch Averil. I'm a friend of Lena's. I was just wondering if you could tell me anything about her condition."

"Sorry," said the officer, clicking the top of his ballpoint pen. "The hospital might be able to give you some info, but more likely, you'll have to talk to her sister."

Butch figured as much. His gaze traveled to the spot where Lena had been found. "I can't imagine how she accidentally fell out of her wheelchair."

"Maybe it wasn't an accident," said the cop. "I hear she'd been drinking. Then again, ladies her age, her condition. I'd say there's a chance it was attempted suicide."

"Nobody is ever going to convince me of that." He'd blurted it out without thinking. The way the cop looked it him now made him instantly regret it.

"You suggesting someone wanted her dead?"

"All I know is, she had plans. She wanted to sell the house and move into an apartment of her own. A few days ago she asked me to find a place in town where she could get a tattoo."

"Are you kidding me?" said the cop. "That ancient old lady."

"Old ladies can't get tattoos? Is that written into the law somewhere? I even found a place yesterday and stopped by to tell her. She was so excited. We were going to make a day of it. Lunch somewhere, the tattoo parlor. She was like a kid with a new toy."

"She was in a wheelchair, pal," said the cop.

"So? I planned to carry her out to my car. Load the wheelchair into the back. She talked about doing some Christmas shopping. She asked me to find a tree for the house. Why would she do all that if she planned to kill herself?"

"Maybe it wasn't a plan," said the cop. "Maybe it was just an impulse."

Butch shook his head.

Hooking a thumb over his belt, the cop studied him. "Well," he said finally. "I guess we'll find out soon enough."

Hearing a car door slam, Butch turned to see Eleanor's pastor friend walk toward the house. He took it as an opportunity to excuse himself. Wading through the snow back to his front steps, he went inside the house and walked straight to the refrigerator, finding a can of beer and cracking the tab. He didn't have much time left to find the "genuine Jenny," as he was beginning to think of her, and yet, for the moment, his thoughts were filled with nothing but Lena.

The Skarsvold house had seemed like such an inviting place to him the first time he walked in the front door. Warm and comfortable. Worn, to be sure, but full of the smell of baking bread, wood fires, or homemade soup on the stove. The two battling sisters were at the heart, with Eleanor's dolt of a son, slovenly and underachieving, on the periphery. They fascinated him. And yet, as he got to know them better, he'd begun to detect shadows in their relationships, drops of pure, corroding acid that suggested a sickness at the core. The keener his observations became, the more he wanted to understand them. Now, with Lena holding on to life by the thinnest of threads, perhaps he never would.

28

After talking to the police, Jane concluded that it was time to come clean to Eleanor about her real reasons for renting the upstairs bedroom. She'd grown fond of the older woman and felt increasingly ill at ease deceiving her, though she also understood that it was part of her job. She would have taken her aside as soon as the police left, except that Eleanor had immediately left for the hospital with Iver.

As Jane entered her bedroom to pack her overnight case, she was seduced by the sight of the bed. It looked so comfortably soft and inviting. She propped herself against a couple of pillows, thinking she'd shut her eyes for a few minutes. Several hours later, she woke to the sun streaming in through the window blinds. She couldn't believe she'd slept so soundly, partly because she was worried about Lena, but mostly because of her concern for Julia. She held her phone up in the air and saw that she had a couple texts from Cordelia and another couple from her restaurant manager. Nothing that couldn't wait.

Swinging her legs out from under the covers, she tapped in the number for the hospital and asked to be connected to the ICU. A woman's voice answered.

"This is Jane Lawless. I'm calling about Julia Martinsen."

"Oh, yes. This is Betsy Williams. I'm the nurse who was just coming on when you were leaving this morning. I'm happy to report that your . . . friend . . . is feeling better. She's sitting up in bed and, at the moment, she's having a light breakfast. Dr. Reid is in with her right now."

Jane was happy to hear it. "Do you know if any of the test results are back?"

"Not yet," said the nurse.

"Could you tell Julia that I'll be there in about an hour."

"She's scheduled for more tests this morning. If you want to spend time with her, I'd say you should wait until after lunch."

Not what Jane wanted to hear. She thanked the nurse and hung up.

Grabbing a towel and her toiletry kit, she padded barefoot across the upstairs landing to take a shower. She stood under the water, allowing the heat and the steam do what several hours of sleep had been unable to do—loosen the tension in her muscles. Feeling reasonably refreshed, she toweled off, pulled on her bathrobe and headed back to her room. As she passed the stairway, she heard the front doorbell chime and, a few seconds after, Eleanor's voice saying, "Come in, Sergeant Corwin. I'm so glad you could come by so quickly."

Jane bent her head to listen.

Iver offered the police officer a cup of coffee.

"No, thanks," came Corwin's voice. "How is your sister doing?"

"Not well," said Eleanor. "She's in a coma. We came home because I forgot to take my medications."

213

Jane removed the towel from her wet hair so that she could hear more clearly.

"So, when you called," said Corwin. "You said you had important information you wanted to give me."

"Yes," said Eleanor, her voice firm. "I do."

Jane wished she could see the old woman's face. At least this conversation wasn't being whispered.

"This has all been weighing on me," continued Eleanor. "Lena, too. It's something we agreed we'd never talk about. A family secret. One we're terribly ashamed of. It's led to so much hurt. You see——" She cleared her throat. "It's about the bones that were found in our garage."

"Go on," said Corwin.

"I understand my niece gave you a sample of her DNA yesterday. Or was it the day before. I get mixed up."

"What about the bones?" asked Corwin, sounding impatient.

"Eleanor," said Iver, a warning in his voice.

"No, I have to do this. You have to let me. The bones . . . you see, they belonged to my niece's——Britt's——father. Stew Ickles. Stewart Neil Ickles. He was married to my sister, Pauline, Britt's mother. He . . . you see he——" She stopped speaking.

"Please, continue," said Corwin.

Again, she cleared her voice. "Shortly after Stew and Pauline became engaged, we found out that Stew and my other sister, Lena, had been secretly involved. Stew was a truck driver for a national company. When he would come through town, they'd sneak off together. When Pauline called to tell us she was pregnant, Dad and I were thrilled. That is, until we learned that Lena was pregnant, too, and that Stew was the father. Lena was furious with Stew, though she swore us to secrecy. She spent days stomping around the house yelling that Stew had betrayed her, used her, that she hated him. Hated Pauline. Hated the world and everyone in it. And then, without telling us where she was going, she left. I didn't see her again until my father died in June of '78 when she and the boy she'd given birth to came back for the funeral."

"And what about this Stew Ickles?" asked Corwin. "Did he come for the funeral, too?

"No. By then, he was dead. You see, in February of that year, four months before my father died, Stew came through Saint Paul and stopped at our house. My son, Frank, and I were living here at the time. When Stew arrived, Dad took him out to the garage so they could talk privately. Stew asked my dad to loan him money. A lot of money."

"Eleanor," interjected Iver. "Please stop."

"No," said Eleanor. "You have to let me finish. Stew used Pauline and Britt as leverage, said that if my father really loved them, he'd bail Stew out of some sort of bad financial situation. They ended up in an argument, one that became more and more heated. Somehow—I wasn't there, so I don't have all the details—it got physical. My father was merely trying to protect himself. You have to understand that. Stew . . . well, he was injured. Mortally. He fell and hit his head. It wasn't my father's fault, but he panicked and buried the body in the root cellar. I'd heard their argument so he had to tell me what had happened. He made me promise I'd never tell another living soul, but when he died a few months later and Lena came back for the funeral, I confessed what I knew."

"Let me get this straight," said Corwin. "Your father and Stew Ickles had an argument in February. The upshot was Stew's death.

Didn't Pauline suspect something was wrong when her husband didn't come home?"

"By that time, they'd been married for six or seven years and the relationship had deteriorated to the point where she wouldn't see him for months at a time. She more or less assumed that he had girlfriends all over the country. When she came for the funeral, she was talking about divorce."

Jane couldn't believe her ears. Was Eleanor actually lying to the police? Some of it fit with what Britt had told her, but much of it didn't.

"So, you're saying your father *accidentally* killed Stew Ickles and hid his body in the garage."

"That's right," said Eleanor. "I'm sorry I didn't tell you right away. Lena and I talked it over. As I said, it was weighing hard on both of us. I may be wrong, but I think what happened last night with my sister was an attempted suicide. We're all so deeply ashamed of what's happened in our family. We all played a part and so, I suppose we all share a piece of the blame."

Silence followed her comments.

"Well," Corwin said finally. "That's all very interesting, but I'm afraid your story doesn't fit the information I was given by our forensic examiner."

"What do you mean?" asked Eleanor, a slight tremor in her voice.

"Stewart Ickles was the victim of a homicide, Mrs. Devine. You got that much right. But not by an inadvertent bump on the head. The man was slaughtered. It was an act of rage. Of obliteration. I'd say that, if your father was responsible, he lied to you about what happened."

"No," came Eleanor's voice. "No, that's not possible. My father would never do something like that."

"However it all shakes out, we'll need an official statement from you. For that, you'll need to come down to the station."

"But I can't right now," said Eleanor. "I have to get back to the hospital to be with my sister."

"Understood," said Corwin. "Give me a call when you can and we'll set up a time for someone to take your statement."

Jane heard chair legs scraping against the floor, but wasn't quite ready to go back to her room. Until this moment, she would never have considered the possibility that Eleanor could lie so easily and convincingly.

From downstairs came the sound of the front door closing and a bolt being thrown.

"How could you do that?" came Iver's voice.

"I had to," said Eleanor. "Don't you see?"

Before he could respond, the phone rang.

"Will you get that?" asked Eleanor. "I'm not feeling very well."

Iver's voice now came from the kitchen. "Hello?" he said sharply, almost angrily.

"Who is it?" called Eleanor from the living room.

"I see," said Iver. "Yes, thank you. I'll let her know."

Jane leaned against the banister and closed her eyes.

"It's Lena," came Iver's voice, weaker this time, all the anger drained away. "I'm afraid . . . she's gone, Eleanor. She was pronounced dead a few minutes ago."

The house grew deathly silent. Jane was afraid to move for fear that she'd give her position away. It seemed like an eternity before Eleanor began to cry.

"I'm sorry, Eleanor. So very, very sorry."

"Oh, Lord," she cried, her voice thick with tears.

"I'm afraid you and I both have a lot to answer to our maker for."

"I never should have involved you."

Jane couldn't help but wonder what that meant. How was Iver involved? What on earth was going on in this family? Whatever it turned out to be, it was far darker than Jane had ever anticipated. She would need to be careful. So would Britt.

29

Frank's meeting with the artistic director at the publishing house was, despite his current state of gloom, a smashing success. He left the office in a great mood. He couldn't wait to tell Wendy what he'd learned, the shape his new career as children's book artist was going to take. There would be more money, but even more importantly, his status in the world would soar. Sure, he was in the midst of even more personal chaos than normal, but he made a decision as he went out to his car. He would put that behind him and move into the glorious uplands of his future. He would become the man he'd always known he could be.

As he drove away from the building, he began to muse on all the smug, overfed, swaggering demigods of his youth. His grandfather had introduced him to John Wayne. Frank had never connected with him. He seemed too old. Too ridiculous and blatant. But Bruce Willis and Clint Eastwood had been an entirely different matter. He fed at the trough of their hard-core fearlessness. While Frank feared everything in his pathetic life—spiders, taunts from fellow students, his growing girth, his mother's expectations——these men feared nothing. He wanted to *be* them. And he loathed them. And that was, in essence, his problem. He'd never had a straight, singular, entirely unexamined thought in his life. He lived in his head, dragging his heart behind him like a forlorn teddy bear. That was going to change.

Glancing at the ax resting next to him, propped against the passenger's seat, he smiled. There was nothing to be afraid of. Not anymore. Everything was the way it should be. He called Wendy on his cell phone. It was just after ten. She was already at school, but this was her free period. He was bursting to tell her the good news.

He waited through five rings until her voice mail picked up. "Damn it," he snarled. Then, remembering that he wasn't going to snarl anymore, that he was in a post-snarl world, he clicked the phone off and called the number again. He did that three more times until she answered.

"I can't talk, Frank. I'm at school."

"But this can't wait. I just got out of an awesome meeting with the art director."

No reaction.

"Wendy? Are you there?"

"Do you have *any* memory of what happened this morning? What you did?"

"Huh? Oh, you mean the stool? Hey, I'm sorry about that. Won't happen again."

"You got that right, buster."

"Buster?"

"I don't know what's happened to you, but you frighten me. I can't live with you, because I never know when you're going to snap."

"I don't believe I've ever heard myself snap." He snickered. He was in such a good mood that even her carping couldn't shake him.

"You're not hearing me. When you put your fist through a wall or throw a chair, you're telling me I could be next."

"Oh, come on. I'd never hurt you."

"Really? Because that's not what I see. It's only a matter of time before the wall becomes my face."

"Calm down. Let's talk about it over dinner. Someplace really nice. How about that sports bar on Lexington."

"I'm moving back in with my parents."

The comment was so unexpected, so utterly ridiculous, that it caused him to run a red light. "What? Say that again?"

"Don't come home tonight. My two brothers are coming by to help me move my things."

"You're not listening to me, Wendy."

"Go stay with your mother. And don't call me again. I can't deal with you right now. Oh, and please, please, Frank. Get yourself some help before you do something terrible."

He'd already done something terrible. Didn't she realize that? It was like asking him to close the proverbial barn door after the proverbial horse—or was it a proverbial cow—was long gone.

"Wendy? Wendy?" He pounded the steering wheel, continuing to shout her name until, with his throat constricting and his heart hammering, he realized she'd cut the line.

30

"Yes, captain my captain?" said Cordelia, draping herself against Jane's office doorway. "You rang?"

"I've never heard anyone combine Walt Whitman and Maynard G. Krebs before," said Jane, closing the cover on her laptop.

"I was quoting Lurch from *The Addams Family*, but it's six of one. They're both famous for the line."

"You are *such* a consumer of mass culture."

"Don't be annoying. I am a creature of the mind, of deep and impossibly lofty philosophic thought. I just happen to watch a lot of TV. Now, you summoned me, but you failed to tell me why." She sauntered over to one of two chairs in front of Jane's desk and sat down. "I hope it's not bad news about Julia."

"No, she's doing much better this morning." Jane wanted to tell Cordelia about Lena, but didn't feel it was right to do it in a text or over the phone. After she delivered the bad news, Cordelia's shoulders sank.

"Such a shame. I liked her. She had 'tude."

"One of the police officers on scene was leaning toward suicide. One of the neighbors, Butch Averil—"

"The muscular one? Kind of cute, if you like good looks and dazzlingly white teeth."

"He said it made no sense to him. She wasn't the least bit suicidal."

"And what do you think?"

"I have no idea. I will say, I don't trust anything that comes out of her sister's mouth."

"Eleanor? Pillar of the Lutheran community?"

Jane spent the next few minutes giving Cordelia a blow by blow of the conversation she'd overheard between Eleanor and Sergeant Corwin of the PPD. "Either Eleanor is lying or Britt is. Their stories can't both be true."

"Wait wait wait. Eleanor admitted that Timmy actually existed?"

"She did."

"And that Stew Ickles fathered both Timmy and Britt?"

"That was the story."

"And . . . and the grandfather accidentally murdered him?" Cordelia fluffed her hair, giving the situation some thought. "That last part seems awfully convenient."

"Isn't it. Britt said she remembers seeing her father after they returned from the funeral. She even has that photo taken at that train museum. If he was still alive then, Eleanor's father couldn't have murdered him."

"So if it wasn't the father, who was it?" asked Cordelia.

"It had to have been someone in the family. With my own ears, I heard Lena say she had nothing to do with it. So, if our time

223

line is right, and Stew died sometime after Britt and her mother returned home from the funeral—when Pauline and Stew were in the midst of a divorce—that only leaves three other people who could have done it. Eleanor. Her son, Frank. Or Iver."

"Well, four if you count the newly arisen Timmy."

"But he was only six years old at the time."

"Perhaps he was precocious. Or big for his age."

Jane shot her an exasperated look.

"I'm just saying it's possible. And what was the motive?"

"I can think of several, but all of them would just be guesses."

"Does Britt know about Lena's death?"

"No, I left her a voice mail message, asked her to call me. This is her last full day at the conference. I'm sure she's crazy busy."

"Boy, the news about Timmy is going to *blow her mind*."

Jane was more worried about how she'd take the news of Lena's death. "Look, the officer I talked to last night pressed me about how long I'd been living at the house. I had to tell him that I was a PI. Or, maybe I didn't have to tell him, but . . . it came out. Butch Averil was there, so I figure it's only a matter of time before the family finds out. I'm busted, Cordelia. I can't go back there. But . . . Olive Hudson can. In fact, she has to."

"Listening at keyholes is a specialty of Olive's."

"That would be good, but there's something else. You know that young blond kid, Quentin Henneberry, the one who rented the other large bedroom?"

"I saw him waft by once or twice."

"There's something odd about that guy. When I was leaving my bedroom this morning, after I'd packed my bag, I noticed something on the floor next to the credenza that sits between my room and his—right next to his doorway. It was a little digital recorder. About the size of a large paperclip. I priced them once because I was thinking of buying one. It can store something like ninety hours of recordings. Why would he put that outside his room? What was he trying to capture? Eleanor? I mean, from what I was able to observe, she goes up to her room around nine, closes the door, and doesn't come out until morning."

"What about secret assignations with Iver? It's always possible. Maybe the kid's kind of kinky and wanted to record a little senior hanky-panky."

"Somehow, I doubt that."

"Well," said Cordelia, slapping her thighs and standing up. "I will head over there tonight, sniff around, do my Olive Hudson routine, for which I expect, at the very least, a Golden Globe nomination, and give you a full report in the morning."

"By the way, I'll need to stop by tonight and pick up my dogs."

Cordelia sighed. "Hattie won't be happy. She'd take in every bunny, chipmunk, squirrel, duck, goose, and raccoon in the metro area if she could. Did I tell you she's talking about becoming a field biologist when she grows up? I suppose that's slightly better than her yearlong infatuation with astrophysics, and the earlier obsession with bugs." She gave a shudder. "Why oh why can't she be interested in, oh, I don't know—Theater of the Absurd, Elizabethan court masques, or epic poetry. Something *normal*. Something *practical*."

"Where there are no wood ticks," said Jane.

"Precisely."

"You're a good auntie, always encouraging her to be what she wants to be."

"Yes, I am," said Cordelia. "I'm a saint." Throwing a grin over her shoulder as she headed for the door, she added, "Saint Cordelia of Thornfield Hall."

Jane spent the remainder of the morning in her office, drinking copious cups of coffee to stay awake while she attempted to catch up on restaurant business. Shortly before noon, she removed her reading glasses, leaned back in her chair and stretched her arms high over her head. Julia was never far from her mind. She had every intention of spending the afternoon at the hospital, though it was too early to leave just yet. She placed another call to the mysterious Dixie in Charlotte, North Carolina, Stew's onetime girlfriend, but once again had to leave a voice mail message.

As she turned her attention to the monthly profit and loss statement, the name Karen Ritter popped into her head. Bringing up Facebook on her laptop, Jane typed the name in and waited for the page to appear. Instead of "friending" Karen, she decided to leave her a private message.

> Karen, hi. My name is Jane Lawless. I'm
> a private investigator. I've been hired by Britt
> Ickles, Lena Skarsvold's niece, to look into
> certain family matters. I understand that you're
> a friend of Lena's. I wonder if there's any way we
> could meet and I could ask you a few questions.

Jane left her cell phone number and her number at the restaurant, and then signed off. She switched over to her own page to see if there were any new posts. While she was reading something from her niece, Mia, she received a response from Karen.

Jane, hi. Karen here. Yes, Lena and I were once great friends. We haven't seen each other in years, but keep in touch via Facebook. Sure, I'd be happy to meet with you. I must admit, I'm curious about what you're "investigating." Tonight would work for me, as long as it's early. I'll be out and about, so I could meet you. Just tell me where and when.

Jane responded, thanking her, suggesting six o'clock, and then giving her the address of her house. Karen might not have much to add to what Jane already knew, and yet finding an old friend of Lena's seemed like something she needed to check out.

31

Looking up at the withered old face reflected in the mirror across the room, Eleanor let the book slip from her hand. She'd been reading Boswell's *Life of Samuel Johnson* for several weeks, never making much progress because she had so many other thoughts pressing on her that she had a hard time concentrating for more than a few minutes at a time. She'd begun reading the book after a friend from church had quoted Johnson to her. "At seventy-seven it is a time to be in earnest." Eleanor had missed the date by three years. Perhaps the time for an earnest evaluation of her life had come and gone. It was hard to look into the darkness surrounding her now and see anything very clearly.

The doctor who had pronounced Lena dead said that an autopsy would need to be performed. As a nurse, Eleanor understood that unattended deaths required it, and yet the thought of her sister's body being put through that kind of indignity made her sick at heart. She pleaded to be allowed to take Lena's body to a funeral home, where she could be prepared for burial. They'd done a blood test and knew she'd had an excess of alcohol in her system. That and a Tylenol overdose mixed with frigid night air had surely been the cause of death. What more did they need?

"Lena," she whispered, looking up. "I'm sorry. For everything."

Eleanor had always felt that, when analyzing a problem, it helped to trace it back to its origin. But that was part of her dilemma. Where had it started? With Lena's bad decision to sleep with Pauline's boyfriend? With Stew Ickles arriving at the house? Was the attempt at a cover-up the beginning? Or, as Eleanor feared, was it the one singular, horrific, self-serving lie she'd told that was the genesis of all that came after. She didn't know. She couldn't say. She began to cry.

Rising from her chair, she drifted to the door and then out into the hall. She didn't see the young renter until she'd almost bumped into him.

"I'm sorry about your sister," said Quentin.

"Thank you." She walked past him down the stairs. She was having trouble focusing. Iver was angry at her. He'd said as much. If she lost him, she'd lose the only thing that kept her going. No, that wasn't true. She still had Frank. Her son had always been the one part of her life she would do anything to protect, no matter what the cost. Now, it appeared, it had cost her everything.

"Mom, are you okay?"

She adjusted her glasses. Frank was lying on the couch in the living room. She hadn't heard him come in. "Oh," she said. "You startled me. When did you get here?"

"I saw that you'd called me a bunch of times. Thought I should come by. Hey, before we get into . . . whatever . . . could you make me a sandwich?"

The ordinary request calmed her. "Of course I can. But all I have is peanut butter or bologna."

"Bologna would be good. With extra mayo. And maybe some mustard. Actually, I'm kind of hungry. Could you make two?"

"Come into the kitchen," she said. She found her apron on the hook behind the door and tied it on.

Frank pulled out a chair and sat down at the kitchen table. He played with the saltshaker as she worked at the counter. "I'm afraid I've got some bad news."

"Oh?"

"It's Wendy. We had another fight. She's moving back in with her parents. I'll go home tomorrow, but I'll need to stay here tonight."

"You can always stay here, you know that. This is your home. In fact, maybe it's time you move in permanently. Now that Lena's gone—"

His head snapped up.

"Oh, honey, I'm so sorry. I forgot that you didn't know. That's what I've been calling you about. She attempted suicide last night. She died this morning."

"Died?"

"Yes. It's all such a shock."

He turned his head, looked out the window. "How'd she do it?"

"Booze. Tylenol. She went out onto the porch and somehow managed to fall off. She landed in the snow."

"Did you find her?"

"No, one of the renters did. Jane." She walked over and set the plate of sandwiches in front of him, along with a glass of milk.

"Thanks."

"You see, honey, there's no reason now why you shouldn't

move in here. This is your house. I don't have much money, so this will be your inheritance. It's what you've always wanted."

"I don't want this place," he said, cocking his head.

"Of course you do."

"I don't." He took a bit of the first sandwich, wiped a hand across his mouth and then downed half the glass of milk. "This house is nothing but a white elephant. A money pit. Why would I want to take that on? In fact, why don't you get rid of it? Move somewhere else. You're too old to take care of a place this big."

"But Frank, this is our family home. It's been handed down for generations."

He stuffed half a sandwich into his mouth, chewed. "Why, of all places on earth, would I want to live here, especially after what happened. Lena was right. It's a freakin' nightmare house."

She couldn't believe what she was hearing. Of course he would live here. This was his birthright. His legacy. She'd preserved the house, scrimped and saved every penny to pay the taxes and keep it from falling into ruin. Everything she'd done was for her son.

"Was that the front doorbell?" asked Frank.

"What?"

"Do you have your hearing aids in?" Looking annoyed, he got up and left the room. A few moments went by before Eleanor heard Butch's voice. She stood and walked into the living room.

"Sorry," said Butch, removing his baseball cap. "I was hoping I could get an update on Lena's condition. Novak was wondering, too."

"She's dead," said Frank, still chewing. "Died this morning."

"Would you like to join us in the kitchen?" asked Eleanor. She could see how upset he was at the news. "I made a pumpkin pie yesterday."

"How . . . how did she die?"

"Pills and booze," said Frank. "And frigid weather. A lethal combination."

"So . . . it was definitely a suicide?" asked Butch.

"What else would it be?" asked Frank, wiping the back of his hand across his mouth. "You think one of us murdered her?"

Butch's gaze slid from Frank to Eleanor. "No, of course not."

"You were here this morning, weren't you?" asked Eleanor. "You talked to the police?"

"Yeah. Mostly the cop wanted to speak to Jane—your renter. She found Lena in the snow. Did you know she was a private investigator? That Britt hired her."

"She's *what?*" said Frank, his eyes nearly popping out of his head.

"A PI," said Butch. "Yeah, it surprised me, too."

Frank turned to glare at his mother. "Did you know anything about that?"

"Certainly not."

"Didn't you vet her? Don't you vet the people you rent to?"

"Well, not extensively."

"You're an idiot. I'm surrounded by idiots." He grabbed his coat off the couch.

"Don't go yet," said Eleanor. "Please. There's something important I need to tell you."

"I better head back to my house," said Butch, looking uncomfortable as he slipped his cap back on. "Will you let me know about the funeral?"

"Just leave," said Frank, stomping to the door and yanking it open.

"Yes, I'll let you know," said Eleanor. "We haven't made any plans yet."

As soon as Butch walked out, so did Frank.

Eleanor sank onto the couch feeling utterly defeated.

32

When Jane returned to the ICU that afternoon, she was told that Julia had been moved into private a room on the fifth floor. She was watching TV and eating lunch when Jane entered with a bouquet of pink roses.

"You look so much better," said Jane, bending over to give her a kiss.

"And you look awful. Like you haven't slept in weeks."

"Caffeine is my friend."

Julia pressed the flowers to her nose. "These are so beautiful. You shouldn't have."

"You mean, I should have."

"Yes, that's what I mean."

Jane was incredibly grateful to see some normal color back in Julia's cheeks. "I also brought a cribbage board—in case you were up for a game." Jane glanced around the room. "Where would I find a vase?" She was about go in search of one when Julia reached for her hand. "Let me keep them for a minute. They're so alive, so fresh. Hospitals are the opposite. Good when you're sick, but never a place to get well."

"That from a doctor," said Jane, pulling over a chair.

"No, sit here. With me." She moved over so that Jane could sit on the bed. "That's better."

"What do your doctors say? Have any of the test results come back?"

"They all tell me I'm better. That, if everything continues to go well, I'll be released tomorrow. Or Sunday at the latest. Can you come pick me up?"

"Just let me know when." She touched Julia's cheek, traced the curve of her lips. "Does that mean they think this experimental drug you're on is working?"

"Someone has to get lucky. Might as well be me."

As they continued to talk, Jane was struck by the casual affection and genuine tenderness in their words. "You know," she said, her eyes shifting to the window, "sometimes I think I've forgotten how to be at peace with myself."

Julia laughed. "You've never been at peace with yourself."

"Really?" But if that was true, then why did she feel that way now?

"Will you do me a favor?"

"Sure," said Jane.

"Go home. Get some rest."

"Absolutely not."

"I'll be fine. Look, neither of us is as young as we used to be. When you're healthy, it seems like a given, like it will go on forever. It doesn't. You've been so generous with me these last few months. Let me take care of you every now and then. Okay?"

Jane didn't want to leave. Being sleep deprived wasn't the end of the world, and yet the way Julia put it to her, that she wanted to give something back, made it impossible for her to say no. "I've got a meeting at six. I'll come by after I'm done."

"Come here," said Julia, setting the roses aside and drawing Jane close. "No long goodbyes, okay. Not ever. Just a quick, passionate one."

Butch sat on the futon couch in his living room, staring out the picture window with the Saint Paul paper open on his lap. His usual morning routine consisted of making coffee and then sitting down to go through each of the local newspapers, which were delivered to his front door. Today, however, he couldn't seem to tame the jumble of thoughts and emotions spinning around inside him. It hadn't helped his mood when the coffeemaker he'd bought at a secondhand store refused to turn on. He hadn't been to a grocery store all week, preferring to eat most of his meals out. Thus, he was reduced to drinking a beer. For some reason it tasted so foul that he got up and returned to the kitchen, pouring it down the drain.

As he sat back down, the doorbell rang and then, only seconds later, someone started pounding. Hearing a familiar voice shout, "Come on, Averil, open up," Butch trudged over to the door. Novak stood outside, his breath coming in visible puffs. "You heard anything more about Lena?" he asked. "I rang the doorbell next door, but nobody answered."

"Might as well come in," said Butch.

He stepped inside. "My God, man, ain't nothing in here. Just a couch."

"I travel light."

"That's an understatement."

Butch scraped the newspapers off the futon, sitting down on one end as Novak dropped down on the other. He sucked in a breath, trying to tamp down his feelings, and delivered the bad news about Lena.

"Aw, nah. Nah. That reeks, man. Suicide?"

"That's what Eleanor said."

"Shit." He pressed the heels of his hands to his eyes. "Wish I had a joint. You have anything?"

"Sorry."

Butch sat silently, refusing to look at Novak, though he could tell the news had hit him hard.

"You know, like, maybe we should smoke a menthol in her honor."

Butch smiled. "I hate cigarettes. Especially menthols."

"Yeah. Me, too."

They each stared at their hands until Butch made a decision about something he wanted to say to Novak. "You burned that garage down, didn't you."

"What? What the hell?"

"It never made any sense to me that you kept pushing Lena to sell her house. I finally figured it out."

"I was just trying to be helpful, man. Help those two old ladies out."

"No you weren't."

"You calling me a liar?"

"You bought that house across the street so you could flip it. What happens when you're ready to put it on the market? Somebody comes through and likes what you did, but when they walk out the front door, they get a good look at the Skarsvold place.

Nobody wants to buy a house across the street from an eyesore. The way that house looks would take thousands off your profit. So what do you do? Burn the garage to the ground. Maybe it scares the sisters enough so that they decide to leave. At the very least, the insurance payout would be enough to repair some of the worst parts of the place. It's win-win for you either way."

Novak's chin sank to his chest. "You think I'm gonna admit to arson, man, you're crazy."

"No, but we both know you did it."

"You gonna say something to the cops?"

"Nope. No interest in that."

"Well then," said Novak, wiping a hand across his eyes. "Ain't nothing more to be said, I guess."

"I guess," agreed Butch.

"You heard anything about a funeral?"

"I imagine they'll have to do an autopsy first. Might take some time."

"Why? If they know it was a suicide, why bother?"

"It's pretty standard."

"It's bullshit."

Butch shrugged.

"She was a friend, you know?" Novak sat for another few seconds and then got up. "I'm gonna be screwed if I don't get back to work. Later, man."

"Yeah, later," replied Butch, watching out the window as Novak headed across the street to his truck. For the next few minutes, he sat motionless, unwilling or unable to move. When he finally picked up the stack of newspapers, thinking he'd try once again to get through them, a snapshot fell into his lap. It was the only picture of Jenny he had. In the photo, a very pregnant young woman sat on a dock dangling her feet the water. Looking at her sad face always made him feel sad, too. On the back someone had written, "Jenny Nelson, June eighteenth. Day after husband's deployment."

From that one stolen photo, Butch had learned four things. Jenny was married. Her married name was Nelson. She had at least one child. And her husband was in the military. Beyond that, he knew she lived in Minnesota, that she had an older brother, and that her father was gravely ill—or had been a couple months ago. Every photo Butch had taken since coming to the Twin Cities had been downloaded into his computer and compared against the picture of Jenny on the dock. A couple of the women had come close, though in the end, none of them turned out to be her. With a name like Jenny Nelson in a state where, if you shook a tree, at least three dozen Nelsons would fall out, finding her was like finding a Norwegian needle in a Lutheran haystack. He'd done his research. Nailed down as many possibilities as he could. But, three weeks in, he was beginning to think that, unless he somehow got extremely lucky, he would never find her.

Butch spent the next few minutes finishing up with the Saint Paul paper. Nothing stood out. Turning his attention to the Minneapolis *Star Tribune*, he scanned each section. He always gave special attention to the obituaries, thinking that, if Jenny's father was ill, he might have died.

"Oh my God," he said out loud when he got to the fifth obit on the page.

Next to a picture of a white-haired man in a business suit was the notice:

EDWARD MYRON JOHNSON, 71, onetime majority leader in the Minnesota State Senate, died on December 11th after open-heart surgery. Ed was a much beloved Republican lawmaker and businessman in the Twin Cities, serving as a state senator for the last twenty-two years of his life. Ed was blessed with a large and loving family. He is survived by his wife of forty-nine years, Emma Thalberg Johnson of Stillwater, his son, Paul Johnson of Minneapolis, his daughter and son-in-law, Steve and Jenny Nelson of Saint Bonifacius, and his three grandchildren, Chelsea, Dylan, and Michael. The family gratefully declines flowers and donations. Funeral information has not been announced.

Butch opened his laptop and typed in Saint Bonifacius. Minneapolis was a city of over four hundred thousand people. He knew because he'd looked it up. Looking for Paul Johnson would take time. Saint Bonifacius, as he now saw, only had twenty-three hundred people. It was twenty-five miles west of Minneapolis. He typed Jenny Nelson into the Saint Bonifacius White Pages. There she was. Her phone was listed along with her address: 19840 Andover Lane.

As he punched the numbers into his cell, his hands began to shake. Four rings. Five. After the sixth, the voice mail picked up. A man's voice said, "You've reached Steve, Jenny, Chelsea, Dylan, and Mike. Please leave a message."

Butch froze. After all this time, he didn't know what to say. Instead of leaving a message, he cut the line, realizing that, now that he'd found her, the one thing he couldn't tell her was the truth. He had to talk to her in person, to finesse the situation to get the information he wanted. And to do that, he needed to think through the possibilities. He was so close now that his entire body began to thrum with nervous excitement. He'd found her. She was the link. His last chance.

33

After picking up her dogs at Cordelia's house, Jane drove home through the sunny winter afternoon. Retrieving her mail from the box inside the front closet, she glanced through it for a few seconds, then headed for the kitchen, where she let the dogs out into the backyard. She watched them out the kitchen window as she made herself a sandwich. When they came up to the back porch, barking to be let in, she dried their feet and put down some kibble and fresh water.

It was going on two. Lena's friend, Karen Ritter, was stopping by around six. Instead of going upstairs to her bed, Jane built a fire in the living room fireplace. She curled up on the couch to watch the logs burn. Mouse eventually came in and took up his usual place on the rug in front of the hearth. Gimlet hopped up on the couch and nestled down next to her, burying her nose under Jane's arm. As the fire crackled and snapped, and the logs shifted in the grate, Jane drifted off to sleep.

She woke several hours later to the sound of a doorbell.

Mouse and Gimlet raced into the foyer as Jane, running a hand through her hair, followed behind. "You two be good now," she said. "Sit."

Mouse sat. Gimlet jumped up and down.

"Gimlet," said Jane, pointing a finger at her. "Sit." They'd been practicing this for weeks, mainly for Gimlet's benefit.

Looking momentarily chastened, Gimlet sat down.

"Good. Now stay." Jane opened the door.

"I'm sorry, I'm early," said a woman in a camel wool coat.

"Karen?"

"Yes, it's me."

"Not a problem," said Jane. "Thanks so much for coming." While she'd been asleep, the bright afternoon had faded into night.

"Oh, you have dogs," said Karen, hesitating.

"I can put them in the kitchen, if you want. Not everyone likes dogs."

"Are they friendly?"

"Very," said Jane.

"Then I'm fine," said Karen. "I wasn't sure I had the right house. The streets get kind of tangled around here."

Jane released Mouse and Gimlet, who rushed up to Karen to sniff and nudge her hands. Once everyone was done saying hello, Jane led the way into the living room. The fire had long ago burned down to ash, though there were a couple glowing coals still giving off tiny bit of heat. As she took Karen's coat and draped it over one of the chairs by the picture window, she motioned her to the couch.

"The reason I'm early," said Karen, sitting down, "is that my daughter called a few minutes ago. She unexpectedly got the evening off and wondered if I'd like to get together for dinner. I said I'd make a meatloaf, so I've only got a few minutes."

243

Jane sat in the rocker next to the hearth, the dogs hunkering down around her feet. "This won't take long," she said, feeling a flutter in her stomach. She knew that, before she could begin the conversation, she had to tell her about Lena.

"Dead?" said Karen after she'd heard the news, narrowing her eyes as she gazed up at the mirror above the mantel. "I . . . I had no idea."

"I didn't want to tell you over the phone," said Jane.

"No, I understand. It's just . . . so sudden. So unexpected." She paused to remove her glasses so she could wipe her eyes. "You said you found her? Was it an accident?"

"I haven't heard the final word on that. One of the policemen at the scene thought it might be suicide."

"Oh," she said, just above a whisper.

"Were you two close?"

"Well, no, not for many years. We were friends on Facebook, though that's not saying much. I haven't seen her in person since— let me think." She glanced down at the dogs. "Probably the mid-nineties. We met when we were both waitressing at the Lexington Grill on Grand Avenue in Saint Paul. Do you know it?"

"I've eaten there many times," said Jane. It was one of her father's favorites.

"We worked together for, oh maybe six months before she quit. Even after she left, we stayed friends. I was a dozen years younger, but it didn't seem to matter because we had so much in common. We double-dated a lot. She always had a new guy. Me, I stuck with the same one."

"What was Lena like back then?"

"Oh, my," said Karen. "Wild and crazy. She had a motorcycle, liked to go off for weeks at a time. She'd work a while, build up her savings, then quit and take off for parts unknown. Sometimes with a guy, sometimes alone. She wasn't the deep thinker type, but she read a lot, mostly science fiction and fantasy. She drank a lot back then, too. She was really beautiful, at least in my opinion. Always reminded me of Demi Moore. And she was funny. Loved music, especially rock. We were always going to one concert or another."

Karen stopped and smiled at a memory. "When I first met her, she was living on ramen noodles and bananas. Hated to cook. She was fun to be around—unless she'd had too much to drink. I never understood that. I mean, she had so much going for her. I know she didn't get along with her sisters. Eleanor was the older one. I met her once and, at least to me, she seemed really nice. She was a nurse, if I remember correctly. Kind of religious, but then, I was raised a Missouri Synod Lutheran, so I had the same background. Never met the younger sister. I think her name was Paula. They'd both gone to college and Lena never had. After a while it occurred to me that she must have felt embarrassed by that, like she hadn't lived up to family expectations. She saw herself as the black sheep, that's for sure, and she was darn sure she was going to live up—or down—to that. I know it hit her hard when her dad died. She'd been really close to him, especially when she was younger."

"Do you know why Lena and Eleanor didn't get along?"

"Some history they had together. Bad blood, you know? It included the other sister, too, although Lena was pretty tight-lipped about it." She folded her hands in her lap. "I just can't believe she's gone. And suicide? No."

"Why do you say that?" asked Jane.

"Just . . . because of something that happened once."

Jane waited to see if she'd elaborate. When she didn't, she continued, "Lena made a friend of one of her neighbors. A guy named Butch. I talked to him early this morning, after the ambulance took Lena away. He said he didn't believe it was suicide either. He told me she had plans, that she seemed upbeat. I suppose it could have been an accident."

"That's more likely," agreed Karen. "Suicide doesn't make sense."

"Why?" asked Jane.

She looked away. "Just between you and me, she tried it once. I suppose some would say that first attempt makes a second attempt more likely."

This was news to Jane. "Can you tell me more?"

"It was such a long time ago." She sighed. "Lena was living in an apartment just a few blocks from my place. We had keys to each other's buildings. They both had security at the front door, with buzzers to let people in. Sometimes the buzzers didn't work. It was a real pain. Lena liked to sit up on the roof. Sometimes she'd sunbathe or read a book. There was a padlock on the door up there, but it was always open. On nice summer evenings when we weren't working, we'd buy a bottle of wine, spread a blanket, and play cards. If I came by and she wasn't around, I'd always go up to see if she was there. She had a fear of heights, but if she stayed away from the edge, she was okay. One night when I climbed the stairs and ducked under the small doorway, I was surprised to see her standing close to the edge. She was kind of swaying, so I was terrified she'd fall. I called out to her to get away, to come back to where I was standing. She didn't turn around and hollered for me to get lost. Her words were slurred, so I was positive she was drunk. I refused to go. That's when she started cursing, yelling about what a loser she was, how she was stupid and worthless, that she didn't deserve to live. She said there was nothing I could do or say to stop her from jumping. I kept talking, kept trying to engage her. It took some time, but she finally backed away from the ledge. I helped her down to her apartment, put her to bed, and decided I'd better spend the night. The next morning we talked about it. She made me a promise that she'd never do it again—not like that." Here, Karen stopped.

"What did she mean?" asked Jane.

"She said that if she ever tried to kill herself again, it wouldn't be during the dark of night after she'd been drinking. She promised, if she did try, that it would be on a beautiful, sunny morning, with the birds singing. She said it was the only way she'd know for sure that she was really serious, that it wasn't just a whim or a momentary bout of depression. She swore it to me, Jane, on everything she held dear, and I believed her."

Jane was still curious. "Did something motivate that first attempt? A bad breakup with a boyfriend?"

"No. I mean, she dated all the time. I would imagine she had her share of one-night stands. She liked the attention, but she never trusted men. If they got too serious, she'd dump them and move on. No, it had nothing to do with a breakup. She never really gave me a reason. Most of the time, you'd get the impression that she thought really highly of herself. But then, when she'd been drinking, the self-loathing would come out. It was hard to watch."

"What caused the rift in your friendship?"

"There wasn't a rift, per se. My boyfriend eventually popped the question. I asked Lena to be one of my bridesmaids. She agreed to do it, but backed out a few weeks before the wedding. I was pretty upset. When I confronted her, she told me that Eleanor had been diagnosed with cancer and that she planned to move into the old family house to take care of her. I couldn't exactly get mad about that, although I didn't really understand it since there seemed to be such a deep level of antagonism between them. And then, after I had my first child, Lena simply evaporated from my life. She'd always been clear that she didn't like kids, and that's what my life revolved around. I guess I just let her go." She checked her watch. "Oh, look at the time. Was there anything else you wanted to ask? I don't really know much about her life these days, just what I read on Facebook."

Jane rose to help Karen on with her coat. "This has been helpful. If I find that I have a few more questions, perhaps I could give you a call."

"Of course," said Karen. As they entered the foyer, she stopped and turned to face Jane. "Tell me this before I go. You said you'd been hired by Lena's niece to investigate the family. I'm assuming you can't say much about that."

"No," said Jane. "I'm sorry."

"Okay, but, can you at least give me your thoughts on Lena's death. Do you think it was suicide?"

Jane figured she owed Karen that much. "You have to understand, this is just my opinion. But honestly? No, I don't."

"An accident then?"

"Possible, but unlikely."

"So what does that leave?" asked Karen.

Jane hadn't yet said out loud the word she'd been thinking quietly inside her mind. Now that she was about to, it took on a horrifying force. "Murder," she said, watching the shock bloom in Karen's eyes.

34

After work, Cordelia made straight for the Skarsvolds' house. She was single-minded. On the hunt. Jane had tasked her with ferreting out who Quentin Henneberry, the elusive young man who shared the upper floor of the house with them, really was. Cordelia assumed he was up to no good and was intent on proving as much.

Because she didn't have her Olive Hudson duds with her, just the blond wig, her idiom for the evening would, of necessity, be a little different. She breezed into the house wearing her tall black Cossack boots and black cape, ready with a story about being mugged by a Russian spy who demanded her clothing in exchange for his, but saw immediately that the only person around was the nefarious Mr. Henneberry, and he was watching TV in the den, unaware of her presence.

Climbing the stairs to her postage-stamp of a room, she whirled out of her cape and readied herself for battle by gazing at herself in the mirror over the tiny chest, fluffing her fake blond curls and applying an excessive coat of dark red lipstick. She stepped out of her room and was about to head back downstairs when she re-membered Jane's comment about the digital micro-recorder in the hallway by the credenza.

Creeping over to it, she got down on her hands and knees to do a thorough examination. The first thing she noticed was that it didn't appear to be on. She put that down to voice activation. Next she noticed a wire coming out of one end. She followed it, her knees thudding against the wood floor, until she located a remote mic halfway up Eleanor's doorway, stuck to the edge of the door frame by a piece of clear tape.

The plot thickened.

"Hey, there, you little pissant," she whispered into the mic. "It's not nice to snoop. Didn't your mother ever tell you that? I may—or may not—report you to the FBI. Consider yourself warned."

Struggling to her feet, she brushed off her jeans, straightened her ski sweater, smoothed each eyebrow, and then, squaring her shoulders, walked with all the dignity she could muster down the stairs.

When she entered the den, she saw that the diabolical Mr. Hen-neberry was sitting in a wing chair, scrolling through various Netflix offerings. She sank down on the recliner next to him. "Good evening," she said, doing her most lugubrious Alfred Hitchcock impersonation.

He glanced at her sideways. "Hi."

"I'm not picky about what we watch. As long as you have good taste."

"You're one of the renters. The one in the small room."

"Let's face it, Quentin. It's a freakin' closet."

"What's your name again?"

"Olive."

He seemed ill at ease with her sitting so close, which was fine with her. This would be a chess game. She would use every advantage to win. If she was lucky, he wouldn't have the brain power to play chess and would end up playing checkers. "You a student at one of our fine colleges?" By the looks of him, she figured he couldn't be more than sixteen.

"I graduated from MIT last spring."

"MIT," she repeated. "You have a degree?"

"Physics, with an emphasis on quantum mechanics."

Okay, so scientists weren't always old or mega smart. He could be an idiot savant. Besides, she'd lived much longer than he had, experienced the world in ways he could only dream about. She remained confident that she could, by force of her razor-sharp intellect, ferret out his deepest, darkest secrets. "Impressive. You from the Boston area?"

"Austin."

"Texas?"

"Minnesota. I'm taking a year off to earn some money. Among other things." He edged away from her. "Before I go off to graduate school next fall."

"Where's graduate school?"

"University of Edinburgh."

Okay, so she was well matched. He would be Moriarty to her Sherlock. She would need to use all her cunning to find out why he'd rented that room.

He clicked on the Netflix original, *Grace and Frankie*.

He didn't seem like the *Grace and Frankie* type. "Already seen it," she said. "Pretty awful about poor Lena," she added, continuing to ease ever closer, invading his space to knock him off his game. "I assume you know what happened."

"Could you stop crowding me?"

"Oh, was I? Sorry." She moved back, but only slightly.

"I hear it was suicide," he said.

"Really?"

"Liquor and Tylenol."

"Heavens. Did you ever talk to her?"

He sat forward in his chair. "She mistook me for a ghost the other night."

Cordelia hooted. "Being a student of physics, you probably thought that was rich."

"Rich?"

"Peculiar. Silly. Uninformed."

"I thought she was drunk." He clicked on *Orange Is the New Black*.

"Already watched that, too," said Cordelia. "FYI, I believe in ghosts."

"So do I."

Her eyebrows shot up. "You're kidding, right?"

He shrugged.

"There's this theater that I . . . where I work. The onetime owners, Gilbert and Hilda King, haunt the place. I know, I know. They're dead. But I hear them on the stairways. They're not scary. They bicker. And there's a ghost cat. You think I'm crazy, don't you. It's okay. I'm used to it."

"No," he said, giving her another sideways look. "I think it's more than possible that this theater is haunted. Is it old?"

"Turn of the century, give or take."

He switched off the TV. Rising from his chair, he dragged it in front of her and then sat back down. "In fact, I'd like to know more about the theater."

"You would?"

"When I was a kid, I had a friend who lived on a farm not far from town. We both liked playing in the barn. We were up in the hayloft one sweltering summer afternoon and because we were thirsty, he offered to go get us some cold black cherry pop from the kitchen fridge. It's always been my favorite."

Her eyes widened. "Seriously? Do you like strawberry?" If she'd been straight, he'd be her dream man.

"Oh, sure. That's the other one. Love the stuff."

He might be Moriarty, but at least he was a fellow gastronome.

"Anyway, while he was gone, I began to feel this presence. It was an old woman. I'm not sure I ever actually saw her, but I sensed her, if you can understand that."

"Oh, I do."

"I was sitting with my back against a hay bale when I suddenly felt my hair being stroked. It was very gentle. Nothing scary. It actually happened a couple of times. She would only come out when I was alone. It was something I never forgot."

"Bet your physics professors wouldn't much like hearing that story."

"You'd be surprised."

This was turning into a more interesting, less adversarial, conversation. Cordelia scolded herself for not challenging him more, not demanding answers. She needed to stay on point, not be sidetracked by their similarities.

Quentin sat back in his chair and folded his arms. "That's why I'm attending the University of Edinburgh. It's the best school out there for people who want to get an accredited degree in para-normal studies. I'm hoping to get my doctorate. But before I dove in, I wanted to have a good grounding in quantum physics. See, at heart, even though I'm what they call a 'sensitive,' I see myself as a skeptic. Quantum theory posits that the universe splits into separate branches, only one of which corresponds to our view of how the world works. There's a bigger connection between science and anomalous experience than most people would guess. That's what I want to spend my life pursuing. It's why I'm here in this house."

Cordelia blinked. Could it be this easy? "Why *are* you here?"

"I don't usually announce the fact that I'm a ghost hunter, but if asked, I wouldn't deny it."

"I'll be jiggered."

"I'm not sure what that means."

"But why here? Why this house?"

"My parents are always on the lookout for stories about haunted houses. My mom read something in the paper about this place, so I thought I'd spend a week seeing what I could track down."

"That's why you set up the digital recorder upstairs."

"Oh, you saw that?"

Trying her best to look innocent, Cordelia said, "I may have whispered something into the mic that wasn't . . . entirely ap-propriate."

He laughed.

"But tell me. Are there ghosts in this house?"

"Nothing conclusive. One cold spot. An odd compass reading. Oh, and there were a couple times when I had the strong sense of being watched. I haven't downloaded anything from the voice recorder yet. I did stand in the middle of the landing upstairs and ask a bunch of questions. I do that every day, when nobody's around. And I took all the normal baseline readings. Relative humidity. Temperature. Normal decibel levels in the house. My feeling is, that yes, the house does have some paranormal activity. As a scientist, I would simply point out that what we don't know is far greater than what we do know."

"So . . . you're not related to the Skarsvold family."

"What? No, of course not."

"And you don't know anything about the bones of the murdered man found in the garage?"

"Murder," he said, sitting up straight.

"Did you see Lena last night while you were out doing your nightly wandering?"

"I didn't see her. I did walk past her bedroom. The French doors were closed, but I could hear her talking to Eleanor."

"What were they saying?"

"Ghost hunters don't make a habit of eavesdropping."

"What time was it?"

"Oh, maybe one in the morning. I spent some time in the basement. I was in bed by two. Before I fell asleep, I heard Eleanor come up and go into her room."

Cordelia would need to run this past Jane, but if memory served, Eleanor had said she'd gone up to bed around eight last night, not two in the morning. If that statement turned out to be accurate, Eleanor had lied to Jane. "You're sure it was Eleanor you heard?"

"Pretty sure. I'm used to hearing her door open and close. Who else would go into her room that late at night?"

Who else indeed, thought Cordelia, drumming her painted nails on the arm of the recliner. The plot, in her estimation, hadn't just thickened, it had completely curdled.

35

Butch sat in his Yukon with the motor running and the lights off. He'd found Jenny's home in Saint Bonifacius without any trouble, though he was a little surprised by how big it was. The house, which sat on a hill that sloped down to a wooded area, looked almost new. It was a two-story with a three-stall garage and a kids' jungle gym in the backyard off a walk-out basement. It wasn't special in any way, but stood out because it seemed so much bigger and more expensive than the houses that surrounded it. Christmas lights had been strung around three pine trees in the front yard.

Both sides of the street in front of the place as well as the drive-way were so packed with cars that Butch was forced to pull up next to a red Jeep so he could use his binoculars to see inside. With lights burning across the entire first floor, he could easily see in. A party, or perhaps more accurately, a family gathering was in progress. People stood in the living room in small groups, eating from paper plates. It might be a pre-funeral event, or a gathering after the funeral had taken place. Either way, he had no business interrupting.

Butch spent the next hour driving around town, getting a feel for the area. He'd always been drawn to small towns, probably because he'd grown up in one. He liked the pace in a place like Saint Bonifacius, and the fact that, if you lived here, you had fewer choices demanding your attention. Maybe that seemed un-American, but it was the way he liked it.

Even though he wasn't particularly hungry, he decided to stop at a bar, one that served food. He had to kill more time before he returned to the house. Sitting down at a table near the door, he ordered a burger and a brew from a pretty waitress who was trying her best to ignore the sexual innuendo coming from two obnoxious men sitting at the counter. They were rough looking, young and greasy, and tossing back shots like they were water, well on their way to a night of alcohol-fueled oblivion. Butch felt sorry for her and was ready to run interference if they kept it up.

And keep it up they did. As she carried Butch's beer over to his table, one of the men got up and made a grab for her. Butch shoved his chair back and stood. "Get away from her."

"Says who?" said the guy, his face puckering into a snarl.

"I got a hundred pounds on you and I know how to fight. You wanna take this outside?"

The guy glanced at his friend. Giving Butch the finger, he threw his leg over the stool and sat back down, turning to hunch over his shot glass.

"Thank you," whispered the waitress as she set Butch's beer in front of him.

"Are they in here a lot?"

"I went to high school with both of them. They're losers. Maybe I'll tell their mothers what they're up to. They both still live at home."

Butch shook his head. Halfway through his beer, the two guys pushed their stools back and got up, tossed some cash on the counter, and sauntered drunkenly to the door.

"Have a nicey-nice night, Kieren," called the one who'd given Butch the finger.

"You got our phone numbers if you change your mind," called the other.

Butch made a move to get up, which sent them scurrying, slamming the door as their last parting gift.

By nine that night, the majority of the cars at the Nelson house had gone. Butch parked across the street and walked up the winding sidewalk to the front door. Even in the cold, his hands were sweating. For just a moment he wondered if he'd gone crazy in some quiet, undetectable way. This was it. Now or never.

He rang the doorbell.

When the door was drawn back, the Jenny in the photo taken on the dock, older but clearly the same woman, asked, "Can I help you?"

"Um, yes," said Butch. "You're Jenny, right?"

She nodded.

"I want to tell you how sorry I was to hear about your dad."

She nodded again, offered a quiet thank-you. When she also offered a kind of half-smile, he saw that her front teeth weren't completely straight. He liked that. It made her seem human, not just a sad, old photo. "Look, I'm wondering if your brother, Paul, is here?"

"I don't think he's left yet," she said. Turning around she called, "Paul. Someone's here to see you."

A moment later, a trim, curly-haired man in a crewneck sweater and jeans appeared at the end of the long entrance hallway, sipping from a glass of wine. "Who is it?" he called back.

"What's your name?" asked Jenny.

"Butch. Butch Averil." As he said his last name, he caught Paul's eyes. "Hi," he said, feeling his entire body tense. "I probably should have called before I came over."

Paul slowly shifted his eyes from Butch to his sister.

"Do you have a minute?" asked Butch. "I was hoping we could talk." The waiting was over. It was now or never.

"Would you excuse us?" asked Paul. "Tell Mom I'll be back in a few minutes."

"Sure, take your time," said Jenny, shutting the door behind them.

Alone on the front steps, Butch said, "Surprise." He hoped his silly smile would break the ice.

"Come here," said Paul, grabbing his hand. They walked quickly to the end of the garage, then down the hill toward the backyard. Pushing Butch against the side of the garage, Paul kissed him so hard and deep that it made Butch's knees nearly buckle. "God, I'm so glad you're here. How did you find me?"

"Wasn't easy," said Butch, his eyes half closed.

"I thought you'd never want to see me again after the way I left. I just got . . . scared. I knew what you wanted—"

"I suppose an engagement ring was the tip-off."

"Do you forgive me?"

"Depends."

Paul scrutinized Butch's face. "But you're here. That must mean something."

"You didn't make finding you easy. All I had was a photo of your sister and a few other facts."

"How—"

"You had a picture of her in your room. I took it."

"I wondered what happened to it." He held Butch at arm's length. "How long have you been here?"

"Three weeks. I gave myself four to find you, and then I was going to head back to Montana. It's the Christmas season. The resort is booked solid. And the skiing this year is incredible."

"Oh, God," said Paul, crushing Butch in his arms. "You don't know how much I've missed you. But I needed this time. I've done a lot of thinking. Dad spent several days in the ICU before he passed. My mom and sister and I sat at his bedside. One night, when Mom was gone, I told Jenny the truth. About me. About us."

"And?" whispered Butch.

"She said she'd suspected I was gay for a long time. She also said she understood how hard it would have been for me to come out."

"Because of your dad."

"Yeah." He looked puzzled. "How did you know?"

"I don't really know much of anything," said Butch. "I'm just beginning to see the bare outlines of your life. I mean, you've been coming to the resort for years. How long have we been together? Four at least. And in all that time, you never told me your real name or anything about yourself."

"I told you everything about me," he said, looking hurt. "Everything that was important."

"Okay, fine. I figured you'd tell me the rest when you were ready. But that time never came. We had what? Maybe six weeks together each year. Two weeks in the summer. Two in the winter. One in the spring and fall. I was happy, but when you came out to stay in October, I realized that it wasn't enough. Not anymore. I wanted a life with you. A real one."

"I know," said Paul, folding his arms over his chest and stepping away.

"You're shivering."

"I'll survive. Look, we need time to talk, but not here. Not now. I'll explain everything. Just give me a chance, okay?"

"When? When will this talk happen?"

"Tomorrow is the funeral. Most of the family will be staying at my mom's house in Stillwater tomorrow night, and then the out-of-towners will leave on Sunday. Mom's planned a meal for those of us who live in the area on Sunday night. I want you to come." He slipped his hand around Butch's arm.

"And how will you introduce me? Your friend? Your old ski buddy?"

"No," said Paul, tugging Butch's arm until they were facing each other. "If you still have that ring, I'll introduce you as my fiancé."

His words gave Butch's heart a hard twist. "Of course I still have the ring."

"Dinner's at six."

"On Sunday?"

"On Sunday. Where are you staying?"

"A house in Saint Paul."

"Give me the address and I'll meet you at your place at four."

"So we can be officially engaged?"

"That, among other things," said Paul, moving in for another kiss.

36

Jane was in a filthy mood. She'd been summarily tossed out of Julia's hospital room shortly after eight because visiting hours had ended. Rules were rules, the nurse had stated. Now home, Jane had been kicking around the house, obsessing over the Skarsvold case, which caused her even more frustration. And then there was Stew Ickles's North Carolina girlfriend, Dixie, no last name, who had never called her back.

Grabbing a couple of marrowbones from the refrigerator, Jane, followed eagerly by her dogs, walked down the hall to her study. The bed they shared in one corner of the room was the only place they were allowed to chew on meat bones. Once they were settled and blissfully content, Jane opened her briefcase and removed the Skarsvold folder. Sitting down, she paged through her notes until she came to Dixie's phone number.

"Let's hope three's the charm," she said to her pups as she picked up her landline and tapped it in. Almost immediately, a woman's voice said, "Hello?"

"Is this Dixie?"

"Speaking."

Jane explained once again who she was.

"Oh, it's you," said Dixie, her friendly tone turning wary. "Yeah, I got your messages. This is about Stewie, right?"

"That's right. His daughter, Britt Ickles, hired me to look into his disappearance."

"Oh, gosh. I'd forgotten he had a daughter."

"So you knew him."

"Yeah."

"You two dated?"

"For a while."

Dixie wasn't making this easy. "When was the last time you saw him?"

"Look, if you think I had anything to do with his disappearance—"

"No, it's nothing like that," said Jane in her most reassuring tone. "I'm just trying to nail down a time line. According to what I've been able to piece together, he went off the grid in August of 1978. Did you know he was married when you were dating him?"

"Well, sure. He never made a secret of it."

"I get it," said Jane, trying to win her over. "I hear his wife was—"

"She was a shrew. Nothing he did was ever good enough for her."

"I've known women like that." Her words seemed to break the logjam.

"She totally didn't deserve him. I met Stew in a bar one night over in Charlotte. He drove a semi back then, came through there fairly often. I mean, we really hit it off. Got serious right away. In fact, I was staying at his apartment in Milwaukee the summer he told his wife he was done, that he wanted out of the marriage. I remember the afternoon he came home to tell me. The whole thing was pretty wild."

"In what way?"

"Well, I mean, I don't remember all the details, but it seems he got his wife's sister pregnant around the same time he and his wife were married. Didn't really surprise me. He never struck me as the till-death-do-us-part kind of guy. His wife had been back home in Saint Paul for some reason or other and had learned about it directly from the sister. I think his wife sat on it for a while before telling him. Honestly, he was totally blindsided. Had no idea he had a son. But let me tell you, as soon as he found out, he was sure as hell gonna claim the kid as his own. I'd forgotten about the daughter because, see, he never talked about her much. But a son . . . that was a horse of a different color, if you catch my drift. Thing is, he'd totaled his car the week before, so he was using mine. He asked if he could drive my Pinto to Saint Paul to get the kid. I said, sure, why not?"

Jane was furiously taking notes. This was exactly what she needed to know. "What happened when he didn't come back to his apartment in Milwaukee?"

"Well, at first, I was confused. He said he'd be back in a couple of days. I waited a full week before I went over to the library and looked up the name Skarsvold in the Saint Paul White Pages. I went back to the apartment and called. Talked to a woman—never got her name. She said she had no idea what I was talking about. She admitted that she knew Stew, but said she hadn't seen him in years. I mean, what was I supposed to think? I called every mutual friend we had, but nobody had seen or heard from him. I contacted the trucking company where he worked. Same thing. He was a no-show. I phoned his wife, told her who I was. That woman hung up on me before I could even ask a question. I didn't know what else to do. After another week, I simply locked the door of his apartment and left. Took a bus back home. I never heard from him again."

"This car you loaned him," said Jane, leafing through her notes. "I don't suppose you remember the license plate number."

"Hell, no. Why?"

"I found a North Carolina plate in the Skarsvolds' garage."

"So he *was* there," she said, her voice filled of triumph. "I knew it. I just damn knew it. That lady. She lied to me."

"I expect she did," said Jane.

"So?" asked Dixie. "If he was there, then what happened to him?"

Jane tossed her pen down. "I don't have all the facts yet."

"He's dead, right? You can tell me that much. Did they do it? His in-laws?"

"Yes, he's dead."

"I hope they burn in hell."

Jane promised that she'd give her a call and explain everything she could, but only after she was able to nail down the full truth.

"You go, girl," said Dixie right before hanging up. "Make sure they get what's coming to them. Nobody's got the right to take another person's life. *Nobody.*"

As Jane returned the receiver to its cradle, she heard the front doorbell chime.

Normally, the dogs would be out of their bed in a flash, but because they were more interested in the bones, Jane was able to close the door to the study before heading into the front hall. She looked through the peephole to see who'd come by so late at night.

Surprised to see Frank Devine standing on her front steps, she opened the door. "Evening," she said.

"Who the hell do you think you are?" he demanded, his face knotted in rage.

Her eyes dropped to the ax dangling from his right hand.

"You're gonna pay, lady. Big time."

As he raised the ax over his head, she slammed the door and locked it.

"Jesus," she whispered, jumping at the sound of a loud crack. The door shook. A second blow caused it to rattle against its hinges. She was so shaken that she was momentarily paralyzed. When the third blow hit, she reached for her cell phone. With the way her life was going, she might as well put 911 on speed dial. She gave her name and address. "There's a guy outside my house attacking my front door with an ax. And yes, I know him." She was glad she'd locked the dogs in the den. Responding to the noise, they were barking up a storm, scratching at the door to be let out.

When there were no more ax blows, Jane rushed into the kitchen to make sure the back door was locked. She checked windows on the way. Back in the front hall, she edged slowly, carefully toward the peephole. It took a few more seconds to brave the distance and look outside. She felt an intense wave of relief when she saw that he was nowhere in sight.

Placing the flat of her hand on the door, she began to examine it, trying to determine the extent of the damage. To really get a sense, she would need to examine it from the outside, something she wasn't prepared to do. Even though she hadn't been able to locate him, he could still be lurking somewhere out in the darkness.

Jane staggered back at the sound of shattering glass. She rushed into the dining room just as Frank's ax came through a second window. "What the hell are you doing?" she shouted at him. "Stop it."

"You're going to pay for what you did," came his muffled voice.

Was he planning to take out every window in her house? Acting more out of anger than better judgment, she grabbed a canister of pepper gel spray from the front closet and raced outside. She stood on the sidewalk, watching him veer away from the second window and wade through the snow toward the third.

"Stop it," she yelled, pointing the pepper spray at him.

He reared back, his eyes wild. Holding the ax in both hands, he came for her. "I'm going to break every goddamn window in your house. Then I'm gonna chop you to pieces and throw your worthless carcass in a Dumpster."

"Don't come any closer."

"You can't hurt me. Nothing can hurt me. I'm invincible." As he tried to push through a mound of snow, he stumbled and fell. Yelling obscenities, he struggled to right himself. "Consider me the grim reaper. The freakin' mouse that roared. I'm done trying to be Sammy Cream Cheese. Mary Poppins. The Quiet American. All this time, I've been living inside the *wrong* goddamn movie." He stumbled again, slipping backward and flipping the ax into the snow behind him. As he flailed around, trying to locate it, he bellowed, "This is *Night of the Living Dead*, lady. *Nightmare on Elm Street*. I am the reincarnation of Freddy Krueger." Displaying a more reasoned tone, he added, "Not that he was a real person. I know that. I'm not stupid."

"Just stay there," ordered Jane. "The police will be here any minute." She prayed they'd hurry.

He crowed with joy when he located the ax, holding it up and waving it over his head. "Great. The more the merrier." On his feet again, he continued to push through the snow toward her.

Pointing the pepper spray at him, she pressed the trigger and released a stream of gel, hitting him square in the face.

With a bloodcurdling scream, he dropped to his knees and pressed his hands to his eyes. "Shit. What did you do? I can't *see*." He thrashed around, scooping up show and crushing big handfuls against his eyes. "I'm gonna kill you. You are a *dead* woman."

Around the corner came a squad car, lights flashing but the sirens off. It pulled up to the curb and two officers jumped out.

Both officers waded into the snow. One kicked the ax away while the other flipped Frank onto his stomach, pulled his arms behind his back, and cuffed his wrists.

"One freakin' night and my life tanked," screamed Frank.

As one of the officers crouched next to him, trying to get him to settle down, the other walked over to Jane. "What did you use on him?"

"Pepper spray gel."

"Do you know the guy?"

"Not well, but yes." She nodded to her dining room windows, and then to her front door.

"He did that?"

"Yeah."

The officer walked up to the door to take a closer look. "Any idea why?" he asked, taking out a notepad.

She explained that she was a private investigator, that she'd been hired to do an investigation into his family.

270

"So you think it was some kind of retaliation?"

"He said as much."

"Did he threaten you physically?"

"He said he wants to kill me." She hadn't been aware of the cold before, but she was now. Shivering, she stood and answered the rest of the officer's questions. "If you let him out, for any reason, will I be notified?" she asked.

The officer assured her that she would. "Do you know anything about his mental health status?"

Jane shook her head.

The officer dealing with Frank, called over his shoulder, "This guy's seriously in the mumble tank."

Up on his feet now, Frank continued to spew his rage. It took the muscle of both cops to haul him over to the squad car. "I'm in the wrong movie," he kept screaming. Right before he was stuffed into the backseat, he looked up at Jane and shrieked, "I am an *avenging angel*."

Jane felt a momentary stab of sadness at seeing him come apart so completely. Then again, the entire Skarsvold family must have been living on a knife's edge ever since Stew Ickles was murdered. Someone in that family had done the deed. After what she'd just witnessed, she felt she had a pretty clear idea of who that person might be.

37

"Eleanor called me last night to tell me about Lena," said Britt as soon as she sat down at the table. She searched Jane's face. "You knew?"

"I did," said Jane. "I didn't want to tell you over the phone. Thought it would be best if I waited until our meeting this morning."

"Well, Eleanor had no such qualms." When the waitress set a menu in front of her, Britt quickly ordered a bloody Mary.

"Make it two," said Jane.

"I gave her my cell phone number last weekend, when she invited me to dinner. But . . . suicide?"

"They're sure of that?"

"Apparently. Alcohol and Tylenol, according to Eleanor. She was found outside in the snow nearly frozen."

"I'm the one who found her," said Jane.

Britt blinked back her surprise. "Wow," she whispered. "You know, I suppose I should feel sad, but the truth is, I hardly knew her. Then again, I've been thinking: You don't suppose my turning up at the house after all these years had something to do with it?"

"Honestly," said Jane. "I think the problems in that family long predated your visit."

"I have to say, Lena didn't seem depressed to me."

"You're not alone," said Jane. "Butch Averil, the guy who lives next door, said he didn't think she was remotely suicidal. Of course, that's a hard judgment call."

Again, Britt blinked. "So what are you saying?"

"It might have been an accident." For now, Jane left it at that. "What else did Eleanor say?"

"Well, I asked her about the funeral. She said that Lena's body hadn't been released yet. She wanted to know how long I'd be in town. My plan was to leave tomorrow. I'm kind of torn about whether I should stay or not, especially since nothing's been firmed up and my department chair expects me back on Monday."

Jane leaned back as the bloody Mary was set in front of her.

"Would you two like to order?" asked the waitress.

"I need more time," said Britt, taking a sip of her drink, then picking up the menu.

Jane had suggested they meet at this particular Dinkytown restaurant because it was close to Britt's hotel, and also because it was one of the few places in the Twin Cities that served a fry-up, otherwise known as a full English breakfast.

As Britt scanned the offerings, Jane continued. "I have a lot to tell you. But first, you should know that Frank came by my house last night. With an ax."

Britt's eyes widened.

"He was furious at me because of the investigation."

"He found out?"

"Eleanor knows, too. And that friend of hers, Iver, the minister. Cordelia, as Olive Hudson, spent the night again last night. Her cover hasn't been blown. I'm sure I'll get a full report later today. She's not an early riser."

"What did Frank do?"

Jane gave her the down and dirty on what had happened. "He's in the Hennepin County jail at the moment, charged with felony assault. It was all so strange. I mean, I don't know him that well, but he was ranting, not making any sense."

Britt gave a visible shiver.

After they placed their orders, Jane took several sustaining sips of her drink. "Before we continue, I need you to refresh my memory. The night Cordelia and I came to your hotel I believe you said that, after you returned home from the funeral in Saint Paul, you saw your father again. Did I get that right?"

Britt swirled the celery stick around in her glass. "You did. It was right around the time Mom asked him for a divorce. We'd been home for a while. I don't think he was living with us then, though I could be wrong. He came by to pick me up and take me to a railroad museum and then out to lunch. I remember wearing this pink sundress. It was my favorite. Mom bought it for me while we were in Saint Paul. It's the dress I have on in the picture I showed you, so it must have still been summer."

"You're sure you saw him after you came back from Saint Paul?"

"Yeah, positive. Why?"

"Because your aunt Eleanor told the police that your dad came to Saint Paul in February of 1978, and asked her father, your grandfather, for money. She said that she didn't know exactly what happened because she wasn't there, but that there was a

274

fight in the garage. Your dad ended up dead. Your grandfather buried him in the root cellar."

Britt seemed confused. "No . . . no, that's not possible. My dad was still alive after my grandfather died. I'm sure of it. Why would Eleanor blame—" Her expression darkened. "She told the police that story to get herself off the hook. That is so incredibly evil."

Evil or not, Jane saw it as self-preservation. "I'm not sure how energetically the police will pursue a cold case—the bones found in the garage—when they have so many current cases vying for their attention."

"She is so two-faced. And here I thought Lena was the rotten core of the family."

"I spoke to a woman last night who was dating your father while he was still married. Her name is Dixie. She's from North Carolina." Jane went on to explain what she'd learned. "He was driving her car when he came to see your aunts. I found a North Carolina license plate in their garage before it burned down. I've got a photo of it, so given enough time, I think we can trace it back to Dixie. But here's what's important. Dixie said she was in Milwaukee staying with him when he went missing. She said it was August 1978. No doubt about that. So if he was alive in August, after your grandfather died, there's no way he could've been responsible for your dad's death."

"That blows Eleanor's story out of the water. She is *such* a liar."

Jane knew her next bit of news would be even more explosive. "I'm sorry that I haven't been able to track Timmy down. That's why you hired me. But I have learned something important. Dixie said that your mother's reason for divorcing your father had a lot to do with something she learned when you two

275

were in Saint Paul that summer. Apparently your father had a sexual relationship with Lena. She was pregnant with his child when your mother announced that she and your dad were getting married. Lena kept it to herself, never told anyone. When she came back to the house that summer for the funeral, and you and your mother were also there, it all came out. That's what caused the rift in the family, why your mother never contacted her sisters again, and why she returned home and asked your dad for a divorce."

"So, you're saying—"

"Timmy isn't your cousin, Britt. He's your half-brother."

Britt's eyes searched the room, finally coming to rest on Jane's face. "I'm . . . absolutely stunned. Timmy is my brother? Seriously?"

"When your father learned that he had a son, he borrowed Dixie's car and drove to Saint Paul. Dixie said he had every intention of claiming Timmy, of bringing him back with him. We know he arrived at the house. What we don't know is what happened after that."

"We have to talk to Eleanor," said Britt, her expression growing fierce. "We need to expose her lies and demand the truth. It's the only way this is ever going to get resolved."

Jane didn't disagree. "When do you want to do it?"

Britt took several gulps of her drink. "Let me think. After I leave here, I was going to finish packing. And then I have a final session at one. I have to be there. It's a command performance. What about four? We could meet over at the house, beard the dragon in her den together."

"I'll make it work," said Jane.

"Wow," said Britt, gazing down at her bloody Mary with a dazed expression. "I mean . . . this is a lot to get my head around. Do you think there's any hope that she'll tell us what really happened?"

"There's a chance," said Jane. "For now, let's hold on to that."

38

Adrenaline pumped through Butch's body as he stood in the hotel hallway and knocked on the door. He'd been thinking about this for days. Now that he'd found Paul, he had the time and the focus he needed to deal with another important matter. Remembering his cap, he pulled it off as the door finally opened.

"Yes?" said Britt, a quizzical look on her face as she peered out at him.

"You probably don't remember me. We met last Sunday night at the Skarsvold house. Butch Averil?" He'd shaved off his beard and gotten a haircut. He wanted to look his best when he met Paul's family tomorrow.

"You look so different," she said, taking him in.

"It's me. Shaved my beard." He felt his face.

"Oh. Sure." She stared at him so hard it made him squirm.

"Can I talk to you for a minute?"

"Well—" She looked over her shoulder. "I was doing some packing, but . . . okay." She stepped back.

Walking into the room, he took a moment to look around. "This is nice. It's a suite."

"The conference paid for it. I was one of the featured speakers."

When he turned back to her, he found that she was staring at him again. She motioned him to the couch and then settled down on a chair across from him.

"Is something wrong? You're looking at me kind of funny."

"It's nothing. You just look like someone I knew—when he was young."

"Who's that?"

"My dad."

"Well, I guess we all have a double somewhere."

"What did you want to talk to me about?"

In a halting voice, Butch continued, "First, I wanted to say how sorry I was about your aunt's death. I liked Lena."

"Thanks," said Britt. "We weren't close."

"No, I suppose not." He thrashed around for how to begin. "Look, I was there when the paramedics took her away. I listened as the police asked the woman who found her in the snow some questions. Jane Lawless. I understand you hired her to find your cousin, Tim."

She hesitated. "Yeah. That's right."

"Well, the fact is . . . see—" He cleared his throat. "I'm Tim."

Her eyes widened. *You're* Timmy?"

He nodded.

"Oh," she said, pressing a fist to her mouth. After a long moment, she added, "I get it now. Wow."

"Get what?"

"Did Eleanor and Lena know?"

He shook his head. With the dam now broken, his words began to tumble out. "I remember the summer when we met. I liked you so much. And I thought your mom was beautiful. Lena and I, we lived on a farm back then. We took this long drive to get to the funeral in Saint Paul. I wasn't happy about it because it meant I had to be away from my dog."

"Where was the farm?"

"Upstate New York. I guess you'd call it a commune. Hippies and whole wheat and stuff like that. I loved it. Lena and my dad and I all lived with a bunch of other people in this big old drafty house."

"Your dad," said Britt. "Tell me about him."

"He's not my bio dad. Lena never told me who that was, probably because she didn't know. Mitch Averil was the guy who raised me. He'd adopted me legally when I was still pretty young. He's a lawyer. He already had an undergrad degree in political science when he met Lena. He and Lena were never officially married. So, after Lena . . . disappeared—"

Britt interrupted him. "She disappeared?"

"Yeah," he said, scratching his head. "We have a lot to catch up on, don't we?"

"I want to know everything."

"Me, too."

"You first. Why did Lena disappear?"

"Well, see, that's where this all gets kind of murky. When Lena and I returned to the farm after the funeral, she seemed really miserable. Sometimes she'd stay in bed all day. My dad came to me one afternoon and told me she'd been in a car accident and was in the hospital. I wanted to go see her, but he said we had to wait. And then, a while later, he came into my room one night, sat on my bed, and told me that she was in heaven. That I wouldn't be seeing her again."

"He lied?"

"Yeah."

"But . . . when you introduced yourself to Lena as Butch Averil, didn't she know who you were?"

"No. She never made the connection."

"But your last name? Didn't that give it away?"

"More hippie drama. At the farm, nobody used their real names. My dad called himself Falcon. Lena was Willow. And if you had a degree, or money, or anything that might set you apart from anyone else, give you more status, you didn't talk about it. So no, Lena never knew his real name."

"Bizarre."

"I know."

"But if you thought Lena was dead, why did you come to Saint Paul looking for her?"

"I didn't," said Butch. "I did come to the Twin Cities looking for someone, but it wasn't her. But since I was in town, I figured I'd drive by the house in Saint Paul and see if I remembered it."

"You knew the address?"

"I looked it up in the phone book. Lena left behind some family photos. My dad would take them out and we'd look at them together. He didn't want me to forget her. One was of the house in Saint Paul. I should tell you that my dad married a woman named Sandy. We all moved away from the farm to go live in Montana. That's where I mostly grew up."

"So what happened when you drove by the Skarsvold house?"

He shrugged. "Maybe it was luck or pure serendipity, but the afternoon I came by, I saw this old lady sitting on the front porch.

281

She was in a wheelchair. I guess I was curious, so I parked and strolled past the house. I'd noticed the 'for sale' sign in the yard next door, so I called to her and asked if she knew how much the house was selling for. We struck up a conversation. I knew almost immediately that it was her. I was shocked and confused. When I got back to the motel where I was staying, I called my dad and demanded the truth."

"Did he tell you?"

"He wasn't very happy about it. The first thing he did was to ask my forgiveness. He stressed that Lena had been fragile—emotionally—and was really struggling when we returned to the farm after the funeral. She thought she was a bad mother. She figured I'd be better off without her. He was appalled to learn that I'd found her alive and well and living in Saint Paul. He asked me what I intended to do. At that point, I wasn't sure. I had some questions I wanted to ask her, but I figured I'd get to know her first. I mean, I toyed with the idea of being pissed at her. Maybe if I'd found out that she'd abandoned me when I was still a kid, I would have felt more betrayed. But I'm forty-five. I know everyone makes mistakes. More than that, I have a great family—my dad, my mom, and two knuckleheaded younger brothers. It's unlikely I would've had any of that if I'd spent my childhood with her. In the end, I realized I was far more curious than angry. What I didn't take into account was how little time I would have with her. And I never expected to like her so much." He squeezed the bridge of his nose to stop himself from crying.

Britt moved from her chair to sit next to him on the couch. "I'm sorry. I really am."

"It's okay," he said, feeling a rush of tenderness toward her.

She reached for a box of tissues on the end table and handed it to him.

He smiled. "Thanks."

"But . . . who are you? Are you married? Do you have children? What do you do for a living?"

"No, not married. No children. I'm gay. I came to Minnesota because the man I'd fallen in love with left me, just when I was about to ask him to marry me. I found out just recently that he's from a very prominent, politically conservative family in Minnesota. I first met him when he began coming to a resort I own in Montana."

"You own a resort?"

"The Spoon Ridge Ski Lodge. It's near the town of Twin Elks. Part of the Beartooth basin in south central Montana. I opened the place in the winter of 1998. I met Paul five years ago. He came to ski one winter and we talked a few times. I wondered about him. He always came by himself. Didn't try to pick up women. Paid for everything in cash. It took a few more visits before I worked up the courage to ask him to have dinner with me. We've been together now for almost four years."

"But you said he left you?"

"It's a long story, but I'll give you the quick version. Paul made it clear right from the start that he wasn't interested in a committed relationship. His life was somewhere else. I knew he was deep in the closet. His cars had Minnesota plates, so I knew where he was from, and I was pretty sure he lived in a city, but he never gave me his real name. All of that put me off, and yet, over time, maybe even against my better judgment, I fell hard for him and I was sure he felt the same way. By the second year, he was coming more often. We even took a couple road trips together, one to San Francisco, and one to Tucson. He was so smart, and so much fun. It was getting harder and harder for us to be apart. But we hit a snag when I asked him to make a real commitment to me. Instead of giving me an answer, he told me his sister had texted him that their father was really sick. He needed to get back home right away. He left that same night without giving me any indication of how he felt about my proposal. I called and texted, but heard nothing back. And then one day, the number I had for him was disconnected. I took that as the answer to my question. I was hurt, deeply angry. I nursed that anger for weeks. And then, one night, I assembled every possible fact I had about who he was and decided to find him."

"And did you?"

"I did. And much to my surprise, I think things are going to be okay with us. When I left Montana, I gave myself a month. I made a deal with the guy who was selling the house next to the Skarsvold place. He wasn't having any luck selling it because, in my opinion, it was a dump and the asking price was way too high. I made him an offer. Minimal rent while I worked to rehab whatever he was willing to pay for. It was perfect because it allowed me to be close to Lena and still look for Paul's sister. I spent each week searching in the metro area, and the weekends in various other cities—Duluth, Rochester, Saint Cloud. The sister—Jenny—was my one and only real link. I was chasing all that down when all hell broke loose at the Skarsvold house. The garage fire really got my attention, especially when they found bones."

"This is critical," said Britt, leaning forward. "Do you have any memories of what might have happened in that garage? The man who died in there, he was my father."

"Oh, jeez, I'm so sorry. I had no idea."

She wrapped her fingers gently around his arm. "We're talking about some hard things here. Surprising things. I think this may be the right moment to tell you something more. The man who died, he wasn't just my father, he was yours, too."

Butch felt as if a firecracker had gone off inside his head. "*What?*"

"His name was Stewart Ickles. Right around the time he and my mother were married, he got Lena pregnant. I don't know all the details, but you and I, we were born within months of each other. At the funeral for our grandfather, it all came out. There was a big family row. When my mother and I returned home, she asked my dad for a divorce. He had no idea he'd fathered a child with Lena. She'd kept it to herself. When he found out, he drove to Saint Paul looking for you. He wanted to take you away from Lena, bring you home to his place in Milwaukee."

"Jesus," whispered Butch.

"Somehow or other, he ended up dead in that garage. Were you and Lena still at the house when he showed up?"

Butch stared into space. "So that's who the guy was," he said after a few seconds. "He was the boogeyman in all my dreams when I was growing up. He scared the shit out of me. See, I have these really vivid but confusing memories that I've never quite been able to place or understand. I remember a man who wanted me to sit on his lap. I squirmed away from his hands and hid under Lena's legs. And then, while we were sitting at the dining room table, he grabbed my arm and yanked me outside. I must have been yelling or fighting him because he hit me across the face, told me that if I didn't shut the eff up, I'd be sorry."

Britt grimaced.

"I remember thinking, this guy's kidnapping me. He seemed

like he was eighty feet tall. He dragged me into this room, began stomping around, like he was really pissed at me. I didn't know what I'd done wrong. The next thing I remember, Frank was carrying me into the house. I think he put me to bed, because I remember him telling me not to worry. The man was gone and was never coming back. 'I took care of him, Tim. He's a goner.'"

In a tightly compressed voice, Britt asked, "Was Frank saying he'd done it? That he'd killed him?"

Butch hesitated. "You know, I've always wondered about that. Yeah, I think he was."

Silence caught and held.

"Listen, I'm meeting Jane Lawless over at the Skarsvold house at four. We've decided that the only way to get answers to our questions is to demand them from Eleanor. She lied to the police about how our father died and we can prove it. I'm hoping it will give us the leverage we need to get her to open up. You want to come?"

"Are you kidding? I want the truth as much as you do."

She squeezed his hand. "Great. Let's go find it."

39

Jane was coming out of her restaurant later that afternoon, heading for her Mini, when the sound of a honking horn stopped her. Squinting into the late afternoon sun, she watched Cordelia's new black Subaru ease up next to her and the tinted passenger's window come down.

"Quentin," said Jane, surprised to see him inside.

"Howdy," said Cordelia. "Meet my new best friend."

Jane had been waiting for a report. This was apparently it.

"I now know all," said Cordelia. "Sorry I didn't get back to you sooner. We both slept in because we were up most of the night."

"You were?" said Jane. "Why?"

"Quentin's a ghost hunter. That's why he rented a room. The house is haunted, you know."

"We can't actually say that," said Quentin, turning to her. "Not until I've studied all the data."

Cordelia tapped a finger to her head. "This is all the data I need. I knew there were ghosts in that house from the first moment I stepped inside. Anyway, we're on our way over to the theater.

I want to introduce Quentin to Gilbert and Hilda King, the official Thorn Lester Playhouse disembodied spirits."

"She said they bicker," said Quentin. "Hard not to want to investigate something like that."

"I expect it is," said Jane. "So the digital recorder upstairs—"

"For recording anomalies," said Quentin. "I ask a series of questions each day and hope to get a response."

"It's all about quantum theory," said Cordelia, nonchalantly examining her nails.

"Okay," said Jane, now completely confused.

"Oh, and I found out Eleanor was in Lena's room talking to her night before last."

"Around one in the morning," offered Quentin.

"Really?" said Jane. "Eleanor said she'd gone to bed early."

"Another whopping Eleanorian fib. Anyway, I'll give you all the details later," she added. "But right now, Quentin and I gotta boogie."

Jane backed up as the window closed and the car roared away. At least Quentin was officially off her list of suspects. Cordelia had been the right woman for the job. And now, she had someone new to play with. A true Hollywood ending, Jane mused to herself. Soon to be a major motion picture.

Big and bare, and empty, thought Eleanor as she sat down at the kitchen table with a cup of coffee. The house she'd lived in and loved for most of her life, the inheritance she'd done everything to protect and preserve, would pass into another family's hands. It never occurred to her that Frank wouldn't want it. The rooms, once so filled with life, were silent now. Lena, looking down from heaven, or more likely, up from hell, would be thrilled.

Taking the note she'd received from Iver out of her apron pocket, she spread it out in front of her, and, with shaking hands, adjusted her glasses to read through it a second time.

Eleanor,

This is terribly difficult for me to write. You know how much I care about you. Ever since that day you came to me so many years ago and told me about the horror of that night, what Frank had done, my support for you and your family has been unwavering. I tried my best to do what you asked, to befriend your son, to be a strong male support in his life. I understood why you and Lena hid the body in the root cellar, and I never once condemned you for your actions. I saw it as an untenable situation. I also knew your only goal was to save your son. It was apparent to me that the lie you told the police officer yesterday—that it was your father who accidentally caused Stewart Ickles death—was also motivated by nothing more than your love for Frank. But that lie, Eleanor. That lie.

I've searched my soul and all I can say is, for me it was a bridge too far. Again, I know you're only trying to protect your beloved son, but I also know that I can't be a party to the defamation of a good man's name.

Maybe I went too far in giving you the benefit of the doubt all those years ago. If I did, it was because I loved you, perhaps too much. We're old, Eleanor. We'll be meeting our maker soon. I would ask you to consider your actions in that light. For the moment, I need to separate myself from you. Perhaps my decision seems harsh, and for that, I'm sorry. I hope we will see each other again somewhere down the line. I don't know how you will resolve what you've done, what you will do to make it right. I ask that you

289

pray about it. God will guide you far better than I've ever been able to do.

Tenderly,

Iver

This wasn't a time to be in earnest, as Samuel Johnson had suggested. For Eleanor, it was a time of endings. There were things she'd never told Iver. If they came out, she doubted he'd ever speak to her again. The man who had saved her, both emotionally and spiritually, the one who had centered her, warmed her as she negotiated a cold, difficult life, was gone for good.

Eleanor's head snapped up when she heard Lena's voice whisper in her ear: "Well, if it's really over, El, my advice is, ChristianMingle.com." Eleanor laughed out loud. So like Lena, and so absurd.

The phone rang.

Straining to rise from her chair, Eleanor moved over to the wall and picked up the receiver. "Hello?" she said.

"Eleanor? Is that you?"

"Yes?" For a moment, she didn't recognize the voice. Then, "Wendy? You sound upset. Is something wrong?"

"It's Frank."

Eleanor steadied herself against a chair. "What is it? Tell me."

"He's been arrested. Last night. He took an ax to someone's front door."

"An ax?" repeated Eleanor, the old nightmare bursting to life inside her mind.

"He hasn't been arraigned yet, but the lawyer assigned to him told me he was being charged with aggravated assault. It's a felony."

Feeling dazed, Eleanor lowered herself carefully onto the chair. "I . . . I don't understand. Why—"

"It was the woman who rented a room at your place under false pretenses. She's a PI. She was spying on you, hired by your niece."

"But . . . she can't hurt us. Britt has some strange ideas. That's what prompted her to hire an investigator in the first place. It's all make-believe, Wendy. Nothing to worry about."

"Stop lying," said Wendy, her voice cold.

A shiver crept down Eleanor's spine.

"I spoke to Frank. He told me everything. Why oh why did you keep this from me? I should have been told. I'm his *wife*, for God's sake, I deserved better."

Eleanor's expression tightened.

"Frank needs help. He totally came apart last night and he's barely holding it together today. His lawyer told me that, after the arraignment, he'll try to get him a psychological evaluation. He's suffering from PTSD, Eleanor. He's a sick man."

"He's not sick," said Eleanor. "Don't say that."

"I am *so* angry."

"Wendy, listen to me. What he told you . . . did he mention any of that to the police or his lawyer?"

Silence. "I never thought to ask."

"Where is he being held?"

"The Hennepin County jail."

"I'm coming right down. There's something I have to tell him. I should have done it yesterday; he left before we could talk."

"Don't come," said Wendy.

291

"You do not tell me what to do when it comes to my son."

"You've been his official fixer your entire life. You've babied him, coddled him. You've waited on him hand and foot. Don't you get it? There are things no amount of mother love can fix. This is one of them. When I spoke to him a few minutes ago, I told him I was going to call you. He had one message: Stay away. He doesn't want to see you."

"No," said Eleanor feeling suddenly desperate. "That can't be right."

"They have him on a suicide watch. Half the time, he's spouting gibberish. The other half, he's so ashamed of what he's done that he can hardly hold himself upright. Give him a break. I understand that you're concerned. I'll call you when I know more. But for now, please Eleanor, respect his wishes."

As she was about to respond, Wendy ended the call.

40

"Before we get started," said Britt, standing next to her rental car with a broad Cheshire Cat smile on her face. "There's someone I'd like you to meet."

"Sure," said Jane, glancing over at the house, wondering if their luck would hold and Eleanor would actually be home and willing to talk.

Britt turned as a truck pulled in behind her car.

When Butch got out, Jane said, "Oh, we've already met. I almost didn't recognize you. You shaved off your beard."

Butch walked up to Britt and linked his arm through hers.

"Jane," said Britt her smile turning to a grin, "I'd like you to meet my brother, Timmy."

Jane's mouth dropped open. "*This* is . . . Tim?"

"Afraid so," he said. "I just found out about the brother part myself. Go ahead and call me Butch. It was a grade-school nickname that stuck."

"I have so many questions," said Jane, shifting her gaze from face to face. Viewing them side-by-side, there actually was a discernible resemblance.

"Look," said Butch. "I don't want Eleanor to know who I am. Maybe I will want that somewhere down the line, but not now."

"Understood," said Jane.

"To be continued," said Britt, leading them up the sidewalk. "Let me take the lead." She trotted up the steps and pressed the doorbell.

Jane didn't have the same kind of anger toward Eleanor that Britt did, though the more she thought about what Eleanor had done, the more it seemed to be building. Still, she hoped Britt would go easy, start slow.

When the bell went unanswered, Britt tried again. She seemed keyed up, jumpy. Butch showed his nervousness by cracking his knuckles.

Jane finally offered to use her key. Once inside, they found the house quiet. "Maybe she's not here," whispered Butch.

"Why don't you check upstairs?" said Jane, moving through the living room. One of Eleanor's favorite spots in the house was the kitchen table. If she'd forgotten to put her hearing aids in, she could easily have missed the bell. But as Jane stepped into the dining room, she saw that the French doors to Lena's bedroom were open. Eleanor was sitting in Lena's recliner, a phone in her lap.

With Britt following close behind, Jane entered the room. Eleanor's eyes were closed. Crouching down next to her, Jane was shocked by how pale and drawn the old woman looked, as if she'd aged a decade in a few short days. "Eleanor?"

Eleanor's eyes fluttered open. She stared straight ahead, breathing softly, her expression unreadable.

Britt moved directly in front of her. "We've come to talk to you."

Eleanor looked up, then tilted her head to watch Butch come in.

"The gang's all here," she whispered.

"When was the last time you had something to eat?" asked Jane.

"I can't remember."

"Let me fix you something?"

"No," she said, more firmly this time. She patted Jane's hand. "But thank you for the kind offer." Removing her glasses, she rubbed her eyes. "You've come for answers, I expect."

"I'm not leaving until I know what happened to my father," said Britt.

Eleanor sighed. "Well," she said, putting her glasses back on, "your timing is perfect."

Britt and Butch looked at each other.

"Sit down," she said, "and I'll tell you a story."

"I don't want a *story*," said Britt. "I want the truth."

"The truth," she repeated with a faint smile. "Well now, that's always a little more complicated, don't you find? A matter of perspective? But yes, I'll do my best."

Butch and Britt perched on the edge of the twin bed. Jane sat down on the floor with her back propped against the wall. Was it really going to be this easy to get Eleanor to open up? All Jane knew was that the old woman's normally cheerful, friendly demeanor was completely gone. In its place, she sensed a terrible weariness, a woman who no longer stood at the edge of a dark and dangerous cliff, but someone who had taken the leap into the unknown.

"Stewart Ickles was the devil," Eleanor began. "He beguiled both of my sisters with a charm I never understood. He got them both pregnant. Lena gave birth to a son and named him Timothy. Pauline gave birth to a daughter and named her Britt. Beautiful children.

"When my father died, everyone came for the funeral. I won't get into the nitty-gritty, but suffice it to say that Lena got drunk one night and let Pauline know who Timmy's father really was. It was awful. I tried to stay neutral, but from the start, it was a losing battle. Pauline left, saying she washed her hands of us. She never wanted to see either of us again. I would imagine that she went home and, whenever she saw Stew next, she told him what she'd learned and that she wanted a divorce. On August seventh, a Sunday—I'll never forget the date—he walked into our house with a handgun stuffed into his belt and demanded to see his son. It was clear he intended to take him away from Lena. In an effort to calm him down, to get him to see reason, I invited him to stay for dinner. Right before we sat down to eat, I realized that Frank was gone, so I went outside to find him. Called his name, said it was time to eat. When he didn't come running, like he usually did, I gave up and went in.

"During dinner, Lena said something, I don't remember what, but it riled Stew up again. He grabbed Timmy and took him out to the garage. We stayed in the house, afraid he'd use the gun if we tried to prevent him from leaving. I had my hand on the phone, ready to call the police as soon as he was gone. But he didn't go. Next thing I know, Frank is carrying Timmy across the grass and into the house. Frank thought Timmy was dead. When the boy opened his eyes, Frank nearly dropped him he was so surprised. I checked him over and sent them both upstairs."

"What happened to Stew?" asked Jane. "Why did he let them go?"

Eleanor leaned her head back and gave another sigh. "The reason Frank disappeared from the house that night was because he'd gone to the garage to stick a knife into one of the tires on Stew's car to prevent him from leaving with Timmy. He made sure the tire was flat and then he hid in the back of the garage. Stew yanked Timmy inside, threw open the passenger's door and told Timmy to get in. But then he noticed the knife and the flat tire. He roared with anger as he pulled Timmy out of the seat and threw him against a pile of junk on the garage floor. Timmy hit his head and passed out. Frank thought Stew was going to beat Timmy up——or worse——so he grabbed an ax that was hanging on the garage wall, crouched down and waited until Stew had turned his attention to the tire. As he was bent down fiddling with it, Frank jumped out and planted the ax blade in his back. And then he picked up Timmy and ran into the house."

Britt chewed nervously on her lower lip. "You're saying that Frank killed my father?"

Eleanor's eyes rose to hers. "That's what Frank thought."

"What's that mean?" asked Jane.

"I couldn't tell him the truth, don't you see?" She began to grow agitated. "He thought he was a hero. I told him as much. Again and again. So did Lena. We showered the boy with praise. I knew his actions might have repercussions, but I would be there for him, I could help him deal with anything. I wanted to give him the whole story yesterday, but he left. And . . . and . . . I mean, how could I tell him that his mother had. . . . no, it wasn't possible. What would he have thought of me if he knew?"

"So what *did* happen?" asked Butch.

"Oh," groaned Eleanor, dropping her head in her hand.

"You've come this far," said Jane. "Tell us the rest."

Eleanor sank lower in her chair. "I suppose it doesn't matter anymore. It will all have to come out. I asked Lena to wait in the house, just in case the boys needed her. As usual, she was more than willing to let me clean up her mess. When I got out to the garage, Stew was on his hands and knees, wailing like a banshee, struggling to remove the ax from his back. It was deep inside him, but I wasn't sure it was a mortal blow. His handgun was on the floor next to him. I rushed over and kicked it away. When he realized I was there, he reared up. It was grotesque. He was like a Frankenstein monster. I looked around, saw our old baseball bat, and grabbed it. As he came for me, I swung it and hit him square in forehead. He went down. I hit him again. And again. And," she said, her eyes searching the air around her, "again. When what I'd just done finally penetrated, I sank down on my knees and pleaded with God to forgive me. I had to do it, don't you see?" She looked imploringly at Britt. "If he'd lived, Frank would surely have been arrested and charged with attempted murder. He was only thirteen, but he was big for his age. I was scared to death. And what would have happened to Timmy?"

"*You* did it?" whispered Britt.

Jane sat up straight, appalled by the revelation. She knew Eleanor was a liar, but this was far more twisted than Jane had ever considered possible.

As Eleanor smoothed her apron and gazed around the room, Butch stood up and crouched down next to her. "Eleanor, you need to finish the story now. I need to know about Lena. Did she really commit suicide?"

Eleanor's eyelids fluttered. "Oh," she said, lowering her head. "God forgive me."

"What? Tell me."

"I . . . I crushed half a bottle of Tylenol and put it in her liquor bottle, sat with her late into the night and encouraged her to drink her fill. It wasn't hard. You have to understand, I was in constant fear that she'd tell you or Rich Novak the truth. I couldn't have that. I wasn't going to jail for something that was *her* fault."

With that one admission, Jane watched a change come over Eleanor. The piece of herself she'd kept hidden all these years—a core of pure hate—finally emerged for everyone in the room to see.

"There it is," said Eleanor, scowling at Butch, then up at Britt. "Eleanor is a monster just like Stew. Just like Lena. We're all monsters. Every last human being."

"No we're not," said Jane.

"I think it's time to call the police." Britt moved off the bed.

In response, Eleanor held up the cordless. "Already did. You can leave now knowing the wicked old lady is headed for prison. Are you happy?"

"No," said Butch. "Not even a little." Turning to Britt, he held out his hand. "Let's get out of here."

Britt stood for a moment, looking down at Eleanor, who gazed back at her with undisguised defiance. And then, without saying another word, she took her brother's hand.

After they were gone, Jane climbed to her feet. "Did . . . did you really call the police? They're actually coming?"

Eleanor glanced up at her. "You don't believe me?"

"Any reason I should?"

With a faint smile, she said, "They're coming, Jane." She paused, then added, "You hate me, don't you? Go ahead. Say it."

Jane was disgusted, repulsed. She imagined Eleanor could read it in her face. "You let your son think he'd killed a man, when in reality, you'd done it. Do you have any idea what that must have cost him?"

Tipping her head back, she said, "Of course I do. We've all paid a price for Lena's sins. You know, I've been thinking about the night that Lena and I drove out into the country to burn Stew's car. You see, I had this idea that if I looked back to watch the fire, I'd turn to a pillar of salt. Are you familiar with the Old Testament?"

"Lot's wife."

"That's right. I wanted to look, but I wouldn't let myself. And from that moment on, I steadfastly lived my life that way, refusing to look back, unwilling to dwell on what had happened. I kept my eyes on my son. On his future. He was everything to me. Still is. I'm turning myself in because it's what I need to do to protect him."

If Jane had learned anything in her life, it was how evil became lodged in the human heart. It almost always started with a story, a fiction that was created out of need and then the individual worked to believe it. Over time, that fiction replaced reality. The moral center collapsed. And ultimately, in the worst instances, *anything* in the service of that story was permitted.

"I'll say it again," said Eleanor, her mouth set in a grim line. "Everything bad that's happened to this family was because of Lena."

Jane gazed down at the plump, sweet-looking old woman, watching her rearrange her face, tuck the hate back inside.

"I should probably take off my apron before the police get here," said Eleanor, touching the pearls at her neck.

"I don't think it matters," said Jane.

"No?" she asked, closing her eyes and folding her hands in her lap. "I suppose you're right."

41

Jane made it to the hospital just after six that evening. As soon as she walked into the room, she knew something was wrong.

"Bad news," said Julia, turning the sound down on the TV.

"What?" said Jane, not wanting to waste a minute on small talk.

"Come and kiss me first."

Jane sat down on the bed, leaned in, and gave her the kiss she'd been dreaming about all day.

"Not bad," said Julia. "But there's still room for improvement. What, no flowers this time?"

"Tell me what's going on."

She released an exasperated breath. "I won't be going home tonight. It's my blood pressure. Reid thought he had it handled, but apparently he doesn't. The experimental drug I'm on . . . they don't understand all the side effects yet. One, at least for me, appears to be very high blood pressure. They're worried I might have another stroke."

"No," said Jane.

"They're trying a couple different blood pressure medications. Maybe it will work, or maybe not. It's possible he'll have to lower the dose of the experimental drug. It does seem to be helping me, so I hope I don't have to go off it. If I do, it could be curtains for old Julia."

She was dealing with her mortality by being flip. In the same situation, Jane wondered if she might handle it the same way. "How do you feel?"

"Now that you're here, I'm much better." She cupped Jane's chin in her hand. "Why are you always so earnest?"

"Don't make fun of me."

"What have we here?" said Julia, glancing at Jane's hand. "You're wearing the ring I gave you eons ago."

It was an Egyptian blue scarab set in gold. Jane had always loved it, but didn't feel she should wear it after the breakup. She'd taken it out of her jewelry box last night and tried it on. As she was about to take it off, she stopped—and spent the rest of the night thinking.

"Does it mean we're going steady?"

Jane had mulled this moment over in her mind all night. Now that it was here, was she really going to say it? "Julia?"

"Yes?"

"I've been thinking."

"That can be good or bad."

"I don't just care about you."

"I know. You admire me. On occasion, you respect me. You're fond of me and you lust after me. All good. I'm not complaining."

"Shut up."

Julia seemed startled.

"Not like a friend," said Jane, knitting her fingers together with Julia's. "Like a lover. Like the woman I want to share my life with."

Julia's face flushed. "Am I hearing voices? Did you just say what I think you said?"

"I can't lose you. You need to do everything in your power to beat this illness."

"I want that, too. More than you know."

Jane let it fill her now, all the emotions she'd kept clenched behind a wall in her mind. She was breaking all the rules she'd so carefully made for herself. Life was too short. Love was rare.

"I've had this dream before," said Julia, taking both of Jane's hands in hers. "Many times. And in my dream, when you tell me you love me, I always say the same thing. It's a quote. Samuel Beckett. 'Ever tried. Ever failed. No matter. Try again. Fail again. Fail better.'"

"Maybe this time," said Jane, bringing her lips close to Julia's, "we *won't* fail."